Brushes

Courtney Pierce

Windtree Press
Hillsboro, OR

Windtree Press
Hillsboro, OR
windtreepress.com

Cover Photo:

The Conversion of the Magdalene, c. 1598
Michelangelo Merisi da Caravaggio
Oil and tempera on canvas
Detroit Institute of Arts, USA, Gift of the Kresge Foundation and Mrs. Edsel B. Ford, The Bridgeman Art Library
Used by Permission

ISBN-10: 0988917513
ISBN-13: 978-0-9889175-1-4

DEDICATION

To my dad, who will forever be the Chief on the immortal printed page, and also to Jake, the world's newest Old Master.

"Every child is an artist. The problem is how to remain an artist when we grow up."

—Pablo Picasso

ACKNOWLEDGMENTS

Thanks, as always, go to my husband, Wayne, whose knowledge of music makes my characters come alive—and makes me come alive too. Inspiration comes from many sources, and a major one for this story was from a gifted young artist, Jake, who happens to be my nephew and godson. His incredible portraits grace the halls of Congress. His guidance on painting techniques of the Old Masters was invaluable.

My editor, Kristin Thiel, at Indigo Editing & Publishing gave me guidance and prodded me to be better. Her instincts were right on the money. I channeled her cat, Izzy, to make sure this book met his high expectations. Cats are hard to please.

Thank you to Dan Bergsvik, Carole Florian, Helen Dupre, Christina Dupre, Debbie Gerber, Ann Hutchins, Martha Baxter, Harry Baxter, Jan Pierce, Doug Pierce, Ann Pierce, Frank Abbott, Annette Beck, and Darleen McDonough for their eagle eyes. All of you were so generous with your time and support.

And, of course, Miss Rosey, who sits under my chair as I write, waiting for her next helping of Forever Kibble. Her quirks and personality are infused into the literary soul of Mycroft.

Lastly, I am grateful for my involvement in NIWA (Northwest Independent Writers Association) and The Attic Institute. They offer a supportive environment in their mission to make independently published books the best they can be.

CHAPTER 1

Living with Magic

Spence Collins liked to do things in person. Milwaukie, Oregon, was a small enough town where business could still be done face-to-face. At sixty-two, he preferred to take his time with the teller at the bank, the checker at the grocery, the manager of the hardware store, and the owner of the pet supply shop where he picked up Mycroft's special diet food. But Mycroft, his and Jean's Maine Coon cat, defied the food's miracle claim to "bring the kitten out of your cat" by continuing to gain weight and extending his sleep hours.

Life had been a bit complicated and downright dangerous after Jean found a magical piece of fabric in an old chest she'd purchased from Mary Coulter's estate sale. But right now, Spence's focus was on Frank, the mailman. He made a point of going out to meet the truck in the driveway. Today might be the day one special envelope from Mary Coulter's lawyer would be among the bills, ads, and charitable requests.

Frank handed Spence a banded bundle of mail. He, too, liked to bypass the impersonal nature of the box, favoring the opportunity to pick up a few chewy nuggets of neighborhood gossip.

"Mostly begging letters today, Spence," Frank said. "I think you and Jean are on every pet charity list on the planet." The man's eyes twinkled as he pointed to the stack. "You got something from a lawyer. Looks important."

The rubber band released with a *pop* and so did Spence's stomach. He fingered through the smaller envelopes on top, trying to act nonchalant. The larger bubble-pack one begged for a squeeze. "Frank, would you believe a house and an old T-Bird are in here?" He shook the envelope to loosen the jingle of keys inside. "A good day, my friend."

"I hope so, Spence. Give Jean a 'hey' for me."

Spence waved and climbed the wide steps to their mid-century modern house. He paused and watched the light dance on the textured glass of the triangle-shaped clerestory windows. This envelope made their inheritance from Mary Coulter a reality, far from the unreal existence he, Jean, and Mycroft had been living over the past couple of months. In an unexpected twist, Mary had left him and Jean her entire estate. She was immortal. The phoenixes in the an-cient Egyptian fabric transformed Mary to an afterlife, and now they were forever bonded with a ghost. They were also bonded to Jon Segert, an agent of the Portland FBI, who witnessed the magic of the fabric. The phoenixes had transformed to a vicious hawk that killed Mary's son, Raleigh.

Spence burst through the front door. "Jean! C'mere!"

"What's up?" she asked, leaning over the railing along the cat-walk upstairs.

The envelope did a little dance as he held it above his head. "Look what came in the mail . . . from the law offices of Landrum and Sullivan."

"No way! We're in?"

"We're in."

Jean Collins turned both sets of keys—one house, one car—over and over in her hand as Spence drove the Mini Cooper to the Irvington neighborhood where Mary Coulter's two-bedroom yellow bungalow had stood since 1921. Their other car, the Volvo, was history; they'd sold it, knowing the T-Bird was in the wings.

She itched to get back inside Mary's house. A multitude of decisions had to be made before selling it. Glancing down at her list, she scanned the day's big items to assess: floors, kitchen, bath, paint, plaster, and cleaning. After the walk-through, she'd turn her lists into a detailed renovation budget.

"What's the first thing you want to check, Spence?" she asked. "I need to spend some extra time with the kitchen and bath. The home remodeling shows say to dedicate a good portion of the whole bud-get to those two rooms. I'm not sure about the roof and foundation."

"No rush." Spence's voice sounded like his mind was a million miles away. "I can come back anytime. We need to hire someone to go through the basement. The obvious things will be easy, but—"

"Ohhh . . . I get it. You want inside that T-Bird, don't you?"

"The car is calling me." He pressed his lips together. She caught the grin he attempted to hide.

Spence turned down Knott Street, their old neighborhood from twenty years ago. Jean gazed around at the historic mix of stately Colonials and grandiose residences. When they approached Nineteenth Street, it was like going home. These houses, mostly smaller bungalows and four-squares from the early 1900s, were charming and approachable. Mary's small bungalow was only two blocks from where they used to live.

"The neighborhood seems bigger with all the leaves gone. When Phil and I were here for the estate sale, you couldn't see the nooks and crannies."

"Nobody's ever messed with this house—all original," Spence said, his eyes dancing with anticipation. "Vintage details have a pa-tina. We have to be careful to preserve that."

The driveway of Mary's house angled upward. Jean smiled when Spence tapped the gas and craned his neck to get a glimpse of the 1963 Chalfonte Blue Thunderbird convertible in front of the garage. He shut off the engine and turned to her. His deep brown eyes held promise. He reached over and tucked one side of her blond pageboy behind her ear.

"C'mere." She leaned over to kiss him. "Congratulations, Mr. Collins." Jean batted her light aqua eyes and dangled the ring with the warm car key over his palm, and then dropped it in his hand. His fingers curled around hers as she said, "I'll be inside doing my thing. Have fun with the car."

The steps creaked as Jean climbed to the expansive porch. The brass key to the front door weighed heavy in her hand and on her mind. *Maybe Mary's here.* She and Spence didn't picture themselves as part of the human pack since experiencing the magic of the fabric. Of course, they were. More like a pair of life spies with secret information. The possibility of becoming immortal was an alluring thought—more like an obsession—but the reality of living forever disturbed them too. The ticking clock provided all the motivation they needed to achieve the dreams they had for the past thirty-two years—soon to be thirty-three. Skipping over life in a fantastical quest to an afterlife seemed wasteful. Selling Mary's house would help to fund their goals in *this* world.

Jean slipped the key in the lock, pushing away the thought of Mary's loss of her husband, Jim. She held the handle and closed her eyes. *Nothing seen. Nothing stirring.* The thumb latch depressed, and the heavy oak door opened without a sound. The aroma of old wood swirled around her as the squeak of her sneakers echoed through the empty living room.

The Craftsman design details revealed themselves in the absence of Mary's furnishings, from the hand-hewn ceiling beams and original amber-glass light fixtures to the natural oak built-ins, right down to the cut-crystal doorknobs. She fixed her gaze on the distinct squares lined up evenly on the faded wallpaper where Mary's framed needle-point birds had hung. The brightness inside the pattern hinted at the room's original cheer. The embroidered robin she'd finished in Mary's honor, adorning the same spot, would be the perfect nod to her life when she staged the house for sale.

"Mary? Are you here?" she whispered, waiting to sense a presence. *Nothing.* Jean's shoulders slumped. She had hoped Mary would be here—needed for her to be here.

Maybe there wouldn't be magic in the house. She pulled the pen and her list from the pocket of her fleece jacket. The saying printed on the top of this one read, *People who hate cats come back as mice.*

"Floors look good. Just need a light sanding and some varnish," she said aloud, making a check mark on her notepad. Two tapered oak pillars flanked the entrance to a small sitting area with a fireplace to the right of the front door. The charming little nook captivated her when she attended Mary's estate sale. She remembered Mary and Jim's Stickley chairs; one had a deeper dip in the cushion than the other. Jim Coulter's valuable collection of mysteries and crime clas-sics had filled the built-in bookcases. Now they were empty. At least she'd saved one of those books from the clutches of the rabid col-lectors who attended the sale. She had tucked away the first edition of *The Maltese Falcon* to give to Spence for Christmas. Jean wrote a note on her list: *Lemon oil all the natural wood.*

She ascended the narrow staircase and examined the scratched pattern worn on the steps. *How many times did Mary climb these? Her son, Raleigh? Jim? Both gone.* She stood on the upstairs landing and assessed the three doorways leading to two small bedrooms and one bath.

"Easy-peasy: paint—maybe a soft sage with creamy-white satin trim." She stepped into the spacious bathroom. The octagon-shaped ceramic tiles were in excellent shape, along with the wide, square ped-estal sink. The chipped mirror, still speckled with dried water drop-lets, needed to be replaced. She made more notes on her list and turned to check the bedrooms.

Mary's bedroom. Jean's throat tightened as her gaze settled on the corner where she'd first seen the chest at the estate sale. When she'd found the magical fabric inside, her and Spence's lives had changed in an instant. Glancing out the upstairs window, she spotted Spence running his hand along the door frame of the T-Bird. The magic was like a drug. *He's feeling a pull.* Magic crept into their lives in unexpected ways when they touched some of Mary's things: they usually experienced flashes of her life. *Nothing here.*

Jean turned from the window and opened one of the two small closets. At the estate sale, Mary's husband's clothes were still hanging inside. Now they hung in a vintage resale shop. Mary had treasured those flannel shirts, cotton trousers, and wool suit jackets for over forty years after Jim Coulter's untimely death. *Time to check out the kitchen.* The tight turn of the staircase allowed her to inspect the plaster on the walls of the stairwell. *No cracks.*

Her steps squeaked through the dining room. Jean rounded the doorway and laughed out loud at the light-blue rotary phone on the wall. It matched the color of the linoleum counter that had a random pattern of smooth triangles.

"Look at *that.*" She picked up the receiver, weightier than the one she remembered her own family had as a child, and listened for a dial tone. *Nothing.* Then her hand went numb. An electrical charge *whooshed* up her arm. She inhaled its magic and closed her eyes as the vision unfolded.

Mary Coulter inspected herself in the mirror of the upstairs bathroom and slid the diamond-encrusted hair comb into the top of her French twist. She dipped her forefinger into a jar of Dippity-do and pressed a few errant hairs into place. The phone rang in the kitchen. She rinsed her fingers of the gel and quickened her steps down the stairs, hoping Jim was calling to say he could get away from the mill for lunch. Mary lifted the receiver and swung the long blue cord like a jump rope.

"Hi, darling! Are you on your way? It'll be just the two of—"

"Mary, Russ here."

"Oh. Hello, Russ." Her jubilant expression melted. Cradling the phone between her neck and shoulder, she stretched the cord to the sink and grabbed a hand towel to wipe her wet fingers.

"Not good, Mary."

"Why? What's the matter?"

"Jim . . . there's been an accident at the mill."

"Where is he? What kind of accident? Is he all right?" Mary

panicked at the assault of Russ's words. "I'll come now. Let me get my purse—"

"Mary! Listen to me for a minute! Jim's gone. It was very fast. I doubt he knew what happened. A pallet fell from the lift. He died before the ambulance arrived. I'm sorry."

"What?" *Gone.* The word made no sense.

"Stay right there. I'm on my way." A click. Silence.

Mary replaced the receiver and focused on unraveling the long cord, anything to escape from the previous minute. As reality took shape in her head, she smacked it away. She slid down the wall and sat on the floor. As though putting the punch line on a cruel joke, Mary raised her gaze to Jim's coffee cup sitting next to the sink, right where he'd left it this morning.

Jean set the phone back on its cradle as the vision dissipated.

"Oh, Mary, I'm so sorry," she whispered. "Why did you show this to me?" Jean sat on the floor in the same spot where Mary had that fateful afternoon. She anticipated something would happen in the house, but never expected to experience a vision of the most painful moment in Mary's life. Jean couldn't tell if the phone was magic or the magic came from . . . *inside her.*

"It's all right, dear." Mary's voice filled the air, coming from everywhere and echoing off the reflective surfaces of the empty kit-chen.

Heat ripples shimmered as the image of a human form gained strength. Jean watched, fascinated.

"Mary?" She blinked away tears and pulled the sleeve of her fleece jacket across her face. "I expected something but wasn't pre-pared for what you showed me."

"I wasn't ready for that call, either."

Mary's visage materialized to full clarity. Her hazel eyes were bright and inquisitive, with a slight bluish halo. A small-framed woman, she appeared younger than when they'd transformed her at age eighty-six. Standing here now, Mary was exactly as Jean remem-bered her in

1991, when she and Spence jogged by her house. About sixty-five back then, Mary had her hair in a perfect French twist.

"How did you ever survive that call?" Jean shook her head and raised her eyes to Mary. "I don't know . . . if that had been me."

"You'd be surprised what you can survive. But live? A piece of me died with Jim the minute I picked up the phone." Mary's ex-pression turned compassionate. The glisten in her eyes radiated a soft, reflective halo. "Even in immortality, I can never get back what I had before that call. In an instant, the chance for Jim and me to be together forever was gone. I couldn't make him immortal. If he could have hung on long enough, I would have been able to tell him I love him and use the magical fabric. He'd be by my side today."

Jean filled her lungs with air. She blew out the breath and gazed at Mary. "Did you and Jim have a plan to become immortal?"

"Yes, we did. We wanted to be with the rest of my family in Richmond. They, too, were devastated by his death. They're all im-mortal . . . with me. Even our dog, Wiley, is immortal. The family home is now run as a Bed and Breakfast, but we're there. The inn is your and Spencer's now too."

"So many memories here. Are you okay with Spence and me selling this one?"

"I moved on after the estate sale. Richmond is home now. As you've just seen, dear, not all the memories here are pleasant ones. Sell this house. Make it wonderful, as I know you can do. Time is short, even with immortality possible."

Jean went silent. What if she or Spence, or both of them, died away from the fabric and couldn't become immortal? The thought made her hollow inside. *Change the subject.*

"And changing the colors upstairs and taking down the wall-paper in the living room?"

"Do what you will. Don't worry one whit about me." Mary's hand swept through the air, leaving a faint, smoky trail.

"Your generosity has humbled us . . . you know that right?"

"I know I made the right decision to have you carry on this legacy. You must come to Richmond to meet the family."

"We will. A trip would be good for us too. We'd love to meet them . . . all."

"Soon, come soon. The inn is a lovely place. Do you love art?—old art?"

Jean glanced up at Mary, curious. "Of course. We breathe it."

"A small painting in Doc's bedroom will make it worth the trip. I should have brought it here after I transformed Birdie, our housekeeper. One of my former life's regrets."

"What kind of painting?"

"A little boy dancing in the woods; quite old. I think you'll fall under its enchantment as I did. Come to Richmond. I'll leave you to your planning. I love you, dear. I can never thank you enough for what you and Spence did for me."

"Oh, Mary . . . we should be thanking—" Mary's image faded in swirls of haze. ". . . you."

The visage evaporated. Only the baby-blue linoleum counter-tops, white cabinets, and the heavy O'Keefe & Merritt gas stove filled her view. Jean wanted to see Spence.

Jean leaned back against the wall and studied her list. The pen quivered as she wrote: *Keep the original phone in the kitchen.*

CHAPTER 2

Rev Up the Engine

Spence knew he had to get the fin fixed on the 1963 Thunderbird convertible, but he was compelled to check out the rest of the car, spend a little quality time inside. His heart became a lit firecracker when Jean dropped the key in his hand. The car was in near-perfect condition, except for a dented back fin. He wanted it in tip-top shape and in the driveway to surprise Jean on Christmas morning. Her new old car. Jean would look hot driving it, especially if she wore those oversize black sunglasses and wound that long turquoise scarf around her head, the one she got in the Cairo Airport. Even after thirty-two years—nearly thirty-three—he still liked to knock her socks off at Christmas. Jean would never suspect, since she expected the Mini Cooper to be hers.

The sun bounced off the small, silver key in his hand. *I hope the Bird starts.* Classic anything could snare Spence in a web, especially albums, posters, books, and cars. They were windows into the past, reflecting the hopes and passions of others—and his own. His dream of opening a vintage record and rock poster store was a juicy peach, ready to be plucked from the tree. Jean had a project too. The renovation of Mary's house was her baby. Once she got the bungalow renovated and sold, combined with the investments Mary had left them, their security would be set.

The bones of the house were probably fine, but the place needed

Jean's decorating touch. She had a knack for those things. He imagined her buzzing around inside with a list. After years in the theater industry, she knew how to stage a room to make the right impression. And Jean needed a new obsession after being so focused on the fabric. And she wasn't the only one who'd been consumed with its magic. The phoenixes' transformation had showed him anything was possible. Now, all he could think about was possibilities —the store, his life with Jean, and their secret knowledge of im-mortality.

Letting go of the bungalow would be emotionally hard, but he and Jean were too attached to their mid-century modern in Milwaukie. The other portion of the inheritance was slated to kick-start the store. He and longtime buddy Bill Flannery had started laying the groundwork for the business when he and Jean moved back to Portland late last summer. Their planning had been waylaid by finding the magic fabric. Bill and his wife, Linda, still didn't know about that development.

Today, though, was all about the aqua T-Bird. This car, in his opinion, was the coolest thing, outside of the magic, they had inherited from Mary. And there it was—begging for him to insert the key. Spence ran his hand along the driver's door. He could already imagine the scent inside. The distinctive aroma of vintage vinyl was equal to that of a brand-new pair of soft leather loafers coming out of the shoebox for the first time.

A swipe of his sleeve across the window rid the glass of water droplets from last night's rain. Spence stared at his mirrored image, unaware he'd been smiling so wide. Little differences, from even a few months before: buoyant, hopeful, and up for an adventure. Different inside, too, since experiencing the fabric's magic—so light on his feet. Gazing through to the interior, he realized the dash reminded him of the puppet rocket ship from *Thunderbirds Are Go*. The stylish, curved panel gleamed but was only one of a multitude of appointments: radio push buttons, vinyl piping around the airplane cockpit-style seats, console switches for raising and lowering the windows and, of course, the famous winged Thunderbird logo on the floor mats.

Spence inserted the small key into the lock. The inside button popped up. He'd been granted permission to enter. The door groaned, releasing a gust of hallowed air. The near-perfect vinyl pro-tested his intrusion as he lowered himself in the driver's seat. With a firm pull of the door, he waited in silence for the stiff vinyl to relax and absorb his body heat. It was going to be a treat to drive the car to the shop.

The engine fired right up as he tapped the gas. The hungry pistons purred as they distributed the cold oil into the engine's nooks and crannies. *Amazing for sitting idle for so many months.* The car vibrated with life as Spence gripped the expansive steering wheel. His fingers fit perfectly in the dips. He sat up straight when his hands began to tingle. The tingle quickly escalated into an electrical charge racing up his arms. His scalp prickled, ordering his salt-and-pepper hair to stand at full attention. *Am I having a heart attack?* He closed his eyes, the car dissolving as the scene unfolded behind them.

Mary laughed as Jim drove the car. Crunchy leaves swirled in the street as they cruised through their Irvington neighborhood. Long, wavy strands of Mary's mahogany hair escaped the confines of her French twist and stretched toward the open window.

Jim glanced at her with a sly smile. "What do you say, Skeets? This is the one, am I right?"

"Oh, you bet," Mary said, smoothing her hair back. She ran her other hand over the padded vinyl ridge along the bottom of the curved dash. "The only car I'll have for the rest of my life. It'll be perfect forever."

"I'm going to give you everything you ever wanted."

"You already have." Mary set her head on Jim's shoulder and tucked her arm around his. "I have more than I thought possible."

"You wait, gal. Life is going to be a surprise." He took his eyes off the road long enough to make Mary nervous and then, grinning and looking away from her again, he announced, "I got promoted at the mill."

"What? I'm married to the most successful lumberman in

Portland? I only ever wanted you, whatever you did, the moment I laid eyes on you." Mary turned her face to the wind through the win-dow. "Doc and Charlotte are so proud of you, Jim. Birdie and Jess are too."

"I love you, Mary Coulter. I still like the sound of it."

"I love you, Jim." Mary trailed her fingers over his on the center console.

"I bought this car just for you, honey." Jim lifted her fingers to his lips.

"Can I drive it? My turn." Mary squirmed in her seat.

"This is your car now. Yes, you can drive, but we need to get you some proper lessons." Jim pulled the car to an open spot at the curb and kissed Mary slow and deep, as if his life depended on it. She patted his cheek and reached for the handle. Jim held the driver's side door open, waiting for her to run around the front of the car. Blow-ing out a breath, she grasped the wheel with two hands. Mary's gaze followed him through the windshield to the passenger side, admiring his rugged build in his plaid flannel shirt.

"Okay, Skeets, take her slow."

Mary lowered the long shaft on the steering column two gear clicks to D. The T-Bird lurched forward as she stepped on the gas a little too hard.

Spence panted, trying to catch a breath and slow the hammering in his chest. He couldn't let go of the steering wheel. It was real. *Did I do that? The car?* The events in vision had actually happened. The last few months showed him the impossible was real. He was slightly embarrassed at being a voyeur, intruding on Mary and Jim's private world. By the time they were married, Doc and Jess had already passed into immortality; Birdie too. That was the fabric's magic at work. *They're all still around . . . except for Mary losing Jim to the accident.*

With shaking hands, Spence turned the key and shut off the engine. He needed to come back tomorrow to sneak the car to the body shop. He couldn't wait to tell Jean what happened. Before the thought left his head, Spence realized she was still rattling around inside the house. He wanted to see her.

"The vision meant something," he whispered. The quiet in the car got even quieter as Spence figured the math in his head: Mary and Jim would have only six years left together after they bought the car in 1963. Jim Coulter would be dead from a mill accident in 1969. Every day had been a gift. If Mary had known what was going to happen, what would she have done differently?

"Hellooo! Where are you?" Spence called out, his voice echoing in the living room as he stepped through the bungalow's front door.

"I'm in the kitchen!"

Spence's sneakers squeaked toward Jean's voice. He approached the kitchen doorway and his gaze traveled downward.

"There you are. What are you doing sitting on the floor?" He grasped her hands and lifted her to her feet. He wrapped his arms around her. "Let's go home."

"Mary . . . was here in the kitchen."

"I saw her too. Mary was driving with Jim in the car, right after they got it. C'mon, let's go. Tell me on the way home."

Spence watched Jean take a long look at the sitting area with its intimate fireplace.

"A lot to do, but doable," Jean said, handing him the front door key and stepping outside. He locked it and jiggled the handle. "The kitchen needs some work, but the bathroom is fine. The rest is cosmetic. I can do the inside painting myself. We should keep the stove. O'Keefe & Merritts are hot right now, especially in a fun color." Jean hesitated. "And I want to keep the original rotary phone in the kitchen."

"Rotary phone? Nobody uses a rotary phone anymore."

"Mmm . . . this one is special."

As he backed the Mini Cooper out of the driveway, he said: "I'll come back tomorrow and check the roof." *And pick up the car.* "We're in rainy season, so I want to make sure there isn't a leak somewhere."

"How's the car, by the way?"

"Faaan-tastic. I touched the steering wheel and got this vision."

"Mary wants us to come to Richmond to meet the *family.* She mentioned something about a painting."

"Oh, she does, does she? Did she call you on that old phone?"

"Stop. No."

"Well, we can't disappoint Mary. Let's go for our anniversary. It's right around the corner. And once you dive into working on the house, I won't be able to pull you away."

"The store too," Jean countered. "That'll be eating up a bunch of your time."

"Then off to Richmond right after Christmas." He drummed his fingers on the steering wheel. "I need another magic fix. How did Mary look, by the way?"

"Wispy and wonderful. She looked just like she did when we lived in Irvington, except for this weird haze around her. She said she was fine with us selling the house."

"That's a relief. I've been a little worried about her reaction."

As he rounded the corner Spence slowed the car to a crawl. A van had parked in front of their house. The letters KATV were paint-ed diagonally across the side.

"Spence, what's going on?"

The rest of the street was quiet. "About us?" They had discussed whether media attention in Egypt, over the fabric and Raleigh Coulter's death, might make its way to them. "Don't say anything. I mean it, Jean, not a word."

"We'll go in the house through the garage." As Spence pulled into the driveway, Jean clicked the remote clipped to the visor.

A reporter jumped out of the van and ran along the side of the Mini Cooper into the garage. Spence sprung from the car when the reporter followed them inside.

"What are you doing? This is private property!" he shouted.

Jean burst from the car and slammed the door, eyes ablaze.

"I just want to ask you a few questions," the reporter said, throwing up his hands. "I'm with KATV. Are you Jean Collins?"

"None of your business!" Jean seethed through a clenched jaw.

"We have information you and your husband were at the scene when Raleigh Coulter was mauled in London. Can you tell us what happened?"

"You have no right to ask us anything!"

"Yes, I do have a right. How did you know Raleigh Coulter? You inherited his mother's estate. Was that a factor? Were you involved?"

Spence wedged himself in front of Jean and motioned for her to stand back. "What a rude thing to ask! Leave my wife alone."

Jean bobbed and weaved around him. He knew she wanted to rip the notepad out of the reporter's hand and smack his head with it—repeatedly. *Stay cool.*

"Witnesses said a huge bird killed him. Is that true? Where did it come from?" the reporter persisted, eager to sink his teeth deeper into their flesh.

"Honey, get in the house!" Spence pointed to the reporter. "You—get the hell out of here!"

Jean raced up the steps to the mudroom. The reporter's voice was muffled, but not gone.

She cracked the door and leaned her ear to the opening.

Mycroft sauntered up behind her and planted himself at her heels, his eyes curious and questioning. "Stay back, Mycroft," she whispered. The cat continued to stare at her, waiting for Spence to come inside.

Spence exploded through the door spitting tacks. "That reporter insinuated we killed Raleigh to get his mother's estate! Can you be-lieve the nerve?" Mycroft turned tail and ran upstairs.

"Where did they come up with that?" Jean flinched when the doorbell rang. She rushed to the peephole. "Same guy."

"Ignore him," Spence said, throwing the car keys on the kitchen island. "He took a string of incidents and found a common thread—

us. A cheap, dirty way to sell the newscast. He doesn't know the real truth would sell a helluva lot more."

"But he mentioned the hawk—and witnesses."

"Getting out of town is a *really* good idea."

"Let's talk to Jon when he and Meg come over for Thanksgiving. If we're being hounded, I'm sure he's feeling the pinch too."

"Hey, you were pretty chivalrous out there. I kind of like this damsel-in-distress stuff."

Spence smiled with an exaggerated puff of his chest. "Where's Mycroft?"

"He ran upstairs. I bet you couldn't blow him out of the comforter with a stick of dynamite."

"Then he's going to have to move over." Spence wrapped his arms around her and kissed her. "Let's go upstairs, right after I take the batteries out of the doorbell."

CHAPTER 3

Giving Thanks

Jean checked her Thanksgiving Day to-do list on the long, skinny pad. This one had a cartoon of a cat's head at the top. The caption read, *Dogs look up to us—cats look down on us.* By her calculation, she needed to take out the turkey in twenty-five minutes, allowing the bird to rest while she made the gravy. Trailing her finger down the list, she ticked off the other items: beans ready to steam; stuffing casserole waiting to go in the oven, the wine breathing, and the table set. She could take a few minutes to foof, including putting on some lipstick.

Spence was humming in the shower when she got to the small master bathroom. Her blond pageboy lost its pouf in the steam the minute she stepped into the room.

"The Kinks—'Waterloo Sunset'," she called out over the spray in their game of can-you-guess-what-I'm-humming. The rules re-quired to state the name of the band *and* the song.

"Excellent!" Spence said, swishing the loofah.

In between swipes of the towel over the mirror, she applied her lipstick and fluffed up her hair.

"What do you think Meg will be like?"

"She's got to be a saint or an army sergeant to live with Jon. I'm sure she'll be wonderful. Jon loves her. You can tell by the way he talks about her."

Jean had a feeling she was going to like Meg—a lot. "You think he told her what happened in London?"

"Let's not bring it up, unless he, or she, does first." After a moment of silence floated up with the steam, Spence added, "Jean, please don't."

"I'm sure she's lovely." She eyed Spence's rippled silhouette behind the glass door, already plotting how to bring up the subject.

The situation would be awkward if they couldn't talk about what happened in London, not only because of how major the incident was but because she and Spence had met Jon—specifically, on the plane to London. They hadn't known at the time, but Jon was an agent with the FBI in Portland. He was tailing Raleigh Coulter, convinced he was trying to flee the country for insider trading. Raleigh needed money. And when he attempted to steal the fabric from Jean, Jon helped them get it back. Jon witnessed the fabric's transformation into the hawk that killed Raleigh in the taxi, but he chose to leave those details out of his report. The only evidence the hawk, which they named Horus after the Egyptian god often depicted with the head of a bird of prey, truly existed was the three-inch talon left in Raleigh Coulter's thigh. The talon's final blow—after the repeated stabbings across Raleigh's body. The hawk had killed him. Jon had kept the talon.

The doorbell released its long, repetitive bong. Though she was happy to welcome their guests, Jean wished Spence hadn't reconnected it after their play date. Mycroft hated the doorbell. He heaved himself off his chair in front of the fireplace and shot up the stairs.

"Spence! Jon and Meg are here!"

She squinted through the peephole. Jon was nervous. He was brushing the top of his sandy-blond crew cut back and forth. Freshly buzzed. He'd gained a little weight too, but he still had the commanding presence of an FBI agent. A steel-belted marshmallow.

"Hey, hi, you two. Happy Thanksgiving!" she announced. "Wonderful to see you again, Jon. Meg, we've been looking forward to meeting you." Jean, herself only five-foot-three, looked down when Meg stepped up in the entryway. She hadn't expected Meg to be so short.

"Jon loves you guys," Meg said. "Who doesn't love magic?"

"Okay . . . yeah, that'll work. I think you addressed our only taboo subject. We're going to have some fun today, right, Jon?" Jean patted his arm. She already liked Meg's candor. A match to Jon's, Meg had smart, vivid blue eyes, but her long hair was rich brown, bouncy and smooth. A shampoo commercial. Trim and stylish, she appeared at ease with herself.

"Yeah, Meg knows everything," Jon confirmed. "She sensed something weird happened to me the minute I got home from London. As you'll find out, I can't keep anything from her. She's has me pegged."

"Well, now we've cleared this up. Can I get you a drink?"

"Absolutely! Smells fabulous in here." Jon gravitated toward the open kitchen and lifted the tin foil on the resting turkey. "Wow, what'd you do, drive over this bird?"

"It's called spatchcocking. Cooks in less than two hours. Lay it flat after you take the backbone out and break the breast bone. Works like a charm and stays juicy. I got the recipe from *Mothra* Stewart."

Spence came down the stairs, smoothing down his wavy-lined sweater and singing the call of *Maaah . . . thraaah*. He beamed at Jon and shook his hand, and gave Meg a hug. Even when he was singing from a kitschy monster movie, Spence could make anyone feel like an age-old best friend.

"Jon! Come help me pick out some tunes. How about a little Charlie Parker at dinner? Nat King Cole now?"

"Sounds good. I've been anxious to go through your record collection." Jon followed Spence into the den. Spence came back out with Nat King Cole's *Stepping out of a Dream* and set the album on the turntable. "Get to Gettin'" filled the whole downstairs.

"This is a fantastic house, by the way. Look at all the angles—totally unique," Meg exclaimed, looking up at the clerestory windows.

"We sure like it." Jean pulled out one of the leather chairs at the expansive island in the kitchen. "Have a sit." While she uncorked a bottle of wine, she shared the abbreviated version of how they'd moved to Portland. She poured and handed Meg a glass.

"So," Meg said, hesitating and swirling the wine, "I didn't believe him at first—and I'm still not sure I do—but Jon's not one to make up a story. Then he showed me the *talon*."

Jean stopped the wooden spoon in mid-stir. Her first response evaporated as the gravy started to bubble. Instead, she said, "Lucky you! You're now a member of the exclusive club of Horus!" She then went serious. "Let's say we have much to be thankful for today. We owe a lot to Jon . . . and that talon. Quite an experience. Life is different now."

"Has anything else happened?"

"The woman who owned the fabric passed away as soon as we got home from Cairo. Spence and I experienced the transformation in Cairo and were able to take Mary Coulter . . . into immortality. Quite something."

Meg's eyes widened. She took a long slug of her wine. "Jon didn't say anything about what happened after you guys left London. I don't mean to be rude, but that's not possible. The talon story was stretching it. Immortality? Pfft!"

Jean turned off the gravy. She refilled Meg's glass as she thought about how to relay the details of their trip to Cairo. "Meg . . . the fabric has the ability to make people immortal. The birds are phoenixes. They transform. Don't repeat this, please, but I think the magic lingers behind in us. Touch can be incredibly powerful."

"Oh, c'mon. Isn't that taking this too far?" Meg pressed, circling her finger around the rim of the glass. Jean waited for the ring.

"I . . . uh . . . don't think so."

"Okay, keep going. If it's magical, then how could you have given it up?"

"We donated the fabric to the museum. Way too valuable—and powerful. It belongs in Egypt, and should be under the watch of someone who truly understands the potential. That's certainly not Spence or me. Anhur Kumar, the director of the Cairo Museum, knows much more than we do. We're going back to Cairo for the gala celebration for the fabric at some point. We're waiting to hear from him, but political unrest may postpone the event. But we're starting to experience weird things since we got home . . . when we touch Mary's heirlooms." She kept her eyes down, waiting for a reac-tion.

"Like what?" Jean watched Meg wrestle with whether she wanted to hear an answer to her question.

"Okay, and don't laugh, but I think you know we inherited Mary's house, right?" Meg nodded, keeping her eyes trained on Jean. "I can see her life. Clear as a bell—and so is Mary. I talked to her when we went over to the house. She appeared to me. She really did become immortal. Spence experiences it too. The magic is lingering inside us. I swear. And the weirdest thing of all—I think Mycroft, our cat, is seeing things. Sometimes he acts like he's interacting with another animal around here. I've seen him bat at the air with his paw."

"Cats do that." Meg shook her head and shrugged, choosing not to acknowledge the more fantastic details.

"I accept what you're saying about Mycroft. He's a nut ball, even without magic. But I'm not imagining the other stuff. Don't tell Jon. He already thinks I'm pretty high-strung."

"Uh . . . okay. Maybe you're projecting these weird incidents because of what happened. The imagination is a powerful thing," Meg said, waving her hand in front of her face.

"I assure you, this is very real." She finished filling the serving bowls and handed the green beans to Meg. "Here, we're ready to eat. I'll get the guys."

"Well, I don't buy it." Meg tapped her nails in a nervous rhythm.

"You will . . . at some point." Jean stepped into the den where Spence and Jon were on their hands and knees flipping through albums. "C'mon you two—we're ready. Spence, can you cut the turkey? Quick, please, while everything's still hot."

"Yepper Depps. I hope you're hungry. Jean beats up on a bird pretty good," Spence said. He slipped two Rolling Stones albums back into the cabinet and pulled out *Charlie Parker with Strings: The Master Takes.*

"I'm starved." Jon led the way into the kitchen, rubbing his hands together. "So, Jean . . . Spence tells me you guys were hounded by a reporter."

"Yes, it's been upsetting. We've been getting a lot of requests for interviews about the donation of the fabric—and that's fine, and those reporters call first—but being questioned about Raleigh threw us for a loop. What should we do? Any backlash against you at the FBI?"

"Don't bite. They'll twist everything you say and put words in your mouth, so best to keep quiet. On Monday, I'll be able to deflect some of the attention when I interrogate Nash Winthrop, Raleigh's inside tipster. He'll sing like a robin in spring."

"You think there's something bigger than his giving information to Raleigh?"

"I'm almost sure of it. And the talon is going to help me get the goods out of him. Can you pass the stuffing?"

Jean and Spence gave each other a long gaze. They turned to Jon and finally trained their eyes on Meg.

"Don't ask me!" Meg said, holding up her hands. "I'm just married to him. I think all three of you are crazy."

Charlie Parker's haunting sax on "Just Friends" hung over the dining room.

CHAPTER 4

Don't Lie to Horus

Jon Segert opened his top desk drawer and carefully plucked the hawk talon from a compartment in the corner. He'd turned in Raleigh's cell phone as evidence in his death but held back the talon. He wasn't sure, yet, what all of the magical properties were. Turning it over between two fingers, he inspected the talon's needled tip. Playing with fire. He couldn't expose the truth. With his own eyes, he'd witnessed the hawk claw up Raleigh. Any hint of the word *magic*, or *supernatural*, would ruin his credibility at the Bureau. He'd be stand-ing alone as an army of one.

He dropped the talon in his suit pocket. Jon would have pre-ferred to use its razor-sharp point to etch the word *cowards* deep into the top of his desk. Jean and Spence were exactly right. Their words, from when he talked with them in their London hotel room, rang in his ears. *Don't take this up the ladder. Do it yourself.* They had told him the higher-ups wouldn't listen. He pulled his cell phone from his belt loop. Forwarding the pictures from Raleigh's cell to his own phone while still in London had been a good idea. He'd entered Raleigh's phone into evidence, but the guts wouldn't work. It had been soaked in blood—Raleigh's blood. He didn't want anyone to discover those pictures. Jon wanted to view them one more time.

A gallery of photos whisked beneath his forefinger: Mary Coulter's bungalow; Mary Coulter in her apartment at Milwaukie

Manor; and Nash Winthrop looking loaded at some bar in downtown Portland. The next one stopped him in his tracks. He remembered with crystal clarity the exact moment when Raleigh took the picture on the plane to London. The huge hawk in the magical fabric. *The talon.* He would never forget the change in the fabric on the back of Jean's denim jacket when she walked past his seat. Before they'd boarded, the fabric had shown the images of the three lifelike phoenixes. But by the time Jean went to the restroom a few hours into the flight, the back of her jacket had changed to show a menac-ing hawk.

"Horus," he whispered.

Jon flinched from his trance when his assistant, Jenny Kowalski, marched into his office. He clipped his phone on his belt. "What's up?"

"The chief wants you."

"Now? I've got to talk to Nash Winthrop in"—he glanced at his watch—"about two minutes."

"Now." Jenny drummed her acrylic nails on the door frame.

An ugly scene with the chief rolled through Jon's head on grainy film stock as he touched the talon's tip in his pocket. "All right. Tell him to cool his jets."

"I'll tell him the first part, not the second part."

This conversation wasn't going to be pretty. The investigation in London had been a disaster. He had to dance like a prima ballerina to protect the Collinses—and himself. Deflecting attention away from those two wouldn't be easy. They wouldn't be able to offer up anything but unbelievable instances of magic. Not an option. At least he'd convinced Scotland Yard and the chief he would question Jean and Spence—but not until he had to. He'd listened to their story in their hotel in London. A doozy too. No way was he going to relay those details to anyone.

The horrific events in Raleigh's taxi couldn't be rationally explained, nor could their deadly aftermath in the emergency room in London where Raleigh died. The doctor didn't want to admit to finding the talon at all. Now Jon had to protect everyone involved: the Collinses, the medical staff, and himself. Those who encountered the magic hunched under a cone of silence, except for the driver of Raleigh's taxi. The man became hysterical when interviewed. His deposition was deemed useless. Jon found himself in the business of hiding evidence, not uncovering the facts, and his goal with this interview was to get back into the role he belonged in. Nash might lead him to the bigger fish.

And he knew just how to do it.

Brushing his hand across the top of his blond crew cut, Jon walked down the long, carpeted hall to the corner office. He knocked.

"Chief? I've got Nash Winthrop in the room. I need to talk with him."

"Who cares? Sit down! What the hell were you doing in London?" The chief wasn't one for niceties and drippy, feel-good exchanges. If one of those was ever offered, Jon would have shoved that hand-dipped truffle in the freezer for a private sugar fix.

"Sorry? You're referring to . . . ?" Jon stalled.

"Look at the expenses I have stacked here! Plane tickets, a fancy hotel, meals, London Underground pass, and nothing to show for it, except a pile of no answers and egg all over my damned face! Scotland Yard said you were being very cryptic about what happened to Raleigh Coulter over there. Yeah, that's the word they used—*cryptic*."

"I can't explain what happened to him. I'm as stumped as they were . . . and you are."

"Well, the driver of his cab wasn't stumped. He said a god-damned hawk was wreaking havoc in the backseat! And where is that couple"—the Chief snapped his fingers—"the Collinses? Yeah . . . Collins."

"They had nothing to do with this. They were in the cab with me, yes, but they were as shocked as I was." Jon's defensiveness churned to defiance. "I spoke with them at length."

"What the hell tore the guy to shreds then? Can you tell me?"

"I wasn't in Raleigh Coulter's cab. I didn't see a hawk when we found him. Right now, my focus is on wrapping up this insider case. I'm getting close. I can feel it."

"You don't *know*," the Chief sneered. "You *feel* it. Well, something tore him up. And I'm tearing myself up trying to cover your ass. If you don't figure this out, then I'm putting Brick on the case."

"Dan Brick? No. I don't have time to baby him. He'll bog me down. Like I said, I'll be meeting with the Collinses again soon. At least they're here in Portland," Jon hedged, trying to move the conversation in another direction. He never disclosed how close he had become with Jean and Spence. "Let me talk to this Nash Winthrop guy. I wanna find out if we have a bigger issue."

"Yeah, go. But I want answers, Jon—and I want them by the end of the week. I'm getting all kinds of pressure. What a flippin' mess . . . huge expenses, no explanations, and one of the suspects is dead."

"Gotcha." Jon blocked out the chief's words.

"Go get that twerp to sing. Get the hell outta here." The chief threw his silver pen down on the desk.

Nash Winthrop picked at the piece of dry skin hanging from his right thumb. He ripped the end off. Blood seeped around the cuticle bed, racing like toppling dominoes. His stomach sank when he thought about the call he'd made to Mayfield Investments and asked for Raleigh Coulter. Transferred immediately to human resources, he was told that Coulter had unfortunately passed away. Dead was more like it. What happened? No future payments would be forthcoming, but at least he wasn't around to dispute the story he was about to tell this yahoo of an FBI agent.

The sequence of events rolled through Nash's mind. How much had the FBI uncovered? He'd need to say that Coulter had found out about the merger from somebody else, not from him. He didn't tell Raleigh to short the VEY Steel stock. He only said there *might* be a merger coming soon and took the money for the tip. Anyone could see the earnings report was going to be down; no secret. Of course, if all had gone according to plan and the deal had gone through, Nash would have made a pretty penny. *I, myself, didn't buy or sell the stock.* Everybody talks to their friends and family about what goes on at work. Standard operating procedure. Hopefully, the FBI didn't know about the others. Maybe this was only about Raleigh.

Nash scanned the walls of the small room, three mostly bare white, except for a phone, and the fourth being a blackened window, a two-way mirror, no doubt. The rest, only a table and two chairs with a camera in each corner of the ceiling. No vending machine. No water. He ran his hand through his hair and turned his attention back to this thumb—this time pressing against the flow of blood and releasing, pressing and releasing. He could feel a headache creeping up his neck from the annoying fluorescent overhead light. The longer the silence loomed, the less sure he was his story would fly. This Jon Segert guy was letting him stew on purpose from behind that glass.

Behind the two-way mirror, Jon winced when Nash pulled the skin off his cuticle. Nash rubbed the back of his neck and then sucked on his thumb. The scene reminded him of a child seeking self-comfort after he gets caught. The body language told him everything.

Jon stood and walked out of the observation room. He nodded at the two officers standing outside the door.

"Stay out here—let me talk with him alone. I'll buzz when I'm done," he said, pointing to the wall phone in the hall. He stepped inside the interrogation room.

"Mr. Winthrop. Sorry for the wait." The door closed with a magnetic click. He sat across from Nash and stared at him. He instinctively fingered the talon through his right jacket pocket. He reached in his left one and set a pencil on top of a blank notepad. "My name is Agent Jon Segert, FBI here in Portland."

Nash Winthrop wore a black cashmere sport coat and a starched white cotton shirt. His dark hair, streaked with gray, was cut short in the back with wavy tufts on top. He was trying, unsuccessfully, to look younger and hip. He still looked every one of his fifty-some-thing years. And he used way too much hair gel. The smell made Jon a bit nauseated. Nash leaned back in his chair, scratched his right eyebrow, and shifted his brown eyes to the corner of the room.

Jon stood, stepped to the camera and gazed directly into the lens. "Give me a few minutes," he said into the microphone.

"But that's not—" the outside voice cut off as Jon flipped two switches: one for the camera and one for the microphone. He pulled out the chair and sat across from Nash.

"Nash Winthrop—that is your legal name, correct?"

"Yes. Why am I here?" Nash searched his finger for a mirac-ulous healing event. "Why did you turn that off?"

"We're going to have a little chat."

"Am I being arrested?"

"No, not unless you think you should be. For now, we're having a friendly conversation, which I hope will help our investigation. Off the record, okay?" Nash's shoulders lowered by a good three inches. His colleagues would be furious at his turning off the camera, and so would the chief when they marched into his office to report the breach of protocol. No doubt led by Dan Brick, mowing down the others to get in first.

"Okay, then. Off the record." Nash swept his hand toward Jon, mocking him. "What can I do to help?"

Jon outwardly ignored his tone but inwardly took note. "You were good friends with Raleigh Coulter, known him since college, right?" Jon's gaze bored a hole into Nash, square in the eyes.

Nash turned his head and scoffed at the question. "Yeah. Because I went to school with him doesn't mean I know anything."

Here we go. Covering defensiveness with sarcasm. "Can you write your full name for me?" Jon ripped a piece of paper from his blank notepad, placed it in front of Nash, and handed him the pencil. He wanted to establish whether he was right- or left-handed. The direc-tion of eye movements and body language would help him interpret Nash's answers.

Nash blew out a breath and wrote his name, right-handed. He gave the paper a shove across the table.

"How often did you talk with Raleigh Coulter?" Jon asked, stopping the page before it slid to the floor.

"Not often." Nash's gaze floated to his right.

Liar.

"A little more than that. You talked to Raleigh practically every day over the past eight weeks." Jon waited for Nash's reaction; his eyes shifted back to center. "You know Raleigh's dead, right?" He took the conversation up a notch. An angry Nash might say some-thing he didn't intend to reveal.

"I had nothing to do with that—nothing!" Nash turned up his own literal volume.

"He's dead partly because of you."

Silence.

Jon leaned back in his chair and crossed his legs. "We have recorded phone calls and e-mails to three investment managers that we know of—one being Raleigh Coulter—about your little inside tip of VEY Steel's pending merger. Corporate information is confidential. Appears we have a timing issue. Yes? No?"

"Hey, I want to get ahead like the next guy," Nash said, changing his tone to buddy-buddy and oversmiling. "Opportunity. What's wrong with that? This is a democracy, the American dream. I didn't sell any stock. I'm not a murderer. I don't beat my wife or kick dogs. Go after those guys."

"No, but you sold the information, Mr. Winthrop." As if connected to a slow drip, a dose of adrenaline coursed through Jon's veins. "That's illegal, not quite a recipe for a batch of American dreams. A lethal layer cake, maybe, with all the ingredients lined up in little cups like they do on the Food Channel. I like the Food Channel—I really do—but it's certainly not going to serve up anything fancy for you. Your version sticks a straw into peoples' bank accounts and sucks until they're gurgling backwash."

"I want my lawyer present for this conversation. You can't record my calls without my knowledge." Nash easily abandoned his buddy-buddy tone.

"Not if the contacts were made from the company's phone and e-mail system. Instant permission—so cut the crap. Answer the question."

"Somebody hijacked my phone and e-mail, pretending to be me." Nash shook his head. "Not me. No, not me."

"You expect me to buy that? Your voice was on the recording. All those little quavers match up like a thumb print—your bloody, disgusting thumb print." *Try it. See what happens.* "Do you believe in the supernatural, Mr. Winthrop?"

Nash stayed quiet. Jon met his gaze and reached in his pocket. He pulled out the talon and tossed it on the small conference table. The clatter echoed around the room as if he'd thrown down the forged brass key to a rusty, dank jail cell. The three-inch claw was thick, heavy, and lethal.

"Meet Horus. If you're not a believer, you're about to be," Jon said, rubbing his chin and trying not to grin.

"What the—?" Nash's eyes widened.

"Frightened? Curious? You should be. This was pulled out of Raleigh's leg in London. He bled to death, Nash." Jon kept his voice smooth.

"Did you kill Raleigh with that?" Nash asked, abandoning his fake resolve.

"No, I didn't kill Raleigh with this. The hawk attached to it did."

"C'mon! What hawk?"

"Maybe he's right here. Could show up at any time."

"You're trying to freak me out."

"Maybe—maybe not. You decide." Jon picked up the talon from the table.

"Screw you! I don't need to put up with this." Nash leaned forward to stand up but stopped.

Jon dragged the curved talon across the palm of his left hand. The point sunk deep in his flesh, opening the skin with the precision of a scalpel. No blood, only the splayed muscle and tendons on full display. No pain. He extended his hand and showed the wound to Nash. The gash slowly sealed, fully repairing itself within thirty seconds. *The magic is awakened.*

They each stayed quiet. Nash stared. Jon swallowed his elation. The talon had cut him when he reached in his pocket back in London after he talked with the Collinses in their hotel room. His skin repaired itself right in front of his eyes. His gut told him this talon would protect him and extract the truth. Its magic was real.

Jon smirked at Nash and made a deliberate show of setting the talon back on the conference table. He stared, willing it to move. It began to vibrate. A clackity rattle. Scaly skin emerged around the talon's thick end. Jon tried to slow the rate of his own breath, just as he'd been trained—he'd never been trained for this. Nash stared, wild-eyed, as the talon transformed.

"Believe me now, Nash?" he said, his words measured. "How much did they pay you for the information? Better tell me—quick."

Small black feathers popped from the leg.

Nash started to shake. "F-Five . . . thousand . . ."

"Each time? Five thousand each time you gave him information?"

"Yeah."

More claws forming.

"Who else? Names—I want names! How many?"

"Two . . . two."

Claws scratching.

"Names—now!"

"Anthony Dromov . . . Kip Forrester . . ."

"You're going down, pal."

The flesh and feathers disappeared, leaving only the talon sitting motionless in front of him. Jon dropped it in his pocket. He stood, walked to the wall phone, and hit two numbers.

"Got it out of him. Read him his rights and get him out of here."

Jon whipped his head around when Nash wretched. He had

vomited all over his cashmere jacket. The two officers stepped in to take Nash into custody. As they walked him down the hall, Nash vomited again and the officers jumped. Jon stepped around the mess and turned right to the chief's office. He stuck his head in the doorway.

"Done—confession," Jon said. "I'm going after an Anthony Dromov and a Kip Forrester."

"How'd you get him to talk so fast?"

"Wasn't too hard."

"Well, I guess we won't know, will we? *Somebody* turned off the video camera *and* the sound. None of this will stick to that little prick. Big, fat waste of everyone's time. The guy's going to get off because you didn't use proper procedure."

"I don't care about Nash. I got an early Christmas present—two names. Besides, the guy's crazier than a loon. He went all freaky about a hawk being in the room. Can you believe that?" Jon traced the toe of his wingtip over the raised squares of the carpet to avoid making eye contact.

"That's a new one. These 'toons will stop at nothing when they're caught." The chief waved him out of the office.

"I know, right?"

"And don't let me hear about you playing Maytag repairman with that camera again. I should write you up for that stunt."

Jon made a talk-to-the-hand gesture and walked back to his office, pondering his next move.

CHAPTER 5

Visions of Sugar Plums

Like a kid's, Spence's eyes flew open at five o'clock on Christmas morning. The early hour was magical at any time of year, but on Christmas, the first few minutes were hard to beat. One consolation prize for not having kids was Christmas morning. Nobody grumbled about him and Jean getting up too early or too late. They didn't have to be wise or behave like adults. They were kids for eternity.

"It's snowing outside. There must be two inches on the bal-cony," he whispered and pointed to the opening in the drapes. Jean's eyes opened wide with amazement.

"Merry Christmas," Jean whispered, turning from the window. "Open the curtains all the way."

Spence pulled back the comforter, stepped to the sliding glass door, and turned on the floodlight outside. He opened the drape and jumped back under the covers. Mycroft scowled at the jostling and tucked his head in his paws.

"That's a wow, am I right?"

"Yeah. Beautiful," Jean stretched her arms and yawned.

The fat flakes raced down like shooting stars. As if Jean knew what he was thinking, she said, "What if each flake was a wish, Spence?"

"Then we have a lot to do. Let's get up!"

"Okay, okay, don't bother Mycroft. He's not ready."

As he dressed, Spence laughed at Jean pulling her sweatpants from a pile of clothes on the side chair. When she missed a leg hole, she fell across the bed. Her hair reached out in fifty directions. Mycroft lifted his head, annoyed at her less-than-mature antics. Spence loved that she could be as tough as nails one moment and then as silly as a teenager the next, even at the ripe age of fifty-two.

"Look, Mycroft," he said, pointing out the window. The cat raised his eyes at both of them, stretched, and went back to sleep. "Nice hair, dear. I think you've finally achieved true pouf."

"C'mon, let's go down. I'll turn on the tree."

Jean's hair provided directional assistance.

Jean pulled on her hooded sweatshirt and paused on the upstairs catwalk. She reached out her hand and brushed the soft tail feather of the clip-on bird on the top of the Christmas tree in the stairwell. Her steps wrapped around it as she descended to the kitchen.

The switch on the power strip illuminated the twelve-foot noble fir. The tree glowed as a narrow tower of white lights and threw the whole downstairs under a soft, ghostly aura. A sweet piney aroma, still fresh, filled every breath. The ornaments she and Spence had collected over their thirty-two years together were cradled in the lit branches, all the way to the ceiling. Her gaze stopped on the large gold ball decorated with Picasso's abstract images, hand painted in shiny black, red, and yellow, and her mind wandered to its origins. *San Francisco . . . 1984 . . . Gump's . . . Right after the Irish coffees in that old pub. Union Square teeming with shoppers . . . Cold wind blowing a damp fog . . . The Christmas in their first house in Redwood City, California. Their private brand of magic.*

Spence slid open the drapes on all three expansive windows in the living room and stood at the center one to marvel at the view. "Honey, c'mere." The backyard was blanketed in white, and the air fuzzy. "Isn't it fantastic?"

"So quiet," she said, as if her voice would break the spell. "Let's go outside and listen."

"Wait . . . Jazz is here. Get his peanuts."

Jean turned her attention from the tree and tiptoed to the floor-to-ceiling window. Their favorite squirrel stood on his hind legs swishing his tiny wet paws against the glass. The little fellow had such a Broadway personality. He was a show-off.

She bent down and tapped. "Hi, Jazz Hands! No wet paws!" Small chunks of snow melted and slid to the bottom of the window. Still in her slippers, she pulled up the hood of her sweatshirt and grabbed the bag of peanuts by the sliding door in the den. She stepped outside and threw a handful of nuts into the air. They sunk in the snow as if she'd tossed out a fistful of dice. Jazz Hands ran over, snatched one, and motored his tiny, razor-like teeth through the shell.

The backyard looked soft and energized. The long branches of the eighty-foot fir tree at the edge of the patio were laden with droopy blankets of white. The air, quiet and insulated, shushed the intrusion.

The snow flew in Portland little enough to make it special, and having a white Christmas was an especially rare event. When a winter storm did reach the valley floor, the city shut down, out of not only safety but awe. Jean stepped back inside and shook off her slippers. She left them by the door and padded to the kitchen in her stocking feet.

"I'll make the coffee."

"I'll light the fire. You should go out and get the paper," Spence said. She caught the slight smile on his face before he turned his back.

"Me? It's freezing outside, and I don't know where my boots are." *Something is up.*

"C'mon. I need coffee first. It'll only take a minute, and then you can warm up."

Suspicious, Jean grabbed her fleece jacket from the mudroom wall hook and slipped her feet into her rubber gardening shoes. She opened the front door and took a step outside. She gasped and stepped back into the entryway. The brass sleigh bell, looped over the handle, gave off a lingering jingle. "What did you do? I can't believe it!"

"You like your Bird?" Spence's wide grin nearly reached around and patted him on the back.

"Isn't that *your* Bird?"

"Yours now."

"C'mon, let's go for a ride," she said, running her hand through her wild hair.

The coffee pot gave off its last burp of steam and, in response, Spence dashed to the kitchen. "Hold on—still dark outside. Take a look and get the paper since you already have your shoes on. We can go after it warms up a bit. Plus, don't I have a present underneath that tree to open?" He handed her a steaming mug. "Here, calm down and take this with you."

Trying not to slip and spill the hot coffee, Jean stepped toward the aqua T-Bird in the driveway. The car waited for her under a smooth pile of white. She swept her hand over the newly-restored back fin, the snow sailing in a rooster tail. The car's red-nosed tail lights reminded her of pump-up water rockets she used to shoot off in the yard when she was child. She took a sip of her coffee, wishing it were hot chocolate. Her wet hand numbed as she picked up the paper, shook off the ice chips, and stepped back into the house.

"Incredible! Absolutely incredible! I'm not sure my gift can top that," she said, kicking off her shoes at the front door. She bounced to the living room.

"Neither one of us needs to top anything. The past few months took care of that." Spence turned the gas crank in the wall and held the long match under the logs. The flames caught and gave him a welcoming Queen Mum wave. "Let me get some tunes."

Jean waited, her knee jiggling in anticipation as Spence raced to the den and dug through the separate Christmas album section in the end cabinet. That was one of Spence's vinyl organization rules: Christmas music wasn't allowed to fraternize with any type of rock music, and neither were her albums from Broadway shows she'd worked on. If they were filed all together, then it was the equivalent of genetically altered corn. Who knows what could result from the cross-contamination of music cooties—Jimi Hendrix dressed as Santa Claus in a Radio City kick line? She smiled at the thought.

They had agreed to exchange only one present each, since they already had too much stuff. But this one would push at least two of Spence's collector buttons: a vintage book, and written by one of his favorite authors. Plus, this particular one might have a little magic inside, just like Christmas morning.

Spence came out of the den with three albums and slipped one of them on the turntable. She had no idea what was going to come out of the speakers—she never did, and that was one of the many joys of living with Spence. Little surprises. He plopped down on one of the leather chairs.

"Here, this one's from me . . . and Mary and Jim," she said, biting her lip. "I think you're going to love this . . . I hope as much as I love mine."

The electric-blue satin ribbon floated to the floor. Spence poked at the indentation on the silver-foiled paper, making a production of taking his time. He pulled back the wrapping and froze.

Jean sprung from the loveseat and knelt in front of him. "This is the 1930 first edition of *The Maltese Falcon*. Nearly perfect condition. I guarantee it's worth more than what I paid for it—*a lot* more."

"This is incredible," Spence murmured, still stunned.

"I can't believe you, of all people, never read this."

"I blew through *The Thin Man* and then moved on to Dickens and Jules Verne. I never went back to read this one."

The image of a black falcon loomed against the original goldenrod cover, next to a woman's elegant hand holding a dangling necklace and gold coins. Spence ran his fingers over the image. The spine crackled when he exposed the book's center pages. He sniffed the aged paper. Jean knew he loved the smell of an old book . . . and brand-new leather shoes. The shopping ritual was a bit embarrassing. Loafers, especially, had to have a special aroma before he would try them on. He was an olfactory man.

"This belonged to Mary? Where did you find it?" Spence trailed his forefinger down the spine. "There weren't any books in the boxes of Mary's things when we picked them up from Milwaukie Manor."

"I bought this from Jim Coulter's collection at the estate sale when I got the chest."

"No way! You've been hiding it all this time?" Spence's eyes went wide as he set his fingers on the inner pages. "It's happening again. Put your hand—right here, next to mine."

Jean set her hand on the book. "Do you think we'll experience the same thing?"

"I don't know . . . maybe."

"Shhh . . . There's Mary—I hear Jim's voice."

"Me too."

"Doesn't get any better than Sam Spade," Jim Coulter said, running his hand over the cover of *The Maltese Falcon*.

"I hoped you'd like it." Mary beamed as she looped the thread through the linen of her embroidery hoop. "If you weren't a lumberman, honey, you'd have been a private eye."

"That would be the life. Snooping around, chasing bad guys . . . yeah . . . and going after beautiful dames like you." He used his best imitation of Sam Spade's voice.

"Sounds dangerous."

"Adventure, Mary—no limit. Everything being perfect can be downright boring. Danger keeps us man animals alert for prey."

"Woof!" Mary quipped.

Jim laughed and opened the book. He took a whiff of the binding. "Mmm . . . I love the scent of a first-rate mystery. This one's good."

Jean raised her eyes to Spence, their hands still on the pages. She moved her fingers to be on top of his.

"Did you see and hear the same thing?" Jean shook her mind clear.

"Jim getting this book?" Spence said, meeting her gaze.

"Yeah—the same. What do you have spinning?"

"My head." Spence blew out a breath.

"No—what album do you have on the turntable?"

"This is *New Wave Xmas*, 'Mary Xmess' by Sun 60. Takes you back, huh? Honey—Jim Coulter smelled the book . . . just like I did. Isn't that weird?"

"Yes . . . too weird. I think you should put on Dean Martin. How about 'A Marshmallow World'?"

"You were supposed to buy this book, like it was prearranged or something." Spence's tone wavered between appreciation and pre-monition.

"And you know what's even weirder? Danger is exactly what Jim Coulter got." Jean used Spence's knees to push herself upright and waited for his next words.

"Don't borrow trouble, you. I'm gonna get me some bad guys, sweetheart." Spence made his voice sound like Jim Coulter's imita-tion of Sam Spade. "This book is going to bed with me tonight."

"Woof! This pup is going to bed with you tonight too, if Mycroft would quit hogging!" Jean laughed, but their shared vision left her more than a little unsettled.

As Jean stepped to the kitchen to make some breakfast, she heard Spence start to laugh. "You have *got* to love this. The first page is a kick . . . Miss Wonderly."

"Don't get too engrossed. Bill and Linda will be here at three for dinner. And remember, by the way, we're going for a ride in the Bird."

Silence. Spence was already chasing bad guys.

"Let's go, Spence! The sun's out." Jean stood in the entryway after breakfast, bundled in her coat, gloves, and boots. "You can read your book when we come back. I have to start dinner in an hour, anyway."

"Coming. Let me get my jacket." Spence pulled on his sheepskin boots. He grabbed the small dust broom from under the kitchen sink. "We need to brush the snow off the car. You okay driving?"

"Sweetheart, we lived in Minneapolis for four years. I think I can handle a little snow." She pulled the small key from her coat pocket. "I'm going in. Meet you inside." Jean knew Spence wouldn't be ready until every snowflake had been removed. The heavy door opened with a groan. The metal-meeting-metal clank of shutting a vintage car door was as comforting as the quiet *phoomph* of a modern one.

Jean's gaze cruised around the dash. *This is the coolest car ever.* She took off her gloves and ran her hand over the steering wheel. Her fingertips prickled with electricity. The tingle became a *whoosh.* She closed her eyes and took a deep breath as the vision sparkled in perfect clarity.

Mary Coulter put the T-Bird into reverse. Two iron poles supported the thirty-foot sign for the Fred Meyer grocery store. With her eyes trained on the poles she didn't notice the shopping cart behind the car. When she did, she gasped and tried to slam on the brakes but hit the gas instead. The car rammed the shopping cart into the post.

"Oh no, no-no. I didn't do this. It's not possible," she whimpered. Defeated, Mary shook her head with her hands over he eyes, envisioning the damage. The perfect Bird was now injured.

Tears welled when she checked the rearview mirror; the shop-ping cart had indeed flown up and dented the back right fin. It was smashed between the car and the post. Fighting a wave of dizziness, Mary forced herself to get out of the car.

"I'm so sorry. My fault . . . my fault," Mary moaned, petting the dent. The horn blast from an enormous SUV startled her. The T-Bird blocked the lane in the parking lot. Mary turned and waved.

"C'mon lady! You shouldn't be driving when you're that damn old!" The large woman hung her arm out the window and tapped the ash from her cigarette.

Mary's heart sank. Maybe that horrible woman was right. But sitting behind the wheel meant freedom, independence, and the ability to make her world seem bigger than it really was.

"C'mon baby. Let's go home." Mary patted the trunk and got back into the car. She turned the key. "I'm so sorry, Jim. Not per-fect."

As Mary pulled away, the bent cart released from the post. It rolled through the parking lot and banged into the driver's side door of a Mercedes.

Jean turned to Spence when he sat in the passenger seat, her eyes watered with tears.

"What? You don't like the car?" Spence said, alarmed.

"I love it, but—" She swallowed her words. "I just saw a vision of Mary."

"It seems this car is full of them. Here." Spence opened the glove compartment and pulled out a pair of aqua-colored, kidskin driving gloves. "Put these on. Maybe they'll help. I thought they'd look hot with that scarf you got in Cairo and those big black sun-glasses."

"Let's go." Jean took a deep breath, slid on the gloves, and put the T-Bird in reverse. The car lurched, spinning the wheels on the ice when she hit the gas a little too hard.

CHAPTER 6

It's Time to Spill

Bill and Linda Flannery arrived with all the Christmas fanfare of Mr. and Mrs. Claus. Six-foot five, bearded, and full of smiles, Bill even looked like Santa. Not having spent thirty years on the railroad, though, Santa's knees weren't as bad as Bill's.

"Come in, come in," Spence said. "The fire's going and Jean's got dinner almost ready."

"Smells fabulous!" Linda slipped off her wool coat and nosed the air.

"Hi, Croft Man." Bill gravitated toward Mycroft by the fire. He leaned way down to softly stroke Mycroft's head. The cat stretched on his side and lifted his front paw to entice Bill to tickle his armpit.

"He'll take all he can get, especially from you guys." Spence said, following Bill to the living room. "So, let's talk about the store."

"Oh, right. Planning meeting. You're the inventory guy, buddy." Bill continued to pet Mycroft. "I'll squeeze 'em to get a good price."

"Okay, smooth talker. I find out who is selling; you make sure we're buying."

"I'll do the deal; you write the check." Bill chuckled. "This is a good guy-bad guy kind of thing. Meeting is over."

"Let's eat." After years of dealing with academics, Spence wasn't used to easy decisions. Plans needed to be hashed and rehashed, preferably with a committee or two attached. "We're good on the name of the store? And the Main Street location works across from Casa de Tamales?"

"Not Fade Away works for me, and downtown Milwaukie will be easy for both of us," Bill said. "Once the light rail is in, we're gol-den. I think you should ask your cat. He's got an opinion about everything." Mycroft lifted and dripped his head back over the side of the chair. "You can't beat we're near the best cook in Milwaukie."

"The tamale guy or Jean?"

"Toss up. Right now, Jean wins." Bill nodded toward the kit-chen.

"Spence? The meat's all rested. Can you slice?" Jean called out. He imagined her in full octopus mode—moving things around so quickly it'd seem as if she had six more arms.

"I think we've got a prime store, buddy." Bill abandoned Mycroft's ears and followed Spence to the dining room.

"Me too," Spence said, beaming. "We're about to have a prime rib too."

"Let's eat. Merry Christmas!" Jean said, pulling the Yorkshire pudding out of the hot oven.

Linda set the casserole dish of vegetables on a trivet and asked, "So where are you going again? You two have taken more trips in four months than Bill and I have over the past four years."

"We're going to Richmond for our anniversary. Can you guys watch Mycroft?"

"We'd be happy to. We love him to death."

"He might act weird, but don't worry," Jean hedged. Spence shot her a look and narrowed his eyes. He knew where she was going.

"What do you mean—acting weird?" Linda eyed her, suspicious.

Spence stayed quiet. Jean didn't.

"He's not sick or anything," Jean said. "He acts like he's seeing something and interacts with it. Weird. No big deal."

Linda narrowed her eyes. "What's up, Jean? What's with all the mystery? All cats hunt imaginary bugs and stuff."

Spence turned to Jean. "Are we going there, honey?"

Jean searched his eyes for confirmation. "Yeah, it's time."

He scratched his nose and took a sip of wine. "Quite a bit is up, actually."

Jean picked up his cue and kept going. "We need to fill you in on what's happened to us over the past couple of months. We haven't been doing all this traveling without good reason. We feel bad not telling you, but we had no idea what we were dealing with until we got back from Cairo."

Linda glanced at Bill, satisfied. "Well, here we go. Let's have it."

Jean swept her hand at Spence. "You can do the honors, dear."

"We're still trying to figure it out. Do you guys . . . believe in magic?" he asked, taking a breath after he released the words.

"Let's eat while we talk!" Jean pronounced, raising her glass. "Merry Christmas, everyone! This is a magical time of year—and about to be a magical conversation. Bill needs gravy for this."

For over an hour, Bill and Linda were quiet as Jean and Spence went through all the events since Jean bought the chest from Mary Coulter's estate sale in September. They left nothing out: finding the fabric and its transformation into a hawk; Raleigh Coulter's horrific death in the London taxi; the fabric's properties and using it to help Mary pass into immortality; their discovery in the tomb of Nefertari; the magical experiences that had crept into their daily lives; and their relationship with Jon Segert at the FBI.

"Jon kept the hawk's talon. We don't know what he's going to do with it," Spence added.

"So," Jean said, slapping her napkin down. "That's what's been going on."

"Bill, we have to go to more estate sales." Linda shook her head. "Wow, I don't know what to say. I have so many questions."

"We do too," Spence agreed, his blood pressure returning to normal.

Bill clinked down his fork and turned to Spence. "Well, buddy, you can wave your magic wand and we'll make a million bucks on the store. Outstanding!"

"Bill, stop! This is a big deal," Linda reproved and wiped her mouth. "You guys are completely serious, aren't you?" She tucked her long brown hair behind her ear and adjusted the top of her peas-ant blouse. "I remember taking this metaphysical class in California, back in the early seventies. I totally believe in the possibility of an altered reality."

"Uh . . . Linda? You were the one in an altered state of reality when you took that class," Bill quipped.

"Possible. But I prefer to think of it as a higher state of consciousness."

"Every word is true," Jean continued. "Everything we just told you really did happen. I know this is weird. You just have to experience it for yourself."

"Okay, show us some magic," Bill said with a chuckle of sar-casm.

"I can't. Neither can Spence." Jean made a swirly pattern in her mashed potatoes.

"She's right. Things just happen. We don't *make* them happen; at least I don't think we do. We're learning as we go. Since helping Mary into immortality, most are related to the things we inherited from her: the car, a book, and Mary's house. But I'm not sure if her stuff is magic, or if something lingers inside us."

"Spence and I both experienced the transformation. Electricity goes up and down your arms." Jean shook her fork at the air. "And when the phoenixes in the fabric came alive . . . amazing. They're so incredibly beautiful."

"This is a lot to absorb," Linda took a gulp of her wine.

"I, for one, think it's cool," Bill said. "Can you can make Mycroft move from in front of the fireplace? Now *that* would be magic." He drowned what was left on his plate in gravy. "After dinner, I'm going to sit by the fire with him. That seems a lot saner."

CHAPTER 7

The Magic of the Old Gaines House

Jean pulled back one side of her blond pageboy with Mary's sparkly hummingbird hair comb, her fingers tingling as she did so, though no vision appeared. The diamonds on the delicate wings radiated a rainbow of colors as she admired the bird in the mirror; a little piece of Mary's spirit twinkling in her hair.

With their anniversary on her mind, Jean imagined each sparkle was a year in her and Spence's life together. The comb was her favorite treasure, besides the Thunderbird, they had inherited from Mary Coulter. Doc, Mary's adopted father, gave the heirloom to her on her wedding day in 1945. Mary told her the story, along with many of her other life experiences, before she passed into immortality. Mary had worn the comb in her hair for decades. Jean, too, would never tire of wearing it.

"Jean! We gotta go," Spence called out from the entryway.

"Coming!" She bounced down the stairs and turned to show Spence the comb. "I'm ready. What do you think?"

"I'm glad your hair isn't long enough to pull up in a twist. Then you'd have me worried." Spence held her coat out as she slipped her arms in the sleeves. "C'mon. The bags are in the Mini Cooper. I don't want to take the T-Bird to the airport."

Jean followed Spence to the garage. The door rolled up as she pressed the button by the stairs.

"Look—there's a van in front of the house," she said. "A different news station—there are antennae on top. They're staking us out."

"When we back out of the garage, don't roll down the windows—for anything. Get in the car. Quick!"

A man got out of the van and ran up the driveway as Spence backed out. A gloved hand knocked on the window.

"Ignore him," Spence warned. "Did you pull all the drapes in every room?"

"I'm trying and I did." She rolled down the window and shouted, "Leave us alone! We have nothing to say to you!" and then hit the switch. It rolled up on the reporter's words

"Jean, don't!"

"Go! Go!"

Spence scowled and squealed the tires of the Mini Cooper as he pulled out of the driveway and gunned the car toward River Road. "Too close."

"Jon said the publicity would calm down. I hope so."

"You know what?" Spence reached out his hand and fluffed the back of her hair.

"What?" She blew out a breath.

"I think Bill and Linda are going to sit and stare at Mycroft until we get home."

"Linda told me she's looking forward to something happening." Jean's mood brightened. The burning image of the reporter cooled and faded away.

Jean dug around for a CD as they drove down River Road. "I'm looking forward to this trip." She pressed the button on the player. The speakers awakened with David Bowie's distinctive cry of triumph and pain as he sang "Heroes."

"Heroes for only *one* day, Mrs. Collins?" Spence smiled and glanced into the rearview mirror to see if anyone was following them.

"More than one day. Hey, who did you say we were when you made the reservation?" They had planned to arrive at their inherited bed-and-breakfast under assumed names, not wanting to upset the innkeepers. This trip would be their introduction to Janet and Doug Parson, the couple who leased the property and ran the inn.

"Patti and Mick Richards."

She rolled her eyes. "Oh, you didn't."

"I did."

Only Spence could come up with an alias of Keith Richards's wife . . . and Mick?

Even in the barren state of winter, the Richmond neighborhood released its preserved history block after block. As confederate soldiers were recovering from their injuries, both mental and phy-sical, these magnificent homes were teeming with craftsmen re-building.

"The sign—on the corner! Just like the pictures," Jean said, shifting in her seat and already unbuckling her seatbelt.

Spence stopped the rental car in front of the three-story white Victorian with a columned, wraparound porch. The oval sign, shiny with fresh paint, swung freely from two black chains: *The Gaines House, Bed-and-Breakfast, 1881.* The setting sun glinted off the reflec-tive scrolled letters.

The expansive, hand-carved oak front door was welcoming, with its etched, oval glass revealing only a glimpse of what was inside. Jean waited for Spence on the porch with her duffel bag. Ever since abandoning him to schlep their bags at the Cairo Museum, she made a point of carrying her own.

"Let's be us . . . just us, okay?" she said as Spence came up the steps and joined her at the door. "We have enough drama without creating more."

"I thought the ruse would be fun."

"It was—all the way here. But now, standing at the door, pretending doesn't seem right." She peered through the prism edge of the oval glass before stepping inside. A quick scan of the downstairs confirmed everything Mary had told them about the house when they sat on her patio. The details almost seemed familiar. A few of Mary's narrative descriptions jumped out at her: the arched window in the parlor; the rich, fruity scent of wood and lemon oil polish; and the welcoming warmth of the blazing fire. The crafts-manship of the carved moldings, sculpted medallions in the ceiling, and gleaming wood floors could only be appreciated if seen in person.

Jean turned to join Spence at the kidney-shaped Victorian desk at the base of the stairs. A tall woman, with a bounce in her step, came down the hall.

"You must be Patti and Mick Richards! Welcome, welcome, to Gaines House. I'm Janet Parson. My husband, Doug, and I run the inn. He's here somewhere, off doing something that'll make me step up the wrinkle cream."

Janet Parson was in her late fifties, fresh-faced and freckled, with a pixie cut of fine strawberry-blond hair. Her friendly, exuberant smile lit up the room. The pretentious fussiness of some B&Bs was conspicuously absent. Jean couldn't think of anyone better suited to run an inn.

"Not really us," Spence said as he handed her his credit card and driver's license. "We didn't want to mess with your routine."

Janet took the plasticized card and examined it. "Collins? Are you the new owners of the house?" She turned as heavy steps clunked and a door opened. "Oh hey, Doug, guess who's here?"

A middle-aged man, tall and slim, strolled down the hall with a wrench in his hand. Jean thought he was Pete Townsend's twin of the Who, only clean-shaven and with wire-rimmed glasses. She would bet money he and Spence would become kindred spirits.

"Doug, come meet the Collinses—or should I say Patti and Mick Richards?" Janet said with a sly smile. "Doug's a Stones fan."

"Yep, sounded a bit 'spicious. What'd I say, Jan? Hi, I'm Doug Parson. Damn good to meet 'ya." He plunked the wrench on the desk and shook Spence's hand.

"Not there!" Janet scolded and picked up the wrench. She shook it at Doug. "Did you get the pressure up on the heater?"

Doug grimaced. "Hot water heat. Love it or hate it. Contraption in the basement is like something out of *The Twilight Zone*." He leaned toward Jean and whispered, "Don't go down there, it'll git 'ya."

"Do I sense a new furnace coming on?" Spence said, laughing.

"Not yet. A few winters left in her, I think, but if you get cold open up the valve on the radiator in your room. Doesn't work, then give it few whacks."

"Well, I'm thrilled you're both here. We've all been anxious to meet you," Janet said, waving them toward the stairs. "C'mon, I'll show you your room."

All? Jean tried to catch Spence's eye, but he'd completely missed the subtle word.

"We're not here to spy on you or anything. Just think of us as any other guests." Spence picked up his duffel bag and winked at her to do the same.

"And we don't want to change a thing," Jean added, looking around the immaculate and tastefully decorated parlor and dining room. "Just keep doing what you do. We're happy the place is so well cared for. I can already tell you love being here."

"We have one other couple staying with us this weekend—the Moores, Andy and Denise. They're ghost hunters," Janet said, widening her eyes and pressing her lips together. "Ever since the article came out, they've been coming out of the woodwork, but the week between Christmas and New Year's is usually pretty quiet."

"What article?" Spence said, catching Jean's eye.

"The one in *Bed-and-Breakfast Magazine* two weeks ago. A copy is on the coffee table. Don't worry, they're friendly."

"Janet? Is that the original bird bath in the garden outside the parlor window?" *The phoenixes appeared for Wiley.* She remembered Mary telling the story of her adopted family's beloved dog being released into immortality, as passed down to her from Birdie. She nudged Spence. His face fell as he made the connection too. They followed Janet up the graceful staircase. Jean ran her hand along the smooth mahogany banister, supporting the balustrades with their hand-carved vine relief.

"Oh, nothing has been touched. We maintain the house pretty well and used to send the bills for any major repairs to Mary. I guess we'll be sending them to you, now." Janet stood in the first doorway and extended her arm. "I'm so glad I put you in Birdie's room. Used to be Doc and Charlotte's, but Birdie was in here for years after Doc passed away. It's the biggest and prettiest bedroom."

Jean breathed deep as she stepped inside. Magic in this room; she could tell Spence sensed the change too. The fabric had trans-formed four lives here. The carved four-poster bed was covered with a thick bedspread of deep-green vines swirling on a soft cream background. Brightly colored embroidered birds—robins, cardinals, woodpeckers, and geese—flocked across decorative pillows. The wallpaper matched the bedspread. An antique rocking chair, with a wicker seat and back, sat at an angle in front of the bay window with a built-in upholstered bench.

Spence gave Janet a sly, conspiratorial smile. "We have an old chest that belonged to Mary. But I think it belongs here. Do you want us to send it back?" he said, pointing to the foot of the bed.

"Oh, I couldn't ask you to do that," Janet said, sounding like she'd wanted to have the chest there.

"No problem. We'll just put the chest on a truck and roll it right on back." His chest puffed with a triumphant expansion.

Jean's eyes teased at him and then they rose to the small painting over the bed. She froze, transfixed by its lifelike quality. *This must be the painting Mary talked about.* The painting, maybe only eight by ten inches, was charged with emotion. The ornate gilt frame added six inches on all sides. A young boy—maybe nine or ten years of age—in suspendered knickers seemed to jump off the canvas in an exuberant dance. His waistcoat conveyed the texture of real velvet. The boy had one bare foot suspended, frozen in space, and the fingers of his right hand were poised in mid-snap. She could almost hear the lute playing behind the trees in the woods. The light and shadow of the boy's face made him positively angelic. The technique was exquisite.

"That painting is lovely," she said, still staring. "Mary mentioned to me she'd wished she'd brought it home to Portland after Birdie passed." Jean waited a beat after Jan uttered the word *passed.*

"Did she really? She never mentioned anything to me. It's been here for 130 years. Wonderful work and quite charming. Who can resist such a lovely dancing boy? But if you're smitten—and the painting is yours, after all—let's consider a trade out for the chest. We need the storage for extra blankets." As Janet closed the bed-room door, she said, "Dinner's at six. Come down at five or so and have a glass of wine in the parlor. You'll have company."

Jean darted her gaze to Spence. "She *knows.*"

"No, I think she meant that couple, the Moores." Spence didn't sound convinced.

"Smells like a fine meal down here," Spence said as he stepped into the parlor before dinner.

Janet handed him a glass of red wine. "Hunter's Chicken—chicken medallions with fresh mushrooms in homemade sauce. Yummy. Served with grits. Gotta love Birdie's recipes. Be ready in half an hour. Where's Jean?"

"She's foofing upstairs. She'll be down any minute."

"I'll leave the bottle and a glass for her on the coffee table. Back to the kitchen for me," Janet said, making a beeline down the hall.

A young, professional-looking couple was firmly ensconced on the couch in front of the fireplace. They had to be in their late-twenties; the woman's fingers flew over the miniature keyboard on her phone. *Texting.* She took the time to fling her long brown hair back, but didn't even raise her eyes when he came into the room.

"Hello, I'm Spence Collins." He sat in one of the overstuffed chairs flanking the fireplace.

"I'm Andy Moore, and this is my wife, Denise," the young man said. "Pleasure." He turned his curly, red-haired head and sea of freckles back to the arched window.

"We have to be quiet. It's going to happen soon," Denise whispered. Without taking her eyes off her phone, she wiggled her hand and pointed to the tall, arched window offering a view of the garden. "I'm supposed to tell my friend back home when it happens."

"I'm sorry?" Spence said, confused and trying not to reveal the shock on his face.

"Aren't you a ghost hunter? This place is supposed to be rockin'," Andy said with an in-the-know nod. "Didn't you read the review from Susan Kent? Her article came out about this inn two weeks ago. We couldn't wait to get here."

"Hi, I'm Jean, Spence's wife," Jean announced as she stepped through the doorway, smoothing the collar of her cream-colored turtleneck sweater. She poured a glass of wine from the bottle on the coffee table. "Who's a ghost hunter?"

"We all are now," Denise said. "We're waiting for 'the show,' as Susan Kent says in her review."

"Who's Susan Kent?" Jean glanced at Spence.

He raised a finger to his lips. "Honey, this is Andy and Denise Moore."

"Nice to meet you." Jean tipped her glass toward them and took a sip. "Mmm . . . nice. Momma needed that."

Spence realized their private magical weekend wasn't going to be so private. An oil spill was seeping into a delicate ecosystem. Containment could be a challenge.

"Susan Kent's a travel writer who wrote a review of this inn in *Bed-and-Breakfast Magazine*." Denise pointed to the coffee table. "She witnessed real-life ghosts in the garden—right out there—about this time in the evening."

"Did she now?" Jean smirked. "Do you believe in ghosts?"

"We'd like to," Andy replied. "The thought is intriguing, but we've never seen one. We make a goal of staying at inns that are pur-ported to have ghosts."

"We stayed at one once—" Denise gasped and pointed to the window. "Look. Shhh . . ."

"Jean, C'mere." Spence stood and stepped to the window.

Jean peered around the edge of the fireplace. "Well, there they are," she whispered.

The group appearing before them resembled the sepia tone photos Mary had shared with him and Jean. Doc emerged first, followed by Charlotte in a wispy blue dress. They both appeared to be in their early sixties, just as in their pictures. Their movements left faint white trails. Wiley materialized in mid-leap, running circles around them, his tail blurred with sparkles. Even though the tem-perature outside was in the thirties, the group wore lightweight cloth-ing more appropriate for spring.

The Moores joined them at the window. "Unbelievable! Denise, get your phone. Take a picture," Andy said, snapping his fingers.

"No, don't!" Spence held out his hand to Denise. He wasn't ready to have what they knew documented by strangers. Recovering from his knee-jerk reaction, he ran his fingers through his hair. "This is one of those moments. A picture can't do the experience justice."

Jean grasped his arm as if to say, *Thank you for saying that.*

Mary appeared behind Doc and Charlotte, just as Jean and Spence had first seen her in 1991 in her yard back in Portland, in her mid-sixties and wearing a calf-length wool skirt and hunting-style jacket. As she strolled beside the couple, Mary's movement, too, gave off a slight white trail. Spence could tell Jean wanted to do a shout-out to her but kept quiet.

"What a sweet little girl. Isn't she cute?" Denise whispered. "And that white dress is lovely—"

Spence whipped his head around to face Denise. Jean turned too, bewildered.

"Girl?" Spence said, wondering if this woman had slipped some-thing in her own wine.

"Yeah, a little girl in a white dress. She's holding a robin." Andy pointed out the window.

Spence stared at Jean. "Do you see a little girl?"

"No, only Mary as we remembered her from twenty years ago—

back in 1991."

"Huh. Me too."

The Moores gawked, confused. "You know those ghosts?"

"No, no—I mean—" His eyes pleaded to Jean for help.

"Uh . . . actually, we own this inn," Jean said, picking up his cue. "We're acquainted with the original family who built the house."

The Moores relaxed but still gave him and Jean a dubious eye. Andy appeared to be calculating the math of time. All four of them turned their heads back to the rippled, lead-glass panes.

The ghostly group moved away from the garden. Doc turned and threw a smirk at the window. He tipped his hat and gave them a slight bow of his head. Wiley jumped up on Mary's skirt, prompting Doc to clap his hands. As he did so, the group faded from view.

"Dinner's ready when you are. Have a seat in the dining room." Janet announced from the doorway.

"Awesome. That was totally awesome," Andy said, squeezing Denise's shoulders and guiding her to the dining room. "Honey, wasn't that awesome?"

Denise snatched her phone from the couch and started texting as she stepped out of the parlor. "Tomorrow we're getting a picture," she said, wrinkling her nose at Spence.

When Denise turned her back, Jean stuck out her tongue.

After dinner, Jean followed Spence up the stairs to their room. Witnessing, and subsequently discussing, such a special moment with two strangers was plain weird. Throughout the meal, they'd listened to all of the Moore's theories about spirits and paranormal activity, trying to be patient. She was ready to burst at the seams, itching to open up about the Gaines family. Instead, she and Spence offered benign historic details and superficial descriptions of who was who. She'd made a promise to Spence to stay quiet about the fabric and their involvement in Mary's immortality. And the last thing they needed was any more attention from anyone in the media.

The radiator clunked and groaned when Jean turned the valve and crawled into the four-poster bed next to Spence. The sheets, clean and soft, had the fresh scent of hanging on the line outside all afternoon in the crisp air and bright sunshine.

"Tomorrow's thirty-three years," she whispered, turning out the Victorian glass bubbled lamp on the nightstand. The room was thrown in a ghostly glow from the moon hanging suspended outside of the window.

"Doesn't seem very long in Gaines years, does it?" Spence patted her behind. "We're newlyweds in their eyes."

"Why was Mary a little girl to Andy and Denise and a grown woman to you and me?"

"I have no idea, but I'm sure we'll find out more over the weekend while we're here," Spence inched over and tried to embrace her. "And you really need to move your leg. You're being crowdy."

"Uh-uh . . . I'm on my side—"

Now wide awake, Jean watched the dark shadows from the tree outside flicker on the ceiling. Something was next to her, and not Spence's leg. She reached her hand on the top of the quilt, next to her knees. Fur—*warm fur*. She froze but her heart raced ahead.

When they stayed in guest houses in Europe, it wasn't unusual for the innkeeper's family cat or dog to take over their bed, but Jean hadn't seen any pets when they'd checked in.

"Who are you, big fella?" she whispered into the dark.

"You haven't called me that in quite awhile," Spence said, chuckling.

"Spence? We're not alone."

Jean smoothed down the fur. Her fingers ruffled the soft tufts behind two floppy, pliable ears.

A dog. Wiley?

"Give me your hand." She guided Spence's fingers, reaching out to feel the dog's head and long snout. "Do you think?"

Spence gasped. "It is . . ."

"Hey, sweetie," she murmured. "You stay right here with us." A long sigh—a dog sigh. A solid rump against her own. *Heat—real heat.*

Jean let go of Spence's hand and rolled over. She froze before she could turn on the light. "Keep your hand on him."

Beneath the moon's blue haze, Jean could make out a large, wispy silhouette in front of the window. She blinked her eyes to focus. The figure was a woman sitting in the rocking chair. The wicker creaked as the form leaned forward and then back. Another hazy figure—tall and muscular—stood next to the silhouette.

A low chuckle prompted Jean to grab Spence's shoulder. He tightened his fingers. She panicked inside—until she heard their voices.

"You tryin' to steal my dog, you are, Miss Jean. Me and Jess been waitin' for you and Mr. Spence to come." The voice came from the large woman. Her words seemed to broadcast from every corner of the room—not loud but ubiquitous.

"I think he like you too," the man said. His voice was deep and resonant, like she could listen to his wisdom for hours. "Wiley don't sleep with jus' anybody—nobody I ever seen, 'cept family. I guess you part of the family now."

"Uh-hmmm, so right. Lotta folk come through here, but Wiley don't bother them in the bed."

This was a ghostly private conversation, but Jean knew who these people were: Birdie and Jess, the housekeeper and handyman for Doc Gaines, Charlotte Gaines, and Mary Coulter—but much more than that, also their extended family. Birdie died in 1948. Jess died in 1931, right before Mary Coulter was married to Jim.

"Birdie, can I turn on the light? Don't go away if I do," Jean whispered, trying to keep her own voice quiet.

"We stay right here. Go on now—all right. Yes it is."

Jean switched on the light. She took a deep breath at the large black woman in the rocking chair and the man standing behind her. The woman's cotton dress had a finely detailed 1940s print of bluebell flowers. The bodice strained across her ample bosom. Her broad smile revealed a row of perfectly aligned white teeth, except for a gap in front. They gave off a slight halo. The man wore a white cotton T-shirt beneath denim overalls, making his muscular arms look even more powerful. He nodded to her and Spence, a gesture of welcome and not judgment.

"Spence?" She nudged him, without taking her eyes off the pair.

"I'm right here." Spence shifted, and she turned to him. He was up on an elbow, and they were both staring along the full length of the muscular black Labrador lying prone next to her leg.

"We should have left you to sleep and done this in the mornin', but we was excited to meet you. Mary told us you was comin'. What you did in Egypt—you done a good thing for Miss Mary."

"We saw her in the garden with the family," Spence said, beaming.

"You did – yes, you did. She saw you too, and so did Doc and Miss Charlotte." Birdie chuckled. "Going on and on about it they did."

Jean hesitated, but then couldn't resist asking Birdie and Jess a question. "So . . . why did Mary appear to that couple, the Moores, as a child? She was an adult to us."

Spence's hand stopped on Wiley's belly as he, too, waited for the answer.

Jess touched Birdie's shoulder. "I'll take on this one," he said. Birdie reached up and patted Jess's hand. "What you seein' is what you know. You never meet Mary like a little girl. But those other folks and that reviewer lady only know Mary from the stories about her comin' here as a little girl, abandon and all. So, that's how they lookin' at her. You jus' know that little dress—some dress it was, right Birdie?—but you never seen how pretty she was inside it. The Mary you know is a woman, all growed up. So, that's what you see. Same with me and Birdie. We're here in front of you, jus' like Mary told you we was. How *she* saw us, uh-huh, that's right." Jess gazed down at Birdie. "Me? My Birdie here like that young girl a seventeen, jus' as pretty as the day Doc set it up for us to get married with the name Gaines. I never looked at her any other way. Always did; always will."

"Mmm-mmm." Birdie nodded. "Never seen my Jess 'cept the man I married. Never did notice all the gettin' old, or gettin' fat, or gettin' sick parts. All those things happen all right, but that's not who Jess is . . . *to me*."

Jean turned to Spence. His face never changed either . . . to her. "What about Wiley? Mary never knew Wiley until she became immortal," she pressed.

"Oh, she know Wiley, jus' not while he was alive," Birdie said, her tone warm and wise. "Mary heard all about him from Doc. And Wiley been in the house a looong time—used to sleep in her bed like he is with you right now. That dog made more healin' rounds than Doc, I'm tellin' you. Doc never stopped going on about that dog, did he, Jess?" Birdie shook her head and laughed, her bosom bouncing in rhythm.

"Mmm-mmm . . . Go on, pet him. Memories are real."

Jean set her hand on Wiley and worked her fingers through the smooth fur on his neck. Wiley kept his eyes closed, but his tail emitted lazy sparkles with every thump on the quilt.

"I think that ole dog be ruined now. He's goin' to be a spoiled rotten turnip while you here." Jess shook his head.

Birdie laughed deep and genuine. "But that's where he like to sleep best—right up against a warm leg. Yes, he does. You can go through my recipes tomorrow. I do miss cookin'. Miss Janet cooks my best ones. I left 'em for her to find in the kitchen."

"C'mon now. These good folks need some shut-eye." Jess touched Birdie's arm, the one with a scar. "I'll show you 'round tomorrow, Spence. Night, Wiley."

Wiley lifted his head and set it back down. The images of Birdie and Jess faded to nothing, leaving behind a faint dissipating mist. Jean watched the rocking chair slow and finally still.

Their hands moved in a steady rhythm over Wiley's soft black fur. Real—but not.

Jean turned out the light. They each dedicated a hand to one of Wiley's ears.

"Jess is going to show you around tomorrow, Spence," she said, "and I get to go through Birdie's recipes. I wonder what else is in store for us."

"Hey, it's already tomorrow—after midnight. Happy anniversary," Spence whispered. "And you know what? You look just the same to me too."

CHAPTER 8

Happy Anniversary!

The next morning, Jean stared at Spence's face as the light in the room brightened. The lines around his eyes or the gray feathering his dark hair disappeared. She only waited for his dark-lashed lids to open and his enormous dark-brown eyes to gaze at her, the ones that met her at the end of the aisle on their wedding day thirty-three years ago.

Jean reached over and opened his right eye with her thumb and forefinger. "Happy anniversary, you. I think I'm going to enjoy every minute." Spence opened his eyes, and her heart expanded.

"Well, the day can't start soon enough. Let's get up now—and go to bed early tonight."

"Speaking of bed . . . where's Wiley?"

"He's gone, but his spot was warm when I woke up about twenty minutes ago. He's off doing immortal doggy things," she said, laughing. "What do immortal dogs eat, anyway?"

"No idea. If it were Mycroft, he'd be eating Forever Kibble out of a bottomless Forever Bowl. C'mon—up! I smell coffee down-stairs."

Jean rolled on her back and spread her arms. "Amazing last night—having Wiley in the bed and seeing Birdie and Jess." She sighed. "Yeah . . . pretty special. I can't wait to chat with Mary again." She stood and dressed in her yoga pants and sweatshirt while Spence shaved. "I'm going down to forage for some coffee. I'll bring you up a cup."

"Perfect," Spence turned back to the mirror and pulled the razor down the side of his left cheek.

Spence stepped out of the bathroom, patting his face with a towel. The quiet in the room loomed large. He stood at the window and studied the houses in the neighborhood through the barren branches of the old poplar tree outside. All the same age, turn-of-the-century. *So much history.*

Sensing a presence, Spence turned. An image shimmered in the sunlight next to him in front of the window. He watched the ripples become stronger until Jess materialized.

"Let's take a walk, Music Man," Jess chuckled and hooked his thumb under the suspenders of his overalls.

Spence dug his yellow sweatshirt and a down jacket from his duffel bag. "Sounds like the trip of a lifetime. Can I get a cup of coffee?"

"Pay no mind of the time. I got nothin' but time. Meet you out front."

"Wait! Won't you cause a ruckus with the Moores?"

"Naw, they can't see me 'less I want 'em to. And I don't want 'em to." Jess's image faded and disappeared.

Spence met up with Jean on the stairs with two coffee cups in her hand.

"You're in a hurry. Where are you off to?"

"Honey, I need a to-go cup. Jess wants me to take a walk with him."

"Jess?"

"I think this is an immortal man-to-man thing. We won't be too long. I know today is special, and you're special, and I hate to leave you, but this is outrageous!"

"Here," Jean said, handing him the mug. "Paper cups are on the breakfront in the dining room." She gave him an air kiss. "Take a muffin with you. Janet just put them out."

"Love you!" He rocketed down the stairs. "Happy anniversary!" The only way he could have bounced higher was if he had Slinkys in his sneakers.

Jean continued up the stairs with her coffee mug, looking forward to lying in a hot bath. *Spence is going out with Jess.* She shook her head, stepped into the bedroom, and closed the door. The wicker on the seat of the rocking chair crunched as she sat. *Birdie sat right here last night.*

The clack of toenails on the wood floor startled her. Snapping to attention, she waited and listened. The answer wasn't in what she heard next—it was in what she felt: warm pressure against her knee. Extending her hand, she said, "Wiley?" A dark visage glimmered by her legs until the dog's full image appeared—his head rested in her lap.

"Look at you. Aren't you beautiful," she whispered, running her forefinger over his pouty brown eyes.

Wiley's tail thumped on the oak floor, poofing up sparkles like tiny firecrackers. She smoothed his forehead. With a long sigh and a groan, he delivered a small pool of drool on her black yoga pants.

"I would love to take you home with me, but I'm not sure about Mycroft. He might throw your sparkles back at you."

Wiley shifted his eyes as she talked and in her silence settled on her with an endless gaze.

"He might just try, young lady," a gentlemanly Southern drawl said. Jean raised her eyes, trying not to startle Wiley as much as she'd been.

"You're Doc, aren't you?"

"I am, indeed." Doc leaned against the frame of the bay window, next to the built-in seat. He had his arms crossed, studying her. "I right think a conspiracy is being hatched, Wiley. You traitor, you." Doc chuckled and fingered the gold chain of his watch in the pocket of his gray striped vest. His hair, wild with shimmering silver waves, framed his warm, dark eyes. He sat on the window seat and crossed his legs, completely at ease. "This type of dog gets attached. You do know that, right?"

"Oh yeah, I'm stuck."

"I'm glad you're his new friend. But he's still my boy."

"Mary wanted Spence and me to meet all of you, and now I understand why. This is a wonderful home—and quite the family here. Do you mind if I call you Doc?"

"Why, if you call me anything else, I'd right consider it an in-sult."

Jean figured she could ask this man any question and he'd pop out with the answer. "Did you always want to be immortal, Doc?" she said, continuing to stroke Wiley's head.

"I did, yes I did. Of course, having Charlotte waiting for me sealed that deal. I continue to help people, but most don't understand my current state of being. I visit the dying, although I don't stop the process from happening. In the final hours, words and touch are more powerful than pills."

"So you're like a guardian from beyond?"

"You might call me that, if you'd like. As a doctor for most of my physical life, I couldn't fix everything. In afterlife, I've never considered interfering in the choices of others. I guess I could. Best to let these modern days play out—good and bad."

"Can't you change the course?" She flashed on a television program in which actors pretending to be historical figures shared their thoughts on today's world. "You've witnessed so much history. I can't imagine what you must think about the changes."

"Good . . . and not so good. Every choice carries risk of consequence and reward. The view appears different depending on what part of the hill you're standing on. The bumpy road of best intentions doesn't take everybody where they want to go. I shouldn't stop the natural course, but I do enjoy the paper-spitting machine on the desk downstairs."

Jean gazed at Doc, admiring his sense of peace. "Can you make people immortal?"

"No, my dear, I cannot. Only the fabric performs that miracle, I believe. But you and Spencer have the option, if you'd like. I'm sure that fellow in Cairo would help you when the time presents itself."

"I won't pretend I haven't had many sleepless nights about that very thought. But I try to live as though I choose mortality—I need deadlines," she said, swirling the fur on the soft spots behind Wiley's ears. "An hour, a year, a decade—Spence and I set goals, plan, and get them done. If I could do something any old time, then I wouldn't accomplish anything."

"Hmmm . . . interesting," Doc said, scratching his cheek. "Not a crime."

"Spence and I want to do important things in *this* life. We have our health, and thanks to Mary—and to you too—we can make a real difference. I don't mean our name in lights on a building. I mean . . . like you did. You changed people's lives, Doc."

"Then you go on ahead." Doc took off his wire-rimmed glasses. The lenses steamed with his breath, and then he wiped them with the corner of his vest. "By the way, you don't need money to make a difference. Happens when you least expect. One person at a time." He winked at her. "You'd be surprised how far a little effort can reach." He looped his glasses over his ears and smiled. "Good deeds take on a life all their own. Hmmm . . . yes," Doc brushed the hair on his eyebrow back and forth with his forefinger. "Personal is better."

Jean hesitated and decided to come out with the question she'd been noodling on all morning. "Does the family expect Spence and me to become immortal?"

"Expect? We don't have cut notions about anything, dear. A bit harder, though, when you have a choice?"

"A big one too." She leaned her head back in the chair. "If there weren't any deadlines or risks to accomplish those things, then . . . well . . . what's the point?"

"Choices and risks, yes. You got me thinking. Maybe I should take some risks again." Doc released a low, playful laugh.

Jean gazed into his eyes, drinking him in. "Change of subject," she said, startling herself back in the moment and turning to the painting.

"Mary told me she regretted not taking that piece of art home."

"Yes, she did always have an attraction for that little fella. He's a bit of an enigma too, that boy. Why, I believe, you might find it important to the next step in your journey—that is, if you want to solve the riddle of who created such a fine work. Then again, no risk if he stays right on the wall." Doc smirked, making her think he already knew the answer to that riddle.

"Are you saying you want us to take it home?" Jean turned. Doc was gone. And so was Wiley. Only the damp spot on the knee of her pants remained as confirmation Wiley had been there.

The afterglow from her conversation with Doc lingered as Jean luxuriated in a hot bath. After drying off and dressing, she flopped on the bed and examined the ornate plaster medallion in the ceiling. The painting again drew her attention, as if it had tapped her on the shoulder. *The next step.*

Jean shifted her gaze back to the medallion, trying not to get obsessed with the painting. Elaborate vines scrolled around plump pears, apples, and cherries. The artisan had been incredibly talented. The sculpted pieces of fruit were as perfect as any she'd seen in the museums in Florence. The lamp hanging from the center had been converted from its original gas jets to clear filament bulbs. The frosted glass shades balancing on ornate brass arms appeared to be quite delicate with their complementary decoration of gold vines. She tried to imagine life with only gaslight. Days and nights must have been so quiet back in the 1880s: no television, cell phones, mowers, or blowers to deliver a constant audio assault.

When they lived in Houston, she and Spence had experienced a similar routine for two weeks after Hurricane Ike. A small window had opened up to allow them to live life a different way, even for only two weeks. Without the sixty-cycle hum of modern conven-iences, neighbors sat on their porches and talked in the late after-noon. House keys were exchanged, supplies shared, and their street became a close community. The world shrunk to encompass only their street.

The whole neighborhood celebrated the instant the power finally came back on, but they were a bit sad too. Their close-knit group retreated back into the hum of modern routines. But the mounds of debris harbored gems of trust. Any one of their neighbors knew they could count on the others to help in an emergency. That kind of camaraderie didn't exist before the hurricane.

"Electricity . . . such a blessing," said a lyrical woman's voice filled with refinement. "We celebrated for Birdie the day the power came on in 1913. She was terrified of gaslight—and for good reason."

A new voice. Jean kept her eyes trained on the ceiling.

"The medallion you're admiring was created by an Italian immigrant Doc hired when we were building the house. Yes, Angelo Mini was his name. He showed up one day at our doorstep, searching for work. Angelo created art in this house, all by hand. Raise your eyes in any room, and Angelo's gift to the house presents itself." The woman's voice was musical.

"Yes . . . and so intricate," Jean said, studying the plaster work with new eyes. "The detail makes you want to view the whole world from this vantage point every day. People don't learn this old-world craft anymore." She lifted her head. The air rippled and glittered by the window. "Are you Charlotte?"

The shimmering image became a dark-haired beauty in a wispy, ankle-length deep-blue dress. Her long hair swept up in a graceful twist, and her crystalline blue eyes reflected a flickering light the exact color of her dress. Demure tear-drop pearls floated from her earlobes like little bells. Her perfect white teeth cast a slight halo.

"Yes, I am Charlotte Gamble Gaines. Thank you for offering to bring the chest back. It does belong at the end of this bed."

Jean pulled herself up and stood with a bit of a wobble. She stepped toward Charlotte, extending her hand. She wanted to be wrapped in this woman's touch. Charlotte's unadorned fingers, except for the thin gold wedding band, were soft and cool. Her un-polished nails were short and smooth. Jean turned Charlotte's hand over and ran her forefinger across the creamy white palm. She did exist. Jean's own finger emitted a smoky trail as she made contact with Charlotte's enchanted skin.

"Thank you for bringing our Mary home. Doc and I weren't able to bare children. Doc raised Mary on his own, with Birdie and Jess, of course. But you know, don't you?" Charlotte waved at the air in front of her face in a haloed arc and smiled.

"Yes, Mary told us before she—" Jean broke off, not sure if she should say the word. "Where is she?"

"Oh, she's here. Mary wants you and Spencer to get acquainted with the family without her." Charlotte had a slight tilt of her head when she talked. She had a natural elegance about her.

"Spence and I already think of ourselves as part of the family. You're with us, making little things happen."

"Yes, we will always be there, but you must live your life, not ours, dear. We don't make things happen, you do." Charlotte started to fade.

"No—please don't go yet! I have so many questions." Jean panicked as she tried to think of what to say. "Do the Parsons know you're here?"

"They know of us. We appear to walk in the garden in the evening. Doc's idea. He thought it would bring more business to the inn. He likes to help people in unexpected ways. And he still has his fun. That's all the Parsons know. We mostly stay out of sight."

Jean smiled as she recalled her conversation with Doc. "How come we can see you now?"

"Why, my dear, you and your husband are chock-full of magic. It connects with us and also in what is connected to you: our possessions, Mary's things, even your own treasures."

"Are you always here—in this house?"

"No . . . we are everywhere. We gather our energy to be here."

"When Spence and I touch Mary's belongings, we have visions *her* history."

"Those are just memories, dear, buried deep in our personal treasures with special meaning. Everyone experiences that magic, I believe. Don't you relive your memories when you touch a sentimental ornament on your Christmas tree? You can go right back to when you first acquired it, and experience again that moment in your life. That's all it is."

Jean paused as she remembered doing that very same thing only last week. "But this is different. We see *your* memories."

"Ah yes, magic, isn't it?" Charlotte paused and gazed out the window. Without turning back, she said, "That only happens to people who have already experienced the fabric's magic. The trans-formation is quite powerful." She turned to Jean. "We had no idea of its true history, other than what was told to us from my father, until you went to Cairo. That painting there . . . over the bed." Charlotte pointed to the young boy dancing in his ornate gilt frame. "It, too, is a very special heirloom. Angelo Mini gave it to Doc and me as a gift for being able to work on this house. Passed through his family for nearly three hundred years before he presented it to us. Memories linger there too."

"Do you know who the artist was?"

"Unfortunately not. We just enjoyed it. But why don't you find out? You and Spencer have demonstrated an ability to solve puzzles. Enjoy your stay—so lovely to meet you." Charlotte faded to a mist and disappeared.

Breathless, Jean lowered herself on the bed and crawled along the green vines of the bedspread. They pulled her toward the painting above the headboard. Now up close, she noticed the young boy's toenails were caked with dirt, and the fine strands of his rich brown hair appeared to be damp with sweat. How did the painter capture the release of sultry heat and childhood exertion? She hadn't noticed it before, but the blurred images of two other young boys bled off the side of the canvas. The technique gave the painting depth and perspective. The work was exquisite.

Who are you?

Jean ran her fingers, with a light touch, along the frame. Her fingertips tingled. This piece meant something, but she had no idea what. She had barely touched the boy's rosy cheek when a flash startled her. Gasping, the rippling rays of golden light released from her fingertips. The intense vibration spread through her hand and along with it an image filled her mind. *Angelo . . .*

"Done? Angelo, the one in this room is the most magnificent in the house," Charlotte said. "I mean—they're all beautiful, but this . . ."

Doc rounded the corner of the bedroom and raised his eyes to the ceiling. "Well, Angelo, what do we have here? You have certainly outdone yourself. If I could reach it, I might just pluck out one of those pieces of fruit to accompany my lunch." He laughed but then went thoughtful as he extended his hand. Doc pulled Angelo in a warm embrace. Powdery dust dotted Doc's vest when they separated.

Angelo's hands were rough and cracked from decades of wet plaster leeching the life out of his skin, but the chalky material couldn't extract his talent. Tears filled his eyes as he stood in front of Charlotte and Doc. Angelo removed his hat and dragged his sleeve across his ragged face. The gray stubble of his beard was rough from three days' growth. He took a deep breath.

"You give to me a gift," Angelo choked in a thick Italian accent. "The chance to work and leave my mark on this wonderful house—I will never forget. A good house with good bones, yes? You welcome me to be part of your family, so now I share with you piece of my family. This for you."

Angelo reached down and picked up a painting that had been leaning against the bed frame. Pride radiated across his craggy face as he held it out to Charlotte.

"Oh . . . Angelo! We couldn't accept such a gift. How can you ever part with this?" Charlotte said and placed her hand on her chest. "From your family . . ."

"Look good in this room. Belong there, over your bed. Make a home there," Angelo pointed to the wall over the tarp-covered, four-poster bed. "I am old man now—no family left to me. Make sure fine things have fine place before I die. Good hands paint this in Italy for my ancestors."

"We will surely be responsible stewards, Angelo. No one owns a piece like this; we only become caretakers. We thank you kindly," Doc said.

"Who was the artist?" Charlotte asked.

"No matter. Art, yes? So full of possibility. This boy inspire me to make my work. We call it *Il Ragazzo del Ballo*, *The Dancing Boy*."

"Hanging here ever since . . ." Jean whispered as the light beams diminished beneath her hand as she pulled away. "What a dear man."

Jean jumped off the bed, put on her white socks, and fluffed her hair in the mirror of the dark walnut dresser. She was filled with answers—and more questions—as her mind raced through a tantalizing list of potential artists who may have painted *The Dancing Boy*: Da Vinci, Michelangelo, Raphael, Bellini, and Caravaggio, among the top candidates. Of course, she was taking things out-of-bounds. She could almost hear Spence's teasing in her head: *Don't go there, Jean.* But a familiar twinge of intuition filled her; the same as when she'd found the fabric, and on that her confidence hadn't been misplaced. In fact, she'd completely underestimated the significance.

The house rested in stillness as Jean padded down the stairs in her socks. She meandered into the dining room and met up with Janet, who had set a tray of sandwiches on the sideboard.

"Time got away from me. I've been puttering upstairs the whole morning," Jean said, smiling to herself and picking up a sandwich. "This house is amazing."

"We love it here. We've met so many interesting people. Overall, running the inn has been a wonderful experience," Janet said. "Relax in the parlor with your lunch."

"Where are the Moores?"

"They went downtown. Enjoy the quiet while you can." Janet winked and zipped back toward the kitchen.

"Janet? Wait! I . . . I heard stories about Birdie's recipes. Do you have them?"

"Sure do. C'mon with me and I'll show you."

Jean set her lunch plate on the coffee table and did a fast walk to catch up with Janet. Her step through the doorway was a step back in time.

"Wow. This kitchen is all original."

"The squeaks and clunks certainly attest to that," Janet quipped. "You'll never find a better stove. Built like a tank." Janet pulled the long, levered handle on the round-fronted refrigerator. "Not the most efficient by modern standards, but they still crank out a lot of meals." She opened a narrow drawer by the stove and handed Jean four banded bundles of three-by-five cards.

"Are those Birdie's recipes?"

"Gold. That's what these are. If you want to flip through them while you eat lunch, you're more than welcome. Then I'll chain 'em up with a padlock."

The stacks were separated by type: Meats, Sides, Baked Goods, and Desserts. Jean fanned them like playing cards and smiled when she saw that several were spotted with oil and crusted with remnants of flour dust. She could almost hear Birdie voicing non-negotiable instructions from their faded, block-print handwriting.

"I'll bring these back after lunch, but I may want to make some copies."

"No problem at all. There's a scanner on the desk in the hall. You can print them out or e-mail them to yourself. Definitely pull out Birdie's brisket and cornbread and her fabulous fall-apart roast chicken."

"I can't wait." Jean grinned as she imagined Doc peering over her shoulder while she scanned the recipes.

Jean strolled back to the parlor and sat on the couch. She set the cards in her lap, ready to dive in. The combination of eating lunch and savoring food descriptions was a perfect follow-up to a magical morning. She reached for her plate on the coffee table and spotted the latest issue of *Bed-and-Breakfast Magazine*. The featured story, "Top Ten

Haunted Inns in the Southeast," immediately drew her eye. She took a bite of her sandwich and ran her finger down the list: first place, the Kehoe House in Savannah; second, the Battery Carriage House in Charleston, South Carolina; third—*the Old Gaines House, Richmond, Virginia.*

She thumbed through the pages until she found Susan Kent's review. Exhilaration and pride turned to protectiveness as she read the description. Even though others had seen the ghostly apparitions in the garden, she still wanted to claim private ownership of the family's existence. *Has the genie been released from the bottle?*

CHAPTER 9

The Ultimate Tour Guide

Spence admired the stately mix of Georgian Revival and Italian Renaissance homes as he and Jess strolled down Park Avenue in the Historic Fan District near downtown Richmond.

"So that's why they call this area the Fan," Jess said, pointing to the confluence of several streets converging at Meadow Park. "A wedge. All the streets spread out like a big fan. Fancy more like it."

"Seems fancy now," Spence said, gawking at the intricate Italianate woodwork on a three-story, brick townhouse.

A woman jogging with an elaborate, three-wheeled running stroller gazed at Spence, curious, as she went by him. He smiled and then his gaze followed her until she was out of sight. "Jess, does anyone else know you're here? Just me, right?" he whispered, self-conscious at how much he talked with his hands.

"Jus' you—that is—unless I want 'em to. We don't work so hard, though, with the magic folk like you. Me and Birdie don't do that show stuff in the garden. Old Doc havin' fun. And for all his serious deeds, he was always havin' his fun. I'll be forever grateful we went to work for him and Miss Charlotte—though I'm not glad for the reason why."

"What happened, Jess?"

"Our first place of work, the old Whitfield house, used to stand right up on the corner. Where me and Birdie met—and we was smitten, yes we was. We destined ourselves be together forever. The house burned down the very same year. The curtains catch fire from the gaslight. Birdie got burned pretty bad on her arm. Reverend Payne took us to Doc, and that's all she wrote. Jus' seventeen we was." Jess shook his head and chuckled. "Doc was jus' startin' out hisself."

"And Birdie was Doc's first patient too, right?"

"Oh, you are so right, so right. Doc and Charlotte more like kids back then. Kindest people you ever did want to meet." Jess stopped as they emerged from the historic neighborhood at an expansive green space. "Now this be Monroe Park. Been here since 1850s. Let's have ourselves a sit."

Jess sat on the wood-slat wrought-iron bench. Time seemed to stand still as Spence sat next to him, as if he, too, were immortal. They both crossed their legs and bobbed their feet in unison.

"You know," Jess continued, "soldiers used this park at the end of the war as a Confederate hospital. Set up tents all over. Did their drills here 'fore they went back to battle. When the war over, they built those houses in the Fan. The big dragon fountain in the middle used to be a tall pyramid. I like the pyramid better myself. I watch it come down in 1903." Jess glanced at Spence, tapped his knee, and said: "They didn't ask my opinion, no they didn't."

Spence couldn't process all the information fast enough. So much history unfolded in front of him from his ultimate tour guide.

"What's the big building on the side over here?" he said, point-ing to the edge of the park. The three-story stucco structure, with ancient-looking embellishments, took up the whole block on North Laurel Street.

"The Landmark Theater." Jess shook his head. "Somebody got way too big for their britches. Started out as a highfalutin fraternal organization. Called the Mosque back in my day. Built in 1926, uh-huh. One fancy place on the inside. All little tiles—a lot of gold paint too. Make you dizzy. Speakin' of that, Dizzy and Ella played the Mosque in 1947. I was there, yes I was."

"Gillespie and Fitzgerald? But weren't you already—?" Spence wasn't quite able to get out the word: *immortal.*

Jess threw his head back and laughed. "Now that's the good part. Don't got to miss nothin', do I? Mm-mmm . . . never heard such music. Saw Louis Jordan and the Tympany Five too, in 1953. Yes, I did. That was somethin'. Even had Elvis here in 1955. He came out right on the sidewalk." Jess pointed to a side door on the building. "Signed his name on the programs of those screamin' girls. Yes, sir, I had to know what all the fussin' about."

"Who was your favorite?" Spence asked, hanging on his every word.

"Aw, no question—Miss Ella. Sang right through me she did."

"Wow. Jean and I have most of her albums. Is it true she could break a glass with just her voice?"

"Bet so. She 'bout broke me, she did."

Spence jumped when he got a tap on the shoulder. He whipped around and stared up into the quizzical faces of Andy and Denise Moore.

"We thought that was you," Andy said. "Who are you talking to?"

"Yeah, who are you talking to?" Denise echoed.

"No one." Spence tried to act casual. "Jean always teases me about carrying on conversations with myself. Well, I'd better be getting back. It's Jean's and my anniversary today, so I don't want to abandon her for too long."

"We'll walk with you then. We were heading back ourselves."

Spence's shoulders slumped. He turned to Jess, torn about leaving. Jess smiled and gave a slight nod, a signal for him to follow the couple. Andy and Denise waited for Spence to join them. He took a few steps and gazed back at the bench. Empty.

Spence spotted Jean in the parlor, staring at the medallion in the ceiling as he came through the front door. She tossed him a sheepish smile.

"Hey, hi! That looks fun," he said, laughing. "You're not even five steps away from where I left you this morning."

"Actually, I've had a wonderful day." Jean sighed. The sigh said more than she did about her day.

Spence shifted his gaze toward the front hall, a signal to Jean for her to stay quiet. She got the hint. The Moores walked by, waved, and proceeded up the stairs to their room.

"I had an interesting day too," he said when the coast was clear. "Jess gave me an incredible tour of the historic part of town. There's an historic neighborhood they call the Fan because the streets radiate out from the center. The houses are incredible. He has so much knowledge—seen all the history." Spence's eyes went wide, and then he whispered, "He saw Ella and Dizzy at the Mosque—I mean the Landmark. It's pretty weird, though, when you're talking with someone nobody knows is there. Then the Moores showed up." He raised his eyes and grimaced at the squeak of the floorboards upstairs.

"I had an experience too, Spence. Check out this ceiling."

"Yeah, beautiful—" Spence studied the medallion of scrolled vines strung in an endless loop held in the mouths of tiny birds.

"An Italian immigrant named Angelo Mini created a totally unique medallion in every room." Jean cupped her hand to her mouth and whispered, "*Charlotte* told me all about it."

"What? You spoke to the illustrious *Charlotte*?"

Jean motioned for him to keep his voice down. "Yes . . . and I had a lovely talk with Doc this morning. Angelo gave her and Doc the painting upstairs in the bedroom. Unbelievably old. I hope Janet and Doug are okay with us taking it home."

"C'mon. Let's get ready and go out for an anniversary drink and dinner. You can tell me everything they said." Spence took her hands and pulled her up from the couch. "You need to move. I've been walking all day."

"Good idea. Should I do most of my moving now, or later?" she said, giving him her best coquettish grin.

"Hmmm . . ."

"Let me show you the painting first. And when you set your hands—"

Spence wrapped her in his arms. He buried his face in her hair and whispered, "The only thing I want to set my hands on is you."

Jean moved the candle to the side of the small table in the intimate bistro. She grasped Spence's fingers after the waiter set down her glass of red wine and Spence's New York cocktail.

"Doc said we can make a choice," she whispered. "I thought we'd feel obligated to become immortal, but now I'm okay if we move forward the way we've always wanted to."

"Those are some important words, Jean." Spence scanned the restaurant for anyone who might overhear their conversation. He released one hand from hers, lifted his cocktail, and clinked her glass. He took a sip. "Damn, that's good," he said, smacking his lips. "One thing hit me as strange when I sat with Jess today. He told me he'd gone into the theater *after* he was . . . you know. And I thought—wow—what an opportunity."

"So are you saying you want to become immortal?"

"No . . . well, yes, at first I did, but I thought about the concept on the walk home. I realized the musicians that captivated me, I've either seen them already or they're dead. The music of the future's just going to be contrived techno drivel. The best of the best have lived for me. Now it's all about geeky gadgets."

"Not all music, Spence, but I know what you mean."

"Jean, c'mon, I hate to even use a cell phone, but can you imagine if someone called me on a wristwatch or put a receiver in my head. I'd self-combust."

"That's what *I'm* saying. Let's enjoy getting to the finish. Maybe we should set up a foundation to continue doing things after we're gone. Let's do something charitable. How does the Mycroft Foundation sound?"

"Not bad. Or the Wiley Foundation," Spence said with a playful smirk. "And focus on music, art, and animals. We can support up-and-coming artists and musicians to keep the integrity for the future. That's one way to become immortal."

"And create a legacy for animal adoption, or a sanctuary or something." Jean breathed a big sigh of relief. "Maybe we can start with the painting. What if it is some important unknown work? Looks like it to me, even without the sparkles and visions." Jean took a sip and swirled the wine in her glass. "Before we leave, why don't you go downtown to an art store and pick up a case. Then we can carry the painting home without bumping it around."

"Did Doc get you all hopped up by what he said to you?" Spence gave her a here-we-go-again look.

"Yes . . . and yes. The painting showed me the vision of Angelo Mini for a reason. I got the sense that Doc's up to something. He knows me—and so does Charlotte too."

"Well, I know you better than anybody, and I think *you're* the one who's up to funny business."

"Spence, we might be able to bankroll our new foundation."

"Wait, wait, wait, you're getting miles ahead of yourself—as usual. Let's order dinner first."

On the last day of their trip, Spence walked into the bedroom with a hard-sided art case.

"This should work. I took measurements. It'll hold the painting and fit in the overhead on the plane."

Jean placed the last of her toiletries in her duffel bag while he opened the case across the bed. "I talked with Janet this morning when you went to the art store. She was great about us taking the painting home. Doug gave me a hard time, but he was kidding around. I really like them."

"I'll get the chest shipped back here as soon as we get home," Spence said. "I wish we were staying longer. I'm not ready to leave yet."

"I know, but we can't tap into Bill and Linda too much. We said we'd be back tonight . . . and you have a ton of stuff to do for the store."

"I left Bill with one of your to-do lists. He called me earlier to say he's found more collections for sale. We need to get estimates."

"And I need to jump on Mary's house. I'm with you, though. I love it here."

Jean turned her eyes to *The Dancing Boy*. She lifted the small painting off the wall. There was a bright square on the wallpaper, revealing the vibrancy of the original color of the green vines. She scanned the room for something of similar size to take its place. A wreath of lavender and dried roses on the wall by the bay window would do. She picked the circle off the hook and hung it over the bed.

"There. Better," she said, making sure the wreath was straight. "Can you help me get this in the case? How do the straps work?"

"I've worked enough poster shows to do this at lightning speed." Spence secured the painting with the adjustable elastic straps and latched the hard-sided case. "The painting isn't going anywhere in this."

"I'm so glad you're taking my boy home. Isn't he wonderful?" Mary Coulter's voice filled the room. Her wavy image materialized by the bay window.

Jean rushed to shut the bedroom door. She beamed at Mary's form clarifying into full view. "Mary . . . we've been waiting for you," she said, trying to keep her voice low. "We only had a glimpse of you when we got here. I was worried we were going to have to leave without talking with you."

"I would never let that happen. I'm delighted you were able to spend time with the family." Mary held out her hands and Jean grasped them.

"Our time has been fantastic," Spence said. "I spent yesterday with Jess."

"Jess is a special man with a heart of gold." Jean's own hands tingled with the memory of holding Mary's as the magic of the fabric coursed through her when they helped her pass.

"I'm happy too." Haloed tears sparkled in her eyes.

Jean watched Spence's expression fall. He wrapped his arms

around her. Mary buried her face in Spence's sweater, his eyes glistening too.

"We're so glad we came here. This is a magical place," Jean said, unsure as to what prompted Mary's tears.

Mary patted Spence's back and released him. "You look well. Both of you. Transitions can be difficult at times."

"I have something for you." Jean dug in her bag and pulled out the hair comb with the diamond-encrusted hummingbird. The diamonds twinkled in opalescent colors in the morning sunlight. Jean slipped the comb into Mary's palm. Her hazel eyes widened as she ran her delicate finger across the glittering stones.

"I have no words."

"A small thing we can give back to you for what you did for Spence and me. I'll miss it, but this is yours. Can we see you all again soon?"

"Of course, yes, of course. And I want to monitor your progress on the house."

"Yes, we have big plans—and for the painting."

CHAPTER 10

The Collinses Get "Yakky"

Tired from the long flight, Jean suggested they put their feet up in their sweats. She pulled two fillets of halibut out of the freezer while Spence went to the store for some vegetables. Jean picked up the phone to call Bill and Linda.

"We're home!" Jean said, when Linda answered. "All go well?"

"Fine, except—" Linda's voice went quiet.

"What? C'mon, out with it." Jean scrolled through a litany of possible disasters while they were away.

"Thanks for the wine you left for us. We drank all four bottles," Linda said, being cagey.

"Linda . . . what happened?"

"Well . . . two things. I got mad at one of those reporter guys. I *may* have said something I shouldn't have. He caught me off guard."

"Don't worry." She tried to make Linda feel better but dreaded what might be coming next. "What did you say?"

"He got out of me that you were in London at the time Raleigh Coulter died. When he asked me about a hawk, I stayed quiet, Jean. I promise I stayed quiet. The reporter took my silence as a confirmation."

Jean closed her eyes. "Linda, all you had to say was 'no com-ment.' Look, you're not to blame. This is our fault for putting you in an awkward position. Honestly, this is just the news of the moment." She tried to convince herself with those words. "Okay, what's the second thing?"

"Last night . . . we were sitting by the fire and watching a movie with Mycroft. Then this black dog was next to him. A big Lab."

"What?" *Wiley!*

"I swear, Jean, he appeared before our eyes. Scared me half to death. We turned off the movie and stared at him. Real sweet dog, actually. He licked Mycroft's face and all these sparkles came from his tongue. Bill and I had no clue what to do, so we just sat and watched them like two crazy-head lumps. My God, was that part of the magic?"

"It is now," Jean said and laughed. Her body filled with warmth as she remembered Wiley sleeping between her and Spence in Richmond. "His name is Wiley. He's an immortal dog."

"Bill named him Sparkles. He disappeared after Bill turned off the fire."

"How was Mycroft with him?"

"Like they'd been together forever. Couldn't pull them apart."

When Jean hung up the phone, Richmond seemed closer than its twenty-four hundred miles from Portland. Wiley had come home with them—and he liked Mycroft. Her feelings bounced between the afterglow of knowing Wiley had been in the house and trepidation about Linda's run-in with the reporter. She jumped when Spence came through the door.

"Here you go. The broccoli was rubbery, so I got beans—" Spence stopped when he spotted the look on her face. "What? Was I supposed to pick up something else?"

"No, they're fine . . . but let me fill you in on my conversation with Linda. We might have a little company."

"Are Bill and Linda coming over?"

"Not exactly. But why don't you light the fire in the living room. Someone you know could show up."

Spence narrowed his eyes. "Let's eat first. I'm starved."

"Uh . . . why don't you turn on the news while I make dinner?" Jean didn't tell him the *other* part of her conversation with Linda.

Spence picked up the remote and turned on the local news. After the lead story about a recall of frozen pizza rolls, her head shot up when she heard the name *Raleigh Coulter*. Then she spotted Linda's face with a microphone in front of it.

"Jean!" Spence stared at the television with his mouth open. The only words he could eke out were "We're screwed."

"We're calling Jon," she said, drying her hands. She scrolled through the digital menu to find Jon Segert's cell phone number. "Here, it's ringing." She tossed Spence the phone like it was on fire.

"I knew you'd be calling me. I happened to turn on the news." Jon didn't even greet Spence when he answered his phone. *That* number meant trouble.

"What do we do now?" Spence asked.

"I told you guys not to say anything!" Jon snapped, his temper flaring. He punched the air and tried to calm himself. This would shine a spotlight on him, and also on the Collinses. Nightmare.

"We didn't, but I guess we should've been more careful in warning Bill and Linda."

"Who's Bill and Linda?"

"They're close friends. They watched our cat, Mycroft, while we were in Richmond for our anniversary."

Spence's voice hinted another nail was sticking up in the road. "How much do they know?" *Silence.* "Spence? How much?"

"Everything."

"Everything-everything?"

"Everything-everything."

"You know what this means, don't you? I have to haul both your asses in here and question you on the record. I can't stop the formalities now."

"When?"

"Monday morning. Be at the FBI offices at ten o'clock. Sharp!"

"Well, that ruins the New Year's weekend. Wait! Can we talk with you beforehand to discuss what we should say?"

Jon tapped his pen on his desk. "Probably a good idea. Meet me at eight o'clock for coffee at GG's Deli on the corner of McLoughlin and Concord. We'll sit in the back room so no one can hear us."

The cell phone clattered when he tossed it on his desk. Jon rubbed his face with both hands, trying to think about how to play this. After his little stunt of turning off the camera on Nash, the chief would insist on another agent being present in the room, probably Brick, and he'd have to make sure the conversation was recorded this time. He might even be cut out altogether.

Jon locked up his desk and patted the front of his center drawer. *No, Horus, you get to stay put for the weekend.* He turned out the light and shut the office door.

"Jenny?" he called out. Her head popped up over her cubicle partition.

"Don't do this to me, Jon! I'm getting ready to go home." She squinted, as if bracing for him to dump a project on her.

"No, don't worry. Relax. Update my calendar, though, would you? I have Jean and Spencer Collins coming in to talk with me on Monday morning at ten. We'll need about an hour."

"Good guys or bad guys?"

"Good guys, but right now I feel like spanking the hell out of those two."

"What'd they do?"

"Nothing. Happy New Year."

After dinner, Jean walked on eggshells around Spence. He'd been preoccupied through the whole meal about what they'd face at the meeting with the FBI.

"Look, I'm not worried, and I don't think you should be either," she said, trying to brighten her voice. "We'll just tell the truth: We were at the museum getting a valuable piece of fabric evaluated; Raleigh tried to steal it from us; we caught up with him; his taxi swerved off the road and he died. Done."

"What if someone asks us about all the *other* stuff?" Spence shot back, not buying her Pollyanna version of events in London.

"They won't. Jon will steer the conversation away from that." Saying the words equaled belief in the words. "Here, let's get our minds off the Monday meeting and focus on this painting. You light the fire," she said, hoping Wiley would show up. She set the art case on the living room floor.

Spence inserted the wall key for the gas fireplace. Jean's eyes locked on his as the valve squeaked. He struck a foot-long match.

The flames *poofed.* She waited. "Well, I don't see anything, do you?"

"Nope. What's supposed to be here?"

"Wiley."

"Don't think so. Let me get Mycroft's chair. I'm sure he'll be down any minute." Spence stood, gazed around, and headed to the dining room.

The Dancing Boy made her smile as she opened the case. Jean imagined the boy being still when inside, but dancing when he was on display. She stared. *So much movement . . . soft and lifelike.* The shadows and light were unearthly. The brush strokes were made with a delicate touch, nearly invisible. At the height of emotion moment was frozen. The boy's porcelain skin pulsed with blood. His pant legs were rolled up unevenly, showing no concern for etiquette of the day. This boy had snuck off to the woods to dance.

Spence set the dining room chair in front of the fireplace. "Take a bet for how long before Mycroft—" Spence stopped. They both heard a *bah-thump* upstairs. "Here he comes." The floorboards squeaked overhead as all twenty-plus pounds of Maine Coon marched along the catwalk and hopped down the stairs. Mycroft an-nounced his arrival with a jaw-breaking yawn.

"What do you think, Mycroft? Should we hang this in the living room?" Jean asked as if she truly wanted their cat's opinion.

Mycroft stood on the top step and stared at the intruder: the painting. Apparently, he couldn't decide either. Mycroft swaggered over to the fireplace but instead of jumping up on his chair he stretched out of the carpet.

Spence watched Mycroft. Jean watched both Spence and Mycroft.

"Okay, well—" Spence searched for an open spot on the walls. "That painting almost requires an English manor house, not a midcentury modern one. Doesn't go. Just my opinion."

"Before we decide anything, let's have it professionally cleaned," Jean said. "I bet it's never been cleaned—ever. Maybe the museum can tell us who the artist is too."

"Remember, we have a house to renovate. And I've got a store to open."

"This painting is the next step. That's what Charlotte said to me."

"Don't get all boo-hooey. I'll call Palmer Norquist for a consult. He's the curator of European art at the museum," Spence conceded. "We're on the Arts Council together. He'll find someone who won't screw it up."

"You think we can meet with him on Monday afternoon? We should be done with Jon by then. I bet we won't be more than fifteen minutes. Bingada-bangada-boom—we'll be out of there. Let's put the painting in the trunk and go right to the museum after the meeting."

Spence gave her a tired scowl. "I'll send Palmer an e-mail."

After meeting with Jon at GG's, Jean checked her lipstick and fluffed her hair in the mirrored visor of the Mini Cooper as they drove to the FBI building near Portland International Airport. They gave Jon a half-hour head start. He wanted to make sure they didn't all arrive at the same time. As she'd hoped, Jon told her and Spence to just stick to the facts—no embellishment. Any talk of the fabric should be kept only to its status as a valuable and historic artifact. Period. Jean felt pretty confident they had their story straight.

After getting to know Jon, both professionally and personally, Jean was curious to be on his turf for the first time—FBI turf. She expected to be treated like a celebrity with what they went through with Jon in London, but nobody recognized her or Spence when she checked in with the receptionist. In fact, the opposite was true: The woman eyed her as a "person of interest."

To relieve some of the tension, Jean picked at the neglected plant on the corner table. She tried to imagine what was happening in the honeycomb maze of puzzle solvers.

"I'm glad Palmer's available this afternoon," she said, fiddling with the dead leaves in her palm. "But they'd better step things up if we're going to get to the museum by one." Spence turned and gave her a sharp glare when she started sucking air in and out of her teeth. "Sorry. Freaky to be in here. So quiet and all."

"They're probably eating Krispy Kremes in the kitchen and taking bets on who's going to win on *Dancing with the Stars*," Spence said, snapping open the well-read copy of the *Oregonian.*

Jean smiled at the image and stood at the window. She watched a jumbo jet take off at the airport, wondering where it was going. She threw the dead leaves in a small trash can in the corner. The memory of working in a glass-lined office with a sassy assistant faded more after each passing day of the last year. She kind of missed the camaraderie but wouldn't trade her time off with Spence for any-thing. The bitterness of being nudged out of her corporate career had receded. She wanted to remember only the good parts.

Expecting Jon to meet them, the surprise on her face must have been obvious when another agent came to get them in the lobby. He resembled a Dick Tracy cartoon: slick-haired, square-jawed and squinty.

"Mr. and Mrs. Collins? I'm Special Agent Dan Brick. Follow me, please." No handshake or warm greeting. No smile or Happy New Year. He gripped a folder in one hand. Jean cocked her head to glimpse at the label. Their full names were typed along the edge, as was Raleigh Coulter's.

The confidence Jean had before coming to this meeting evaporated with every step as she followed Spence and Agent Brick to a small office, apparently unoccupied. Her mind raced through the morning's conversation with Jon. He said he'd be on the other side of the two-way mirror, observing, but not with them in the room. At least that was hopeful.

"Monday, January 2nd. Interview with Jean and Spencer Collins," Agent Brick said in an officious monotone. Jon had warned them their conversation would be recorded. "We have reason to believe you have information about the cause of Raleigh Coulter's death." Brick shifted his gaze from her to Spence. "Did you know Raleigh Coulter?"

Spence gestured for her to open the conversation.

"Well, we didn't *know* him," she said, glancing at the mirror. Spence kicked her foot for her to keep her eyes straight ahead. "We were acquainted with his mother."

Spence jumped in. "He broke into our house to steal something my wife bought from his mother's estate sale. A police report was filed about the incident."

"Yes, I have a copy of the report here. Says you bought a chest belonging to Raleigh Coulter's mother."

"Right." Jean nodded. "We had no idea who he was at the time. I found a valuable piece of fabric inside the chest after I got it home. We went to London to have it evaluated by the Victoria and Albert Museum. Unbeknownst to us, Raleigh Coulter followed us."

"The report also says Coulter was pretty badly injured at your house too. Did you have an altercation with him?"

"Absolutely not!" Jean's temper flared. *Keep cool. He's trying to knock my guard down.* Spence put his hand on top of hers. She lowered her voice. "Our cat, Mycroft, was defending his turf."

"I'm not accusing you of anything, Mrs. Collins. I'm just trying to establish the relationship. Nothing more." Agent Brick made a note in the folder. "Sounds like you didn't much care for Raleigh. Am I right?"

"A gross understatement," Spence said, rolling his eyes. "Look—let's not make a game of this. Raleigh Coulter broke into our house to steal a valuable artifact my wife found in a chest she bought from Raleigh's mother's estate sale. When he couldn't find it among her things, he tracked us down."

"Tell me more about this artifact." Brick acted as though he already had the answer.

"Like I said, the fabric was extremely old." Jean crossed her arms. "Turned out to be quite valuable."

"Raleigh broke into our house," Spence continued. "We weren't home, by the way. Then he followed us to London to try and steal it. When we came out of the museum, he practically assaulted Jean. In fact, he knocked her down on the steps. She could have been seriously hurt. It was a damn good thing Jon Segert was following Raleigh. Jon was with us when we followed Raleigh's taxi after he fled. The car crashed. He was killed. The end."

"Not quite, Mr. Collins." Brick studied Spence's face. "What about the hawk?"

"The only hawk in that taxi was the one on the fabric," Jean interjected, not giving Spence a chance to answer.

Agent Brick narrowed his already-narrowed eyes. "The driver said a real one was in the cab . . . and it killed Raleigh Coulter."

Jean sat back in her chair to act casual, but her palms went damp. "Now really, do you honestly think a hawk came out of fabric, flew around in a cab, and clawed up Raleigh? Ridiculous!" She made an exaggerated laugh. "You are too much!"

"Why did you leave the scene before anyone could talk to you?"

"We didn't," Spence said, throwing Jean a glare. "We talked to Jon Segert . . . extensively. Nothing more to say. He was with us. We had to catch an early flight to Cairo the next morning. We wanted to protect the fabric. It's extremely valuable."

"Yes, let's move on to Egypt. I read about your donation of the artifact to the Cairo Museum. Quite generous. What—getting rid of the evidence under the guise of benevolence?" Agent Brick pulled out a piece of paper from the folder.

Even turned around and printed on cheap stock, the images of the three phoenixes jumped off the page in a spectacular array of colors. The image had obviously been downloaded from the museum's website. She pictured the mercury bouncing upward on a blood pressure machine. The toe of her loafer found Spence's shoe. Their conversation with Jon hadn't covered this particular morsel of information.

"You know what I find interesting?" Brick continued, tapping the page. "This picture shows the artifact with three birds of a dif-ferent kind. Am I blind? No killer hawk here. How do you explain this?"

"I . . . I don't—" Jean choked on her words. "Interesting . . ."

"Yes, quite interesting." Brick made another note in their file. "How about you, Mr. Collins? Do you find that interesting? Your wife here says the fabric showed a hawk. What kind of bird did you see here?" Brick held up the picture and pointed to the phoenixes. "The three pretty ones like these or the mean, hawky one your wife described?"

Jean winced when Spence's expression changed at Agent Brick's mocking tone. She hadn't intended to blurt out anything about the hawk. She wasn't sure if Spence's slow burn was prompted by her words or the agent's, but he was going to ignite if Brick didn't cut the sarcasm. Blatant disrespect and abuse of animals were the two top violations that could make Spence highly combustible. Brick now was fully aware of one of them.

"I don't find this interesting, *Dan*," Spence seethed, his color a reflection of the hot coals glowing inside his gut. "I do find what you're implying to be shocking." Spence tried to keep his voice calm. "Jean meant none of us, including agent Segert, saw a *real* hawk when we got to the taxi. Are you suggesting a piece of fabric attacked Raleigh Coulter? C'mon." Spence gave the agent an unyielding stare.

Agent Brick broke his squinty stare-down at Spence and made a note in their file.

"God, we have a flipping FBI file. I've never even had a speeding ticket," Jean snapped, slamming the door on the Mini Cooper. "And another thing—that Brick guy was mean and snarky. His tone was uncalled for."

"Jean, why did you have to say anything about the hawk on the fabric?" Spence chided when he started the car. "A damned set up. Brick was well aware of what the fabric looked like all along."

"How could I have been so stupid?" Jean rubbed her forehead with her knuckles. "I caved. I wasn't thinking. I wish Jon had been in the room. Believe me—you handled that meeting much better than I did."

"I almost think they set up Jon too. Maybe they didn't tell Jon about the picture. He would have said something this morning."

"Spence, our donation wasn't exactly a secret." Jean sighed. "Brick knew we went to Cairo after we left London. I'm sure he had a record of our plane ticket. I counted on everything staying with Jon. Stupid, stupid, stupid."

"We have to find a way to make this up to him. He's being squeezed because of us."

"Yeah, we do." Jean dug through her purse, searching for a solution but not finding one. "We'll think of something. I'm glad we're going to the museum. The painting will be a good distraction."

"Doubtful."

Palmer Norquist held open the door to one of the museum's consulting rooms. The light inside was flattering, both to human skin and to the art. The relationship Spence had with the Arts Council gave them a red carpet of direct access to the curators in all of the departments of the museum.

"How are you both?" Palmer said, shaking Spence's hand. He turned and gave Jean a hug. "I haven't seen you since the fundraiser last August."

"We've had a busy fall. The holidays were packed." Jean shifted her eyes to Spence. "But we're excited about our latest acquisition. This is something we inherited."

"I hope you can help us with the painting in here," Spence said, thumping the art case. "Jean, do you want to tell Palmer what you found out?"

"The artist is a mystery, but the piece originally came from Rome several hundred years ago. We do know the history to that point from a family member of the original owner." She hesitated before continuing. "The painting's been in private ownership of only two families: the Mini family in Rome, and then given to the Gaines family in Virginia in 1881. We brought it home from the house we inherited, the Old Gaines House in Richmond."

"Well, you certainly have my interest piqued. Don't keep me in suspense." Palmer had the look of a pirate getting ready to open a treasure chest from a sunken hulk.

Spence unbuckled the case and opened it. Palmer stepped forward but didn't make a move to touch the painting. He stood stock-still.

"Do you . . . want to see this out of the case?" Spence asked.

Silence.

"Palmer?" Jean pressed. She couldn't quite read the expression on Palmer's face. *Awe? Skepticism?*

Palmer seemed to jump from his thoughts. "Yes, please . . . carefully."

The elastic straps *thronged* as Spence lifted the painting out of the case. Palmer eyes trailed the piece to the felt-covered table as if the canvas might explode.

"What is your goal?" Palmer asked.

"We need it cleaned first, and then we want to know who the artist was," Jean said.

"Do you want to sell? Possibly make a donation of it to the museum?" Palmer gave her a sheepish smile. "Kidding. I thought I'd give you the option."

"You wish, Palmer. One step at a time," Spence said.

"Beautiful frame. Let's take a closer look."

Palmer pulled a headpiece with magnification light from a shelf below the table. Leaning over the painting with the focus of a surgeon preparing to make the first cut, he lowered his enlarged eyes to within a few inches of the surface.

"Hmmm . . . I'm not quite sure. The brush strokes are fine, without a doubt, but inconsistent. Not all the same technique. Italian . . . no . . . maybe Dutch, from the complexion of the subject's skin and his bone structure. The eyes . . . yes . . . are definitely Dutch. Interesting combination of detail. Old . . . very old. Late sixteenth or early seventeenth century, I believe, from the patina and aging of the paint. The light and shadow, *chiaroscuro*, technique is impeccable. Egg and olive oil—maybe linseed oil. No signature of the creator, but not unusual." Palmer inspected the design on the wood. "The frame is not as old as the painting. Mid-1800s. The gold leaf is exquisite."

Palmer gasped.

"Something pricked my finger, like static. How odd. The boy speaks!" Palmer laughed but seemed nervous. "Can you excuse me? I need to consult with someone. Make yourselves comfortable." Palmer trotted from the room and closed the door.

Jean turned to Spence. "What do you think he meant? I wonder if our *Dancing Boy* got yakky with Palmer like he did with me."

Palmer's hand shook as he picked up his office phone and called Franco Machelli at the Northwest Institute of the Arts. Only one person could be trusted to tell him, without question, what this painting was. The execution had all the qualities of something important. He wanted the piece in his collection, no doubt, but he was more curious about *who* painted it.

"Franco—Palmer here. Can you send Dillon to the museum? Immediately, please? I need his opinion on a painting that was just brought in. Seventeenth century—I think Italian or Dutch, but I'm not positive. The clients are here now; they're waiting. Have Dillon come as soon as he can. Call my cell after you talk to him."

He set the receiver in the cradle. Palmer double-checked to make sure his cell phone was charged and spoke aloud to himself. "Many paintings speak to me, but this one . . . And what on earth was that static?"

CHAPTER 11

The Man

Dillon Davis swirled the delicate bristles of his thin brush in the glass jar of discolored turpentine. He examined the reflective quality of his subject's inner eye on the canvas as he pushed a long, baby-fine tendril of dark hair behind his left ear. Other strands fell in front of his face. The Man peered at him from behind a scrim.

The Man's soul still eluded him. Dillon had been working on the fleshy folds of skin of eyelids for over an hour now. They needed more texture. Hundreds of crevices made up just one wrinkle in an old person's lids, crevices only seen through a magnifying glass. The effect, when viewed from a distance, would be stunning and alive.

Dillon stepped back from the canvas. *Paint wisdom, man. Where is his soul?*

An impossible assignment. At nineteen, paint wisdom? The exercise, as presented, allowed him access to the real-life subject for only thirty minutes.

His brush touched the canvas, the human model long gone. Dillon realized he had missed one vital piece of information about this man.

Most students painted what was in front of them, fast as furious, and took advantage of their time with the Holy Trinity: subject, canvas, and paint. Not Dillon. He didn't work that way. He'd spent the precious minutes with his subject only in touch and visual study. He'd combed his fingers through the Man's wild, wavy gray hair to sense its weight and texture. He allowed his thin forefinger to graze over the flesh of the Man's lined and complicated eyelids. The Man's eyes weren't only wide and brown; they were the color of amber, flecked with honey and dark chocolate and had a distinct black limbal ring. *They are so intricate.* Dillon liked to study his subjects this way—he learned to appreciate the details. He may be struggling to paint now, but he would bring the Man to life again.

His passion also lay with the painting process. Dillon could prove to himself, and to everybody, he was the best. The youngest student to ever have received a full scholarship at the prestigious Northwest Institute of Art, he had survived into his second year. His professors labeled him a prodigy, but he had no idea what the word meant. Most painters didn't achieve fame, or become profitable, until they died. His reputation had blossomed with well-respected mu-seums around the country: The quiet, weird kid who authenticated and identified Old Master works. He kind of liked the label.

The latest trend was for students to do edgy, abstract work, with themes of being pissed off at life. *Cool-to-be-tortured nonsense.* Dillon wanted to go down a different, more difficult path, an unpopular path. The realm of genius wasn't just a goal but had become an obsession. All or nothing. Relative to the number of painters, only a handful had achieved greatness in the last five hundred years.

For the introverted Dillon, thank God the world of Old Masters was a quiet one. When he wasn't painting, Dillon sat on the floor in the art section of Powell's Books. He was unable to afford the elaborate reference books detailing the intricate techniques that unveiled the whimsy of Rembrandt, the haunting realism of David, and the chiaroscuro of Caravaggio, but he learned without buying. The light and shadow of Caravaggio's work, especially, mesmerized him to no end. He pored through the complete works of Da Vinci to memorize every line and brush stroke, and his eyes misted when he stared into the souls of Velázquez's subjects. As had and would be many humble viewers, he, too, was touched to his core by the quiet solitude of Vermeer. Book after book, hour after hour, Dillon studied on the floor of Powell's, while customers stepped around him in frustration.

Landscapes were all right, but the art of the face raced through his veins. A whole life, with its achievements and failures, emerged in just one eye. He could create the emotions of arrogance and vicious-ness, or make someone kind, humble, sick, or plain worn out with life's challenges. Eyes—the windows to a soul.

The Man was emerging on this canvas, in fine shape by anyone's standards, but capturing his soul stumped Dillon. This model had been strong, unflinching when he touched him. The Man was in control—had always been in control, in person and now on this canvas. Secret keys lay in his knowing smile and the subtle arch of his bushy left eyebrow, the way he took off his glasses and gazed at Dillon with a touch of humor. The Man had an aura about him. Dillon had never been at a disadvantage before. Who was he? Where and how did he live? Was he regretful of misdeeds, or proud of what he'd achieved? There was something special about *this* Man. He needed to think on these questions before he could dip the brush in any more paint. Who was the Man . . . *inside.*

Someone had entered the studio. Dillon didn't need to turn his head—he sensed the slight vibration and change in the atmosphere. Still, he flinched when a hand appeared in front of him with a note: The hand of his teacher and mentor, Franco Machelli. Those specific lines around the knuckles and the deep moons of his fingernails were the identifying markers. Dillon took the paper.

Can you go over to the museum right away? Palmer Norquist needs a consult.

The walk through the Park Blocks would help him to think about the Man. Dillon raised his thumb in approval.

"Thanks, Dillon," Franco said, returning the gesture.

Dillon pulled a paint-stained sheet over the Man. After meticulously cleaning his brush and capping the paint tubes, he wrapped his long Indian-print scarf around his neck. Glancing out the lead-paned window in the studio, he noticed a cold drizzle falling outside. He unwadded his rain jacket and slipped his arms into the sleeves. As he swung his knapsack over his shoulder, he stopped and glanced at the sheet-covered canvas. A man under there—a fine man. At the least, Dillon would make him fine.

Jean's antennae went on full alert. Art filled the air. This painting had the smell of history. She basked in the vision she'd seen and also about Charlotte's comments. *Italy. Hundreds of years.* Mystery pulled at her, pushing her accelerator from zero to one hundred.

Spence's face registered it too. He had that same star-struck gaze as when they were at the Prado in Madrid, the National Portrait Gallery in London, and the Accademia in Florence. And she had the same thrill as when she saw Lincoln's portrait at the Smithsonian in Washington, DC. Every one of the US presidents showed the weight of responsibility to lead a country, but none did like the details of Lincoln's. She cried when she stared at the sole of his shoe, with the leather separated from the toe. It spoke volumes about the man. Some art moved her, and moved Spence in the same way.

"Sorry, I had to get a pad of paper and call a colleague," Palmer said, stepping back into the viewing room. He placed the paper and pen next to *The Dancing Boy.* "Franco Machelli, at the Art Institute, said Dillon is on his way. I must warn you, though; Dillon is not what you think. Don't judge his abilities by his appearance, or his youth. He's highly intelligent and incredibly talented. I have a doctorate, and even I'm intimidated by the depth of his knowledge."

"Eccentric artist types are cool," Spence said, turning back to the painting. "Let me tell you, I've seen my share in the rock art and album collecting world." His face changed from amusement to thoughtful. "Being human—that's what this picture's about; a boy full of hope in a lively moment of no disease, no greed, and no hunger. He's full of music."

Jean turned and stared at Spence with wide eyes. His ability to pop out insightful pearls of wisdom never ceased to amaze her.

"That . . . and this painting has a quality I can't put my finger on.

This is as good as anything we've seen in museums in Europe, Palmer." Her gaze shifted back to the canvas. *And its magic*, she added in her mind.

"I agree. Qualities in this that are unique," Palmer said. "The light emerges from the canvas, making the subject appear natural and three-dimensional. Difficult to achieve, by the way, even for a master. Also, the skin on the boy's face—it's so"—Palmer rubbed his fingers together—"soft-looking."

All three of them went quiet . . . waiting.

The door to the small gallery opened. In walked a kid—a soaking-wet kid with long, dark hair, shorter on one side than the other, purposeful in its cut at an odd angle. A wet tendril hung over his right eye. He reached up and tucked the strand behind his ear, revealing angelic eyes, like a Kewpie doll's. The skin on his fine-boned face was porcelain-white and flawless, as if it had never been touched by the sun. Whiskers were few. The blank canvas of his face bore no expression. He raised his hand as the only gesture of greet-ing.

Jean studied the young man as he took off his dripping jacket and set it next to his knapsack by the door. Worn Keds squeaked as the wet rubber gripped the varnished wood floor of the gallery. With no acknowledgement of Palmer, Spence, or her, the young man walked right up to the painting, put his hands in the pockets of his jeans, and stared. The air was charged and still for a moment, and then the kid lowered his eyes to within six inches of the canvas. Jean heard herself breathing. Spence started shifting, self-conscious, from one foot to the other, as though he'd sipped too much espresso. Palmer pulled at a single hair on his left eyebrow.

"This is Dillon Davis," Palmer said in a barely audible whisper. "He's deaf." He handed Dillon a black felt-tipped pen. Dillon uncapped it without taking his eyes off the painting.

Pulling his own pen from his breast pocket, Palmer leaned over the pad of paper and wrote, *Dillon, this is Jean and Spence Collins. The painting is called* The Dancing Boy.

Dillon dismissed the note. He only had eyes for the oil-based boy on the canvas.

Jean stared at Dillon's hand when he took it out of his pocket. The hand of an artist. Her pulse raced in anticipation of what he would write on the paper. He scanned the canvas, inch-by-inch, with the pen poised, ready to give ink a voice.

With a hint of a smile, Dillon lowered the pen to the lined paper. The graceful, fine bones of his creamy-white hand moved as if the first notes of a Mozart concerto. Dillon wrote the words in perfect, calligraphy-like penmanship.

Caravaggisti

Dutch . . . maybe Italian

Can I clean it? Dirty.

PLEASE?

Palmer raised his eyes, seeking approval.

"Who's Caravaggisti? I've heard of Caravaggio but—" Jean said, thinking she must have skipped out on an important art history class in college.

"Not *who*, Mrs. Collins; a *what*. The Caravaggisti were a group of painters who were followers of Caravaggio, or M to his closest confidants. Artists flocked to Rome between 1600 and 1610 just to watch the man paint and learn his technique. I'm sorry to say, it all ended in violence. Caravaggio was forced to flee Rome after he murdered a man—ugly and tragic. He was gifted—no question—but a gifted thug."

Spence's stunned expression superseded his attempt to stay cool. She kept a calm exterior, but wanted to jump up and down with the confirmation their little painting may be important.

"We have to trust someone with this, Spence. He obviously knows more than we do."

"I feel the same way." Spence turned to Palmer. "Please make sure he takes good care of it."

Palmer leaned over the pad of paper and wrote, *Yes. You can clean it. Do you know the artist?*

Not sure. I suspect but want to spend time with it before I say.

Palmer raised his eyes with an anxious smile. "Well then, we have to wait. This is exciting. We may know exactly who it is very soon. Now that I have more clues, I'll do some research myself."

"How do we know it'll be safe?" Spence asked.

"The painting won't leave the building. Dillon can work here in the museum. He's a focused and intelligent artist. If this were my painting, I would trust him. And my life, I'd trust him with that too."

I'll start tomorrow afternoon. Here? Dillon wrote.

Studio three. I'll have a key card made for you.

Thank you! Jean wrote. She extended her right hand to Dillon; compelled to touch the hand that so captivated her. As soon as their fingers met, Jean felt a raging current of energy shoot down her arm, not up as she experienced before. Her head shot up against the stream. She locked her eyes on Dillon's. As he grasped her hand, the expression of surprise on his face told her that he experienced it too.

CHAPTER 12

Could It Be?

Dillon entered the museum the next day and tried to shake off the experience of holding Mrs. Collins's hand. He'd never experienced such a sensation. If he'd ever been Tasered, then he might have had some frame of reference. The energy of that moment had swirled in him all the previous night and throughout the morning in class. He felt a weird connection with that woman.

After checking in and picking up his key card, Dillon stepped into studio three. He set his knapsack down on the floor at the foot of the easel. He stared at *The Dancing Boy*, liking the name. The gilt wood frame, heavy and ornate, told him nothing. The small, flax-based was canvas stretched over a simple piece of seventeenth-century oak. The insert on the back indicated the painting had been framed in 1854 at a shop in Philadelphia. *Interesting.* The canvas itself was older, much older.

Once he removed the canvas from the frame, it felt light and free. He set it on the easel and took three steps back. The frame seemed to be nothing more than a distraction.

Speak to me. Who are you? Dillon ticked through the list of Dutch Caravaggisti: Gerrit van Honthorst, Hendrick ter Brugghen, Dirck van Baburen? Yes, one of these. Each an interesting prospect.

Neutralize and preserve the varnish. Never mess with the original varnish. The gift wrap of the painting. Just remove the yellowed dirt and years of grit and fireplace smoke.

Pulling the stool to the table next to the easel, Dillon surveyed his tools and solutions. For his first step, he selected a soft, dry brush to remove any loose dirt. *Work in small sections.* He shook his mind like an Etch A Sketch. The Man, and Mrs. Collins's hand, must be shed for now. He'd go back to think about them later. *Focus.*

Dillon brushed in short, soft strokes and became convinced two different styles of painting had been used. A suspicion yesterday turned to conviction today.

Start with neutralizer. Dillon picked up a cotton swab. *Let the picture emerge from the grime one small section at a time.* He dipped the end of the stick in the solution, soaked up the excess in a cloth, and paused over the upper-left corner. *Less is more. Don't rush.*

Is it possible the hand of genius had touched this painting? The telltale strokes were staring back at him. *A story; this boy has a soul.* Like Sherlock Holmes, make the conclusion based purely on empirical evidence.

Dillon's hand trembled as he moved the swab to the top left corner, where the deep green leaves hung over the massive rock behind the boy. He'd always broken with convention. Today proved no different. He must work from the outer edges of the painting to the inside—less risk when testing the stability of the paint . . . but the boy's image pulled at him.

As soon as the cotton touched the canvas, Dillon's hair rustled from a breeze. He gasped. No windows in this studio. He dipped the swab in the solution again and *heard* the breeze—the rustle of the leaves—he remembered the sound. The leaves grew greener as the tip yellowed to a dark amber hue. The breeze escalated to be a light wind. He sat back in the chair and took in a deep breath. *Is this painting speaking to me?*

He plucked a fresh swab from the work table. The bare toes on the boy's right foot drew his eye. Dillon dabbed at them as his own hair blew back from his face. The surface dirt lifted to reveal the microscopic earth painted at the base of the boy's toes. *Music . . . lutes.*

Heat. Dillon began to sweat.

The stick became a barrier between him and the painting. He reached out his hand. The two-inch area he had cleaned around the boy's toes illuminated as he touched the image with the tips of his fingers. *Light . . . golden light.* The beams escaped out of a small window from the past. The whole painting unfolded in front of him. *Voices . . . words of history. A man's voice.* This dancing boy knew. He had wisdom. And had secrets he wanted to tell . . . *to me.*

Hendrick ter Brugghen smiled as he finished the last touches of the soft blue velvet on the young boy's coat buttons. He was satisfied with the shine of the delicate toenails on the boy's right foot, bending to support the weight of elation, ready for the next downbeat. It had been the correct choice to loosen the britches to accommodate the movement, and the uneven roll of the pant legs projected freedom of spirit. *Secret dancing . . . in the woods.* A clandestine tryst with musical instruments. The élan on the face reflected a sense of movement as the young boy danced to the melody of the lute. The expression came through just right. He would call this commission for the Mini family . . . *The Dancing Boy.*

He stood back to admire his joyful work, Hendrick thought about Caravaggio and the brawl in the tavern last week. He, himself, couldn't possibly paint the brutal anger Caravaggio had exhibited. He recalled the vile words M had hurled, without instigation, at the poor waiter. "You damned fool! Do you think you're serving some kind of vagrant?" M had stabbed an artichoke with his sword, grabbed the waiter by the hair, and slammed his head against the table. He pointed the sword at the waiter. "Smell it, you ass. Butter or oil?" Hendrick was sure the man had been marked as a dead. In the end, Caravaggio only smeared the cooked artichoke over the waiter's face to humiliate him. M used power as a weapon.

Yes, perhaps he should add the tiniest grains of dirt between those delicate toes. That is what M would do. Dishevel his hair a bit more. A pounding on the door. Hendrick jerked his head toward the intrusion.

"Brugghen, my man! Open this door!" the voice bellowed.

That voice meant trouble. Hendrick dropped his brush in the jar of olive oil and rushed to the door.

"Come in, come in, M."

Running wild-eyed past him, Caravaggio snapped his fingers for his wiry-haired black dog to follow him. He then kicked the heavy wooden door so hard it slammed behind him. Hendrick flinched. The rush swirled around the room.

"They want my head, Brugghen! Give me haven. That ass respects me now. The air is filled with death tonight—I couldn't breathe its life in fast enough. I've never been more alive."

"Yes, of course, stay as long as you wish." Hendrick immediately regretted his words. "What has happened?"

"Coward . . . Tommasoni." Caravaggio spat as he said the name, shooting a glare at Brugghen. His coal-black eyes were ablaze; his long, wavy dark hair was wet with sweat. "He betrayed me with Fillide. He made me blind with rage, I tell you. We dueled. My sword ended him where he deserved. He won't even be able to walk among the gods."

"Dead? Blood on your hands, M?"

"Yes—and quite a bit of it."

Hendrick feared this would happen. Caravaggio had been arguing with Ranuccio Tommasoni over Fillide Melandroni's affection for weeks now. Fillide certainly was a beauty. She was made for the love of a painter. Paint loved her—and so did M.

"Crow! Sit!" Caravaggio shouted at the dog. He slumped in the heavy chair at the long wooden table. "I'm starved. I need something to eat. And my beast needs to eat."

"Take the amount of fruit you require. Fresh pears there; dried meats on the sideboard." Hendrick filled a bowl with water from the white ceramic pitcher and picked up the plate of meats. The bowl clinked against the tiled floor in front of the dog. He smiled as Crow lapped with such force the water puddled around it. He fixed his eyes on Caravaggio as he slid the plate across the table. "Here, my friend."

"What do you say, Crow? Give our Hendrick some thanks. Dance, Crow, dance!" The dog froze, stood on his hind legs, and turned in a hopping circle. Water dripped from his panting tongue. A perfect hoop of droplets circled on the floor.

Taking a bite of the pear, Caravaggio stopped laughing and gazed at Crow with a thoughtful expression. "*Nec spe, nec metu.* Without hope, without fear, Brugghen. You must love this dog, yes?" He took a deep pull of wine from the open bottle, swallowed hard, and, as if magnetized, locked his eyes on the painting. "What is this rubbish?"

"My latest. Nearly finished, I think. I call it *The Dancing Boy.*"

"Good God, man." Caravaggio stood and moved toward the easel, as if stalking it. He studied the image as he took another bite of the pear.

In the tense silence, Hendrick's knees weakened as he awaited Caravaggio's approval.

"A disgrace! Where is the dirt on this boy? Exceedingly sweet and fresh. Life isn't so rose-colored, Brugghen. Give me the damned brush!"

To take over his painting was the pinnacle of arrogance. But exhilaration coursed through him too. A master painter lived in Caravaggio. He stopped himself from shouting his objection. While he called M a friend, he could be dangerous and unpredictable. Hendrick hated to admit fear held him back from countering the request.

Caravaggio grabbed Brugghen's brush from the ceramic jar, wiped it on his filthy linen shirt, and dabbed in a blur on the palette. The colors remixed and emerged in a completely different way; they came alive.

"Smell the earth," Caravaggio muttered. A hint of dirt appeared in the crevices of the boy's dancing feet. "Feel the heat." Sweat from exertion soaked the silken strands of ragged, dark hair that framed the boy's cherubic face. "Cool the air." Movement of a breeze flowed in the haziness of the blight-spotted, deep green leaves on the branch above the boy's head. The expression began to change as the music inspired the boy to overcome his shyness. Blood gorged in the plump cheeks as the brush in Caravaggio's hand unleashed energy through oil-based veins.

Hendrick stared in silence and awe. His throat burned as Caravaggio achieved, in only forty minutes, what he, himself, wasn't able to do in a month of working on this painting.

"Now, my friend, you have a dancing boy," Caravaggio boasted. "Humors—all that was needed. I'm sorry to say, this work is most excellent now."

There was a noise outside. Caravaggio turned from the painting, following Crow's throaty bark at the door. Caravaggio's eyes grew wide. He threw down the brush, dashed to the table, and put a pear in his pocket. After he held out a strip of the dried meat to Crow, he stuck two in his own mouth. "Come, Crow. We must go," Caravaggio mumbled, snapping his fingers. "Brugghen, you shall never see me again."

As Caravaggio and Crow slipped out the back door, Hendrick turned to his painting. The air of genius gusted, slowed, and then settled. The room went still. He stood in front of the easel, stunned; his gaze filled with the organic, pungent aroma of damp earth; the refreshing breeze rustling the trees of the shaded wood; the rosy luminescence of the boy's heated energy in his skin; and the resulting dampness cooling his overheated body. *Earth. Air. Fire. Water.* As much as he wanted to put his name on this painting, he could not. This dancing boy was no longer his to sign.

Dillon sat on the heavy wooden stool—frozen. This wasn't just a Hendrick ter Brugghen—a Caravaggio too, right here in front of him. Both great painters had come alive under his brush, preserving the past and uncovering secrets. It had wisdom and soul. The painting was beautiful and important, but under the additional strokes of Caravaggio . . . magnificent.

Hendrick ter Brugghen created only forty paintings in his lifetime. Today, the number clicked over to forty-one.

The world turned silent again as Dillon continued to clean the painting for the next four hours. He sensed the door open to the museum studio. The vibration of the floor, or maybe it was the grumble of his stomach. He was starved—starved for more of this magic. Turning, Palmer's beaming face nodded his enthusiastic approval.

Dillon took the pad of paper and the pen from the work table. He held them out to Palmer. He uncapped the pen and wrote, *Magnificent.*

Yes.

Do you have an idea what it is?

Brugghen . . . and Caravaggio . . . together.

You think? You know?

I know.

Should I call the Collinses?

No, I'll go to their house tomorrow. I need more.

Time to stop. The museum is closing.

Dillon raised his thumb.

Palmer retreated from the studio.

After he cleaned up his tools and capped the solutions, Dillon pulled on his rain jacket. Before he left to get a bite at one of the food carts downtown, he took out his cell phone. He used it exclu-sively for taking pictures and texting.

Dillon snapped several photos of *The Dancing Boy* from different angles and distances. He dropped the phone back into his knapsack and strolled out of the studio.

I can do this. I can do it better.

CHAPTER 13

The Whisker

Dillon hopped on the bus, which took him down 99E to Milwaukie, about eight miles south of downtown Portland. The last leg had been to walk down to River Road and finally to the Collinses' house. He pressed the doorbell and waited. He waited some more. He pressed again.

Spence answered the door, his expression relaying surprise. He called to Jean. As Dillon stepped over the threshold, he realized they were eating dinner. *Cool house. Old and modern. So open—no boring squares: trapezoids, rectangles, stone, and diagonal images. The details are a little off center. Their poster art is impressive. Good color—lots of movement.*

Jean ran to get two pads of paper and pens. *Cool of her.*

She wrote, *You hungry?*

No, thanks. Food cart before I came.

He kind of regretted just dropping in on them, but his news would eclipse this faux pas.

Do you use sign language?

Never learned. I have something to tell you.

Let's sit in the living room.

He followed Jean and sank into the soft, sage-green loveseat. They had an enormous fluffy cat that followed the three of them down the steps and jumped next to him to investigate his scent.

His name is Mycroft. He likes you! Spence wrote.

The cat rubbed his arm with his muzzle and stretched out across his lap. *Mycroft. Sherlock Holmes's brother. Do you like mysteries?*

Very much.

So soft and trusting. I love this cat, he wrote.

Mycroft is the boss around here. Jean smiled and nodded.

Dillon rubbed Mycroft's spine as if preparing to give him a chiropractic adjustment. *Cats like massage.* A deep purr vibrated his hand down the cat's back through to the end of his substantial tail. He pressed his finger across Mycroft's broad face in short strokes to simulate the licks of its mother. Cats liked it. Mycroft responded as if he'd been trying to get Jean and Spence to do that for years.

He' purring, Dillon wrote on the paper

He's purring all the way over here, Jean wrote, laughing as she sat on the opposite loveseat.

You have something to tell us? Spence prompted.

Hendrick ter Brugghen . . . and also Caravaggio.

????

His eyes began to water and his throat burned closed. Dillon swallowed hard as he continued to stroke Mycroft. The cat gazed up at him, almost willing him to continue . . . to tell the truth.

Have you ever had a painting speak to you? Dillon wrote.

Yes, that painting you're cleaning did. Jean gave Spence an odd glance.

It spoke to me too, Dillon wrote.

I'm so pleased.

No, you don't understand.

"Honey, I think something's happened," she said to Spence. Dillon interpreted the words. Spence understood too.

Hendrick ter Brugghen, but Caravaggio enhanced it. This painting is important. I listened to the whole story. Saw every detail.

Jean studied him and bit at the inside of her cheek as she waited for him to continue writing.

Voices and music when I started cleaning the surface. And light. The painting spoke to me. What should I do?

Jean and Spence believed him. They had that insider reaction. He was a foreign entity in their lives, but they trusted him and, some-how, understood more about him than he did himself. He felt something for these people he could describe only as respect.

Dillon, do you believe in magic? Okay if you say yes, Jean wrote.

He stared at both of them. Dillon watched the silent exchange between them. The shift of their eyes spoke the words. He continued to stroke Mycroft, who vibrated and turned over in his lap. The fur was so soft. Dillon rested his hand on Mycroft's stomach and picked up the pen. He reached for the paper.

Yes, he wrote.

The burn swelled in Dillon's throat again. He hadn't cried in years. He was beyond crying, but the tears spilled anyway. With these people, he let them flow.

Spence jumped up and left the room. He came back with a box of tissues and went behind the couch to wrap his arms around Dillon's shoulders. Spence's whispering breath as he talked. Jean had her head in her hands. He grasped Spence's arms, his thin fingers holding on for life. Okay to let go, but he would never let go.

Jean reached for the pen. *Magic is real. We believe you!*

Every muscle in Dillon's body relaxed. He wasn't going crazy. This did happen.

Spence handed him a tissue and wrote, *Yes, I'm sure what you experienced was real. When you're ready to talk about it, we're here.*

Who are you? Who's Dillon Davis, Jean wrote.

Dillon set down the pen. His finger grazed something stiff poking from the upholstery. He pulled out a long, ejected whisker. Holding it to the light, he studied the graceful sweep of nature's design. A feline antenna. Its fine end disappeared to become air. *Can I have this?*

Of course. I'm sure Mycroft would be happy to gift it to you, Jean wrote.

Mycroft studied him as Dillon stroked the length of his tail. The cat chose to give up about ten long hairs into his hand. *Do you have a small baggie?*

Spence dashed to the kitchen and came back and handed Dillon the plastic bag. He placed the whisker and tail fur inside. Heaving

Mycroft from his lap, he kissed the cat's forehead and set him down on the couch.

We'll talk again. The painting is magnificent. More later.

Reluctant to leave, but not knowing what else to do, he strolled toward the front door. Mycroft followed him, winding himself around his legs. He leaned down to stroke the cat and raised his eyes to Jean and Spence. Dillon lifted his hand, stepped outside, and closed the door.

Jean knelt to comfort Mycroft, who continued to stare at the front door willing Dillon to come back.

"It's okay, sweetie. He'll visit you again." She straightened and turned to Spence, who was still reeling from Dillon's written words. "I think I did something to Dillon when I shook his hand at the museum."

"No doubt." Spence ran his fingers through his hair. "I need to get in on that. But, my God, Jean . . . a Caravaggio?"

"I knew that painting was special, and not just because of the magic. I knew it!"

CHAPTER 14

Damn Straight It's Good Work

Dillon fingered the baggie containing Mycroft's ginger-colored hair and single white whisker. The ultimate challenge could be to breathe life into his version of *The Dancing Boy*. No harm. Copies of famous art pieces were made by students around the world every day. The copy could be destroyed after he was done. *You can wait, Mr. Knowitall.* He eyed the Man who waited for him under the paint-stained sheet. *We're taking a break, okay?*

The cavernous walk-in storage closet held stacks of old canvases, boards, and cast-off frames. He pawed through the inventory and found one to be of similar size. Four pieces from a pile of aged wood sticks, which when nailed together, would support a canvas. The institute kept stacks of rejected student art and donated canvases for the purpose of other students reusing them.

Yuck, an ugly bowl of flowers—and not very good ones. They deserve to be painted over. Dillon left the studio and went down to the school's small kitchen. With an egg, two glass bowls, and a bottle of extra-virgin olive oil jumbled in his arms, he scanned the counters for anything else he might need. Satisfied, he took them back to the studio.

Time to get to work. Dillonaggio coming up.

After he painted over the entire flowered image with a neutral wash, he set his phone with the picture of *The Dancing Boy* on the easel. Caravaggio dove right in to paint what he envisioned inside. He never sketched. The master's paintings emerged from nothing. He needed to do the same.

Dillon cracked and separated the egg. He pulled up the yolk, the sac remaining protected in nature's delicate balance of fragility and strength. A slight poke released a thick golden string on the mixing wood. He discarded the rest of the yolk once the sack yielded the appropriate amount. A dollop of black, brown, cream, blue, and red from the paint tubes dotted the palette. He began to mix the exact hues which would become *The Dancing Boy.*

After working through the night, Dillon tented the painting. He'd spent over four hours on the boy's face, with an hour on each eye alone. The edges of the canvas matched to the pictures he'd snapped with his phone. He needed a break to work on the original. *Take a nap and go over to the museum.* The chance to make a final in-spection of the folds of the brown linen of the britches would help him finish the copy, but the cleaning of the original painting was nearly done. Class had to wait. He'd catch up.

Dillon picked up his knapsack and strolled to his small apart-ment a block from the school, thinking about the next section to paint. He flopped on his bed, exhausted but energized. The ceiling drew his gaze, imagining the sound of the cracked plaster lifting away, like trying to watch a flower open. *Does it move microscopically, im-perceptible to the human eye? Or does crack wait until no one is looking and quickly separate and freeze, playing a game?* He drifted off to the melody of lutes and tiny, dirty feet stomping at the hard earth.

The bright light in the museum studio revealed the tiniest bit of shine on the toenails as Dillon's swab stripped away the haze. For over four hundred years this boy had gazed out into a soft, veiled world. Not such a bad thing. With the curtain lifted, though, Dillon wanted to memorize every revealed detail. The longer he stared, the more ingenious facets emerged. Tiny spokes in the irises of the boy's crystal-blue eyes conveyed clarity of sight and depth of soul. They held a secret life that couldn't be tied down.

Dillon jerked up his head. The door had opened behind him. He turned to find Palmer Norquist with his teacher, Franco Machelli.

Franco's curious about what you're working on, Palmer wrote on the notepad.

He nodded his approval. The buzz of their voices excluded him from the exchange. *They didn't know the first thing about this painting.*

Franco leaned in, violating his space, to inspect the canvas with a magnifying loop, forcing Dillon to move aside. *The Dancing Boy's* eyes were eerily enlarged under the loop's lens. *Curious. Aware.* He pulled his gaze away and studied his teacher. The slightest hint of a smile crossed Franco's face. Dillon had disappeared. Invisible.

Franco straightened and wrote, *Good work, Dillon. We'll leave you to it.*

Dillon turned to the painting and rolled his eyes. *Damn straight it's good work.*

Franco Machelli walked back to the Art Institute through the downtown Park Blocks. The churning clouds signaled rain, or possibly snow. The air had a damp chill, which got deep inside his core—just like that painting.

Locking his knees became his only defense to stay upright when he examined the image. As soon as the lens went over those eyes, he was bewitched, obsessed. The same sensory overload engulfed him the moment he saw the Turner that old woman wanted to sell. She didn't know what she had.

Other painters attempted to capture the *Sturm und Drang* of weather on the seas or on the land, but none like Turner. The boiling clouds in Turner's sky gave him the same strange sensation he had now, a stillness right before a tornado hits. The painting hung over the old woman's fireplace for more than sixty years. When she was getting ready to go into a nursing home, she called him, out of the blue, to make an appraisal. He offered her ten thousand for the piece on the spot—she took the money. The man who ended up buying it was Gerrod Barnes in London, who paid two million.

A single transaction made him a wealthy man. And just this week, Gerrod had e-mailed, inquiring as to whether he had anything interesting to offer for sale. If Palmer didn't convince the Collinses to donate that painting to the museum, he might get them to sell it to him. They probably had no idea how important the piece was. Gerrod would be extremely interested in a Hendrick ter Brugghen, but a Caravaggio would have him shouting to the rafters. That choice nugget of information Palmer had passed to him changed the game. Even a mention of Caravaggio catapulted the little painting into the ranks of an elusive, and exclusive, club.

CHAPTER 15

Without Hope, Without Fear

Like a worm on a hot rock, Jean couldn't contain her anxiousness. She hated the thought of everyone around her knowing more about her stuff than she did. A bad place to be in business; a bad place to be with that painting—*their* painting. Feeling protective, she set out to find out everything possible about the artists of the Caravaggisti.

Dillon had inspired her to be better. His focus and commitment were qualities which made people not only accomplished but truly brilliant at what they do. Is this why the painting had come into their life? They were supposed to be doing something important with it—more than make mere money. This painting wasn't about money. Well, maybe a little bit.

"Hey, Spence! I need to go to the bookstore. Want to come to Powell's with me?"

"Sure! A biography on Duke Ellington just came out," Spence called back from the den.

"Let's take the T-Bird."

Jean pulled on the aqua driving gloves and backed out of the driveway. Spence dug through the glove compartment for a CD.

"The stereo you installed in here sounds great. How about some Rat Pack?"

"Hmmm . . . I've been jonesing for The Rumour," he said, pulling out *Purity of Essence* from the bottom of the stack.

"Good choice. I wish you'd turn Dillon on to them. He'd probably love that band. I can't imagine not being able to listen to music. You think we can do that for him? I transferred something into him when I shook his hand. He said he could *hear* that painting."

"I don't think he actually heard it. Inside his head possibly, like I did in this car and with the book."

"What's the difference? How about sharing the music with Dillon in the same way? I bet you can do what I did. Reach out to him."

Spence glanced at his watch as they stepped through the Powell's entrance. "Meet back here in an hour?"

"Sounds good. One hour. I'll be in Art."

"I'll be in Music."

Jean ran her hand over the spines along a whole shelf of tomes on Caravaggio. She pulled the heaviest ones out and set them on the floor. She sat, cross-legged, next to the stack and dug in for the fifty-seven-minute haul. The first picture to catch her eye was *The Lute Player*, painted in 1596. A similarity in the hues of the face of *The Dancing Boy*. The boy held the lute like the instrument was the most beautiful object he'd ever created. The fabric of the boy's sleeve hung as if weightless on his arm. Delicate dirty fingers. *Don't read into this. This is what you want to see.*

She focused on pictures of those paintings echoing youth, music, and movement. Some of the others were too serious and scary to compare to *The Dancing Boy*. She touched the picture of *Amor Victorious*, painted in 1602. This boy was naked but as joyous and precocious in his expression. *Curious.*

"Excuse me, please—can I get by?" some guy said.

Jean raised her eyes and flinched at the row of fishing lures dangling from his eyebrows.

"Sure. Step over me." She lowered her knees.

Dillon stood in front of his secret copy of *The Dancing Boy*. Exhausted, he was glad now to have pushed himself to finish in only two weeks. A few final touches to fix Brugghen's missteps. If Caravaggio had taken more time with the enhancements, the original painting would have been as alive as this one. Caravaggio didn't work on the boy's ears. They must not have been important to Brugghen, either, but Dillon knew about ears. He fixed those in his version, making them softer along the rim and more defined inside. The earlobes needed to be soft and squishy, spongy if pressed between two fingers. The extra detail corrected his own shortcomings to make this boy perfect in every way.

The baggie waited for him in his knapsack. Mycroft's single whisker was a gift of nature; his tail hairs were soft and embedded with interesting, variegated shades of persimmon and cinnamon. He extracted the tail hairs from the bag and rolled them in his fingertips. He kept rolling, rolling, rolling while he stared at the painting. To check the tightness of the twist, he examined them in the natural light.

Barely touching the ends in the dark-chocolate oil paint, he poised his hand over *The Dancing Boy*'s hair. His left hand reached for the magnifying glass. He held the round lens in front of his eyes. Inside the soft wave of the boy's locks, along one strand, Dillon painted minute word *Collins*. He feathered the letters to them blend in. He set the twist of tail fur on the palette and picked up Mycroft's whisker. He dipped the fine end in the marine-blue paint, one slight shade darker on the buttons on the boy's jacket. With his other hand, he moved the glass over the velvet coat. On the first button, he painted, in tiny letters, *Nec*; on the second he painted, *Spe*; on the third, *Nec*; and on the button of the boy's suspender he carefully wrote, *Metu,* in the soft color of dark linen. *Without hope, without fear.*

He stepped back from the painting. The codes appeared invisible, merely enhancing the reflection and texture of the original buttons.

The final step: he needed to create the appearance of age.

For the next few days, Dillon switched his focus to the Man and to catching up on his studies.

When the paint was at least surface dry, Dillon eyed the black coffee that had gone cold in the paper cup. He picked up a wide, soft brush. A swath of the rich, dark Sumatra Lintong ought to add the right patina of age. He dipped the bristles in the coffee and swished the tip over the entire painting in graceful movements, barely touching the surface. The colors mellowed as if hundreds of years passed in front of him in mere seconds. Crevices filled, and the boy's skin took on the tone of a Merchant Ivory film.

Hmmm . . . take that Caravaggio! Time to get something to eat and take a walk.

Franco Machelli entered the school's studio to search for Dillon but found the room empty. The draped painting leaning against the wall under the window drew him forward. Franco lifted the sheet and inspected the portrait of Dillon's anonymous human subject. He could have sworn the subject's eye moved. *God, Dillon is good.*

Stepping to the easel, Franco raised the sheet. *What's this?* His heart started to thrum in his chest. *The Dancing Boy.* Why would Dillon bring such a valuable painting here? It should be at the mu-seum, locked in the conservation studio. What was Dillon thinking?

Franco re-draped *The Dancing Boy*, pulled the canvas off the easel, and set it on the floor against the legs. He lifted the portrait of the sitting subject by the window and moved it, still covered, to the easel. *This would serve Dillon right for being so irresponsible.* The definition of genius didn't always include common sense.

He picked up *The Dancing Boy* and walked out of the studio. If Palmer found out, Dillon's reputation would be ruined. But uncomfortable questions would arise if he waltzed in the museum with the painting, so he took it back to his apartment. He needed some time to ponder his next move.

Franco scanned his living room for inspiration about how he could return the painting to the museum without drawing anyone's attention. His eyes stopped on a large coffee-table book containing the complete works of Leonardo Da Vinci. He lifted the heavy tome from the shelf. The size was a good approximation for the dimen-sions of *The Dancing Boy. A belated Christmas present? A New Year's present? A thank-you gift?*

The painting and the book appeared to be comparable once both were wrapped in gold-foil paper. Remembering he had a heavy, Christmas-themed shopping bag in his coat closet, Franco wrapped the book and then the painting – side by side, they were identical – and slid them inside the bag. He took a Christmas card and an en-velope from his desk and addressed them to Palmer.

"Happy New Year, Mr. Machelli," the security guard said with a lilt in his voice. "They're calling for snow tonight."

"Yes," Franco said, trying not to make his smile appear faked as he signed in at the front desk. "That's why I wanted to come over and give Palmer a gift this afternoon. Is he here?"

"No, sir, he's still out of town for New Year's. Went to visit family in Michigan."

"Ah . . . well, I'll set this at his office door then. Just a book; a belated Christmas present."

"I'll take it. Leave it with me."

"No, don't you worry yourself. I have to write a note to him, anyway. You can put it inside his office when you get a break. Only be a minute."

Franco sensed the security guard's eyes on his back as he walked through the main lobby of the museum. As he stepped down the marbled stairs, he passed an older man who tipped his hat. *He's familiar. Where do I know him?* The man nodded his head and smirked as he went by. *Odd.* Franco swiped his key card and entered studio three. He flipped on the lights and froze.

Under soft illumination, *The Dancing Boy* stared back at him on the easel. *What the—? Are there two? What's going on?* This changed things altogether. The original must have never been removed from the museum.

Unwrapping the painting from Dillon's studio, Franco compared the canvases. He couldn't decide, so he turned over the one on the easel. The wood on the back was at least four hundred years old. He could smell the age. *When in doubt, inspect the side people don't see.* Satis-fied he had the original, he slipped it in the shopping bag. This was an opportunity too good to pass up. He decided to leave the frame leaning against the table. It would give the one he'd originally thought was the masterpiece and which he left on the easel, more authenticity. Placing the wrapping paper over the painting, he stepped out of the studio and jiggled the handle to make sure door was locked.

Palmer Norquist's office was dark. He reached into the bag, pulled out the heavy wrapped book, and leaned it against the door. He set the card against the book.

Franco breezed past the security guard at the main entrance and dashed up the stairs toward the main entrance.

"One more stop to make and then I'm done," he called out over his shoulder. "I left that book next to Palmer's office door."

"No problem. I'll put it in his office on my break." The security guard watched the art professor walk out the door with his shopping bag.

CHAPTER 16

Let's Have It!

Dillon rushed into the museum, unable to catch a breath. *Must be here.* He opened the conservation studio door and breathed a sigh of relief when *The Dancing Boy* smiled back at him from the easel. Why would someone steal his copy from the school? To what end? *Someone.* Franco Machelli, the only one at the school who was aware of the original painting. He was also the only one who deemed him-self eligible to violate the invisible lines of privacy at the Art Institute. Dillon sat at the work table and calmed himself. The copy had been just an experiment.

Selecting the right brush for the final phase of the cleaning, he leaned in to examine the painting up close. His hand paused over the buttons of the britches. He sucked in a breath. *No, no, no! This one's mine.* He set down the brush, screwed the lid back on the solution jar, and slipped his arms in his jacket. He grabbed his knapsack and locked the studio door. A bus would connect him to Milwaukie in ten minutes. He might get to the Collinses' house by two o'clock.

When Franco Machelli returned to his apartment, panic crept up his throat. He turned the painting over, yet again, to satisfy himself: yes, the wood appeared to be of sufficient age. He inhaled a deep whiff. *This is the original.* He rushed to his desk and pulled out the glossy business card. The elaborate cursive letters, framed with an image of Gerrod's storefront window, said: *Barnes & Company Fine Antiques, London. Buy, Sell, Consign.* The thrill of the chase coursed through him from head to toe. The recognition he deserved in the art world was within reach—benefactor, collector, and discoverer of something new. Good would come from this money.

Franco flipped the card and fixed on Gerrod's personal cell number handwritten on the back. He checked his watch and picked up the phone. Why not? He'd bet his life Gerrod wouldn't ask too many questions. They had mutual interests: art and money.

He jumped when Gerrod came on the line. "Barnes & Company Fine Antiques, this is Gerrod Barnes."

"Gerrod? Franco Machelli in Portland."

"Yes, what can I do for you this evening? I'm pleased you caught me. Just locking up. Auction tonight, you know."

"Sorry, I'll be brief. I have something you might find interesting . . . quite interesting."

"Do you now? Let's have it, then."

"A painting. Hendrick ter Brugghen . . . and Caravaggio. An undocumented joint work."

"Surely you jest, Franco. Both in one work? I've never heard of such a piece. How did you come by this painting?"

"A bit of a long story. How much is Brugghen going for these days?"

"Well, Brugghen wasn't the most prolific of artists, but Sotheby's sold his *The Youth Playing a Violin* for over three hundred thousand—American dollars—back in . . . 2003, if my memory serves me."

"You don't say"

"Where does Caravaggio come into play?"

"This is not a portrait. The piece is an image of a young boy dancing in the woods. I have reason to believe Caravaggio had a hand in creating it."

"That would certainly make the piece interesting—up the stakes, indeed. Brugghen, of course, was part of the Caravaggisti. E-mail me a photograph. We can talk again after I've had a look-see, shall we?"

"I'll send you pictures tonight." Franco ended the call. He removed one of his own pieces from the adjacent wall, a small Leonardo Da Vinci etching, and replaced it with the unframed canvas of *The Dancing Boy*. The pin spotlight showed off the vibrant hues in a pleasing radiance. Now that Dillon had removed the hazy dirt, the painting was spectacular. It had come alive.

Franco held up his phone, clicked several pictures at different distances, and e-mailed them to Gerrod at the address on the card. Gerrod would be able to review them in the morning, maybe even tonight.

Gerrod Barnes stood at the back of the auction room to assess the crowd. He kept his eyes on several serious collectors—ones he knew would spend whatever necessary to acquire what they wanted. He had three pieces consigned by a client in tonight's sale: a small Rembrandt etching, a rare Whistler print, and a set of three excep-tional bookplates by William Blake.

The thrum of his smartphone signaled the arrival of an e-mail. Glancing down, Gerrod straightened when he spotted the name Franco Machelli—with attachments. He appreciated Franco's sense of urgency, a sign of a true art lover and fellow opportunist. One after another, Gerrod stared in disbelief as he pulled up the pictures. He flinched and broke his gaze when he realized he'd nearly missed his lots being called. He'd never seen, or even heard of, Franco's piece. That fact was both a challenge and an opportunity. The image was attractive, extremely well executed, a perfect size, and exuded positivity in the subject, all pluses to a collector. As a Brugghen the work was valuable, without question, but if the provenance could be tied to Caravaggio—well then, that was another matter altogether. Even through the small image on the screen, the play of shadow and light certainly appeared to be in the Caravaggio style. This very well might be what Franco said it was. He fired off a return e-mail as he monitored the hammer price of his lots.

Overnight this piece to me. So far, Mr. Machelli, the work is excellent . . . most excellent. Do you have a solid provenance for this painting?

"Sold!" the auctioneer announced as the gavel banged.

Spence returned to the living room as Dillon wiped his eyes with the sleeve of his jacket. His heart sank. In an attempt to console him, Spence sat on the hassock and searched Dillon's face for clues to what had happened.

Let's start at the beginning, Jean wrote on the paper.

Your painting was switched with mine, Dillon wrote. *Yours is gone.*

What do you mean by your painting?

I made a copy. Mine, not the real one, was at the museum. Your painting is gone.

"Jean, did you know about this?"

"I had no idea." *Who took it?* She held out the pad to Dillon as if the paper demanded an answer.

I'm sure it was Franco Machelli. He had access to my copy at the school and access to the museum to switch the painting. No other student has that kind of clout. No one at the museum knew about my making a copy.

Spence raised his eyes. "Good God, this is serious. If that painting gets on the market . . ." He turned to Jean "We need to figure this out."

"And we damn well will," Jean said, fuming. "I'm calling Jon right now." She ran up the steps to the kitchen.

Who's she calling?

Jon Segert. He's a friend of ours with the FBI. He'll help us, Spence wrote.

I screwed up. I wanted to see if I could do it better.

You did a good job.

Jean stood on the top step to the living room with the phone in her hand. "Okay—Jon's on his way over."

CHAPTER 17

Who's Up First

Jon sat in his office at the FBI and pored through a dizzying number of websites and news stories on the Internet. The glazed doughnut sitting on a napkin next to his computer drew his gaze. Then he noticed the middle button on his white shirt shouting out a protest chant that it had exceeded the limit of restraint. He switched his focus back to the screen to find anything interesting, beyond the FBI's own records, about Anthony Dromov and Kendrick "Kip" Forrester. Sometimes the public websites contained tidbits of tabloid information overlooked by the internal FBI databases.

Two computer screens worked simultaneously—his desktop for Dromov and his laptop for Forrester. He squeezed his eyes and rubbed them until stars floated behind his lids. After a year of being in denial, maybe he did need glasses. They say the body starts falling apart after fifty. Meg poked him about the glasses and pants-letting-out again this morning. As the stars cleared, Jon stared at the screen. The doughnut remained in his peripheral vision. Nothing wrong with that particular part of his eyesight.

Anthony Dromov was fifty-five and ran his own investment company, the Dromov Fund, with assets of $150 million. His pas-sions were fast cars and art with a pedigree—a lot of art. He liked to live well and used his public lifestyle to attract wealthy customers. Wealth attracted wealth. Dromov had offices in Portland and New York. An online article showed a picture of him beaming for the cameras and holding up a painting, a small Vermeer, after he paid a record $40 million for the piece at auction.

Kendrick "Kip" Forrester, forty-five, was a trader worth about $10 million, who loved to cozy up with stars: rock stars, music legends and Barbie-doll women. He lived in Seattle, but his client base stretched up and down the West Coast, most of them clustered in Los Angeles. Kip collected famous instruments and memorabilia. His personal collection was exceeded only by the Rock and Roll Hall of Fame. Kip collected fame. On the screen was a picture of Kip with his arm around some big-busted babe on the red carpet at a music awards ceremony. How does a mere trader make that much money? Jon was certain the spoils didn't come from stellar research and brilliant hunches.

Neither one of these guys smelled right. Anthony Dromov had the aroma of a Ponzi scheme, which always destroyed the lives of its victims. They ended up getting pennies on the dollar, if they got anything back at all. Kip Forrester went to the bank on insider tips, stepping on the heads of those who played fair. In the end some-body, or multiple victims, got screwed.

Jon created two files, jotting copious notes in each one. The key to bringing these guys down was through their passions. The money was a means to get what they wanted. At that point, smart guys turned stupid. Flaunting their greed made them feel invincible and fed their insatiable egos. These two yahoos would never be able to get enough, but they'd eventually crest the hill and stumble into his net. Jon's eyes tick-tocked between the pictures of the men on each screen. *Who's the lucky guy who wants to go first?* He reached for the doughnut.

The desk phone yapped. Jon jumped and yanked back his hand, imagining Meg on the scolding side of a doughnut cam.

"Jon! Thank God you answered. Jean here."

"Oh hey! What's up?" He picked up the doughnut and took a bite.

"We need your help. A painting's been stolen—our painting. This is too complicated to discuss on the phone. Can you come over to the house now?"

"Slow down. What do you mean 'complicated'? How complicated? Why don't you call the police?"

"Big implications . . . yeah . . . big. Only *you* would understand."

The tiles on the dropped ceiling drew his gaze. He could only imagine what—No, that was the thing with the Collinses. He couldn't imagine. "Can you give me an hour? I'm kind of buried in something big."

"Any sooner? Please?"

"Okay, stay at the house. I'll be there in half an hour—forty-five minutes tops."

"We'll stay right here. Thanks."

Jon hung up the phone and shook his head. He took a big bite of the doughnut and stopped mid-chew. The computer screen pulled his eyes as if he'd been hypnotized. *Painting?* He bored a hole into Anthony Dromov's picture. He swallowed hard and licked the glaze off his thumb. "Jenny?" he called out. "Can you come in here?"

"Yeah, Jon, whatcha got?" Jenny said from the doorway, between furious chomps of her gum.

"This guy—I want everything you can find on this guy." Jon tapped the computer screen several times. "Tax returns, audit reports of his company, client lists and their account balances, phone records . . . and arrange for e-mail access. I want the works—ASAP."

Jenny walked over to his desk and leaned in to the screen. "Forward the link of that article to me. I'll get started, but I doubt they'll give us the client list and balances without just cause."

"Get what you can. I'll work on the just cause. First, check if any client complaints have been posted to any watchdog sites or con-sumer advocate groups about the Dromov Fund."

"Got it. Yea! New bad guys! I'm tired of the old ones." She disappeared from the doorway.

Jon grinned and resumed staring at Anthony Dromov's round, olive-skinned face and coal-black eyes on the computer screen. He tapped the image, leaving sugary fingerprints on it.

"You first."

CHAPTER 18

Anthony Dromov

Anthony Dromov stepped out of the glass-walled shower and wrapped an oversize Turkish towel around his considerable hairy frame. His wet feet left a trail of water on the Brazilian wood floor all the way down the hall of his Park Avenue penthouse.

A demure espresso cup waited under the nozzle of the machine in the kitchen. Anthony took a sip and stepped to the Vermeer hanging over the fireplace in the living room. The soft light from the pin spot, installed specifically for this exquisite painting, made the haunting image appear to move. The folds of the girl's wrap draped like real silk. The creamy skin of her face and pouty eyes mesmerized him every time he stood in front of her. The young girl sat at a piano; the wood's freshly polished shine reflected the natural light.

Holding up the espresso cup, Anthony toasted the painting. "Thank you, Mrs. Goldsmith, for making this moment possible."

Too bad Coulter, who'd referred Goldsmith and her millions to him, was dead. For the past three years, the relationship with Coulter and Winthrop had been a boom to his company. Those two, in particular, provided a steady stream of new investors coming through the door. The secret was new wallets, and also keeping his high-profile reputation intact. If he didn't get an infusion of cash soon, he'd need to shut down the whole fund. Since Raleigh Coulter's death, his clients were nervous and wouldn't stop calling the office to request the withdrawal of their money. And new money wasn't coming in—a severe developing gap.

Anthony had always wanted to get here—well, ever since fifteen years ago when he stood on the beach in the Hamptons and admired a singular, magnificent house, a billionaire's weekend mansion. As a young broker starting out, Anthony realized if he acted the part, then why not *be* the part. He could be a country club guy. He'd done his homework and researched who owned the house. Over the course of six months, he'd followed the billionaire to see what he did to get his money, joined the same clubs he belonged to and frequented every establishment where he shopped, ate, and drank. He'd actually met the man a few times, even played a round of golf with him once. That was a million-dollar day. At least he'd felt like a million bucks.

It hadn't been easy to emulate everything that guy did, and he'd racked up a mountain of debt in the process. That all changed when he met Raleigh Coulter. Raleigh taught him about human nature. Old people were predictable and wanted something for nothing. Smooth charm and the promise of high returns and security in a shaky market opened up wallets. Massive equity lingered, unclaimed, in homes with no mortgages; the cash waited for him to pluck it. Start clients out with a decent return, pennies on the dollar for their first payment, and spend the rest. A taste for the promise of big profits—on paper. All he needed to do was pay the promised interest to his existing clients out of the new money pouring in. New investors were man-datory to keep his life going.

When he gazed at that house, he coveted a lifestyle defined by those modern lines and numerous balconies facing the ocean. The whole mansion had been lit up from the inside in a soft gold glow. The light showcased the spectacular art on the walls, all Renaissance oils in ornate gilt frames: portraits, hunting scenes, floating angels, slices of life in another time. History smacking the face of modern-ism. Money could buy respect, status, cars, and art.

Fine art created a fine man. Class had a price tag. Raleigh had enlightened him on the cheat sheet of gaining trust. In the initial days of setting up the fund, his investment advice had been stellar. Once he attracted elderly wealthy clients, though, the hook easily pene-trated the flesh.

The intercom buzzed by the front door. Anthony pulled his gaze from the painting. He pressed the button. "Yes?"

"I've had your car brought around, sir. Out front, whenever you're ready."

"The Lamborghini, like I asked?"

"Yes, sir—the yellow one."

"Thank you, Henry. I'm still dressing. Give me about twenty minutes."

Anthony handed the valet his briefcase, a fifty dollar bill wrapped around the handle. He ducked into the yellow Lamborghini. The valet opened the passenger door and set the briefcase on the seat—without the fifty dollar bill—and waved Anthony out of the garage.

The morning commute in Manhattan could be a bear, but not when accompanied with the soaring strings of Vivaldi's *Four Seasons*. Stopping at the intersection of West Fifty-seventh and Park Avenue, Anthony glanced over at the clean-cut man in black sunglasses sitting in a BMW 750i. The guy smiled, stuck up his thumb, and nodded. *Yeah, buddy, you only wish you could own this car.*

As he pulled up to the modern glass building in the Financial District, Anthony wasn't sure if he'd be coming here in the next few weeks, or to his office in downtown Portland, Oregon. He hadn't been back to Portland since Raleigh Coulter's death. Things were tense with those clients. He had to keep them appeased for a little while longer, especially Judy Hawkins. She'd been particularly annoy-ing and rude in her persistence to reach him. The nastier the calls became, the less likely he'd even make the effort to return her call.

Preparations to flee had already begun. The new passport arrived yesterday. Three major tasks remained: shred, ship, and book a flight to Amsterdam. He'd already started shipping his art to his apartment in the ancient city. The Vermeer would be last, but it belonged in Amsterdam, away from the noise of New York. In the meantime, he had to keep the appearance all continued to be normal.

"Good morning, Mr. Dromov," the parking attendant said and opened the driver's door.

"Hey, Jack, you been good?" Anthony handed the young man a twenty and grabbed his briefcase. "Be gentle with her, buddy."

"Gotcha covered, Mr. Dromov."

Whirling out of the revolving door, Anthony strutted through the marbled lobby toward the bank of elevators for the upper floors. A gathering of worker bees, sporting sneakers for their pedestrian trek from the subway, waited with him for the first elevator to arrive. He chuckled to himself. *At least they'll all get out before me.*

"Hey, Diane," he said to his assistant, trying to get past her to shut himself in his office.

"Stressed. Salena Steward is on three. I told her you'd have to call her back, but she insisted on holding. We're now up to fifteen minutes and she's driving me crazy!" Diane made an exaggerated growling noise. "Will you just talk to her *please*?"

Anthony rolled his eyes and sighed. "All right."

He shut the mahogany door behind him. The script formulated in his mind as he threw his briefcase on the leather chair in front of his desk. His hand grasped the receiver. Before he picked it up, he smiled to prepare for the show.

"Mrs. Steward! So good to hear from you! How have you been?" he said, keeping his voice bright.

"Yes . . . oh yes, Mr. Dromov, I've been trying to reach you for weeks." Salena's voice sounded frailer than the last time he'd talked with her.

"I know. So sorry. I've been out of town. I'm glad you called because I was getting ready to call you about a new opportunity. Quite exciting."

"Mr. Dromov, I need some of my money—no—all of my money. My daughter needs help her with her son. He's autistic, you see. I . . .

her husband left her and she's—"

"Ooh. I'd be happy to, but we have to wait until the audit is complete. We're going through our annual audit right now. They won't allow us to make any withdrawals until their work is done. I'm sure you can understand the accounts can't be changed while the process is taking place. It'll be fine, not to worry." He tried to keep his voice calm and soothing.

"I don't care about any auditors. You tell them I need my money!"

"I'll call you as soon as they're done, dear, and then we'll make the transfer. I promise. Shouldn't be more than six weeks or so." By saying those words, he'd just created a self-imposed deadline to tie up the loose ends. *Dammit!*

"Six weeks? Mr. Dromov, I can't wait that long! Oh no, I need my money now."

"You should be happy we're being so thorough with our compliance procedures. You watch the news, don't you? We have to adhere to those *very* strict regulations. Like I said, I'll call you as soon as we're cleared to make the transfer. If it's sooner than six weeks, you'll know right away." *He had to get off this damn call.*

"But—"

"I have the auditors sitting in my office right now, Mrs. Steward," he said, cutting her off. "I really need to go, dear. Please give your daughter my best." He hung up the phone.

I have six weeks.

CHAPTER 19

You've Got a *What*?

Jon waved at the peephole in the Collinses' front door, knowing they'd check before opening to his knock.

"Oh thank God, Jon. You got here so fast," Jean said and gave him a hug. "Come in, come in."

"Yeah, no problem. What's this about?" he asked.

"We need your help. A painting was stolen."

"Yours? Why didn't you call the police?"

"We called you first. This is a bigger issue than the police."

"What does that mean?" Jon narrowed his eyes, knowing full well he'd be spinning down the rabbit hole with the answer.

"Our original was stolen. We have a fake. Sit down. You need to meet Dillon Davis, the artist of the fake. He's also the one who cleaned our original."

Jon stood at the top step overlooking the living room and studied the couch. He didn't count on seeing a kid to be sitting there, but the actual creator of the fake was the last thing he expected. Cross that off the list of things he had yet to experience. "What was it? Don't tell me . . . a Rembrandt or a Michelangelo?"

"Not to far off from a Michelangelo—more like Michelangelo da Caravaggio . . . sort of."

Jean casually rolled the name off her tongue like a snooty museum docent. Jon turned and gawked at her with his mouth open.

"A Caravaggio? Are you kidding? God, you guys. Where the hell did the painting come from?"

"From Mary Coulter's estate. Inheritance." Jean threw him a sheepish smile with a hint of pride.

"I bet Raleigh wasn't aware that existed. If he had been, he wouldn't have given two hoots about the fabric. Magic or no magic."

"No doubt! And one more thing—" She hesitated. "Uh . . . this one's magical too." Even though Jean had said the words under her breath, she might as well have used a bullhorn.

"Of course it is . . ." Jon stepped down into the living room and eyed the kid, sizing him up. Spence sat in one of the chairs with a pad of paper in his lap.

"And Dillon knows the painting is magical . . . the original," Spence said. "Dillon had a vision, a noisy one, when he started cleaning the canvas. The whole history spoke to him as he worked on it. And Jean had an experience too before we left Richmond. Light came out of the image—swear to God. Jean thinks she transferred something in her to Dillon."

Jon stared at Spence with a deadpan expression, but his mind raced.

"Now can you understand why this is a rather delicate matter?" Jean added. She darted her eyes to Spence. The gesture didn't escape his notice.

"This is Dillon Davis. He's deaf, so if you want to talk with him you'll need to write your questions down," Spence said. "Have a seat, my friend. This is a good one."

"I have no doubt."

"Can I get you anything?" Jean offered. "Coffee? An iced tea? Spence picked up these tasty shortbread cookies with a blop of dark chocolate."

"No, nothing, thanks. I'm off sugar."

Jon sat on the hassock and faced Dillon. He listened to Jean and Spence, noted Dillon's expressions, and wrote on the notepad for nearly an hour as the whole story was unveiled. Jean's right; his was complicated and, yet again, an unbelievable circumstance. And the kid was being truthful too. No mistaking the tell in his eyes. Dillon had seen Caravaggio; he was convinced. At first, he doubted this kid, but something was odd about him. *Purity? Honesty?* He was one of those "art for art's sake" kinds of geniuses who were showcased on public television.

"Do you have pictures of the painting?" Jon asked, and then wrote the question on the paper.

Dillon dug in his knapsack, pulled up the pictures, and handed his phone to Jon.

Swiping his finger across the phone, Jon examined the pictures of *The Dancing Boy*. His body tensed as he handed the phone back to Dillon.

"Yeah, the police would get us involved, anyway, with a name that significant—even without all the magic ooga-booga." He twirled his forefinger for emphasis.

"Now what?" Jean asked.

"Okay, here's what we can do. The FBI has an art crime team and an internal NSAF database, the National Stolen Art File. The woman who heads it up is a friend of mine. I'll enter the details in there first. Then we need to make sure the title and artist get into the Art Loss Register. That's the public database the legitimate auction houses and dealers use to check when a piece like this turns up for sale. But the painting could end up going through a network of underground collectors. Then it slips into dirty hands, or sometimes innocent ones, depending on how unscrupulous the dealer is. Art fraud is big money, guys—six billion a year and growing. And that's only what we know about. I expect the activity is much bigger." He shook his head. "Can you believe some really valuable works of art end up in thrift stores because they're too hot to sell? The stupid thieves realize they'll get caught and dump priceless works for twenty or thirty bucks. No small crime, though. Let me see those pictures again."

Jon scrolled through the images one more time. He sensed three pairs of eyes trained on him.

"Okay. Jean and Spence, you stay here." Jon stood and pointed to Dillon. "He needs to come with me." He took the notepad and wrote, *You need to go back to the museum with me.*

Am I being arrested?

No. I want you to show me your painting. The fake.

The silent air inside of the Crown Victoria became supercharged as Jon drove Dillon to the museum. *A kid . . . he's only nineteen. An art expert at nineteen? And he's deaf—great. Why is nothing straightforward with the Collinses?* He glanced over at Dillon, who stared out the window, closed off in a world of private thoughts. Jon turned his gaze back to the road, his own thoughts whirling at a thousand miles an hour for the quiet twenty-minute drive. All of these puzzle pieces would reveal something—but what?

Jon took note of Dillon's body language as they walked through the main entrance of the museum. The boy's shoulders slumped; he seemed defeated. Reaching out his hand, Jon squeezed Dillon's shoulder for reassurance. The gesture wasn't acknowledged.

"Hey Dillon!" The security guard waved from the main desk. Dillon raised his hand to return the greeting. The guard eyed Jon and pushed a clipboard for them both to sign in.

"I'm Special Agent Jon Segert, FBI. I'm here with Dillon. He's going to show me the painting he's been cleaning for Jean and Spencer Collins." Jon pulled out his ID and turned it on the counter to face the guard.

"Is there a problem?"

"Don't know."

"Well, I'm not sure about this." The guard hesitated and darted a protective gaze at Dillon. "No one gets access to the conservation studio without Palmer Norquist's approval."

Dillon leaned over the desk and picked up the pen. *He's OK. A painting like the one I've been working on was stolen. He needs to check it out.*

"Can you get Mr. Norquist for us?" Jon asked, thinking Dillon was on the ball. It was as if Dillon knew what he, himself, would have said. *Nice going, Dillon.*

"He's not here. Out of town, but I guess it'll be all right, as long as I accompany you." He motioned for his colleague at the front entrance to join him at the desk. "Take over while I escort Dillon and Agent Segert downstairs to the studio."

Jon and Dillon followed the guard. He opened the third studio door, near the administrative offices.

"Please leave your coats and bags in the hall. I'll stand out here. Be brief."

"No problem. We'll be ten minutes max," Jon said.

The guard's eyes narrowed when he spotted Jon's gun in the body holster. Jon tapped Dillon's shoulder and pointed to his knap-sack and then to the floor. Jon took off his jacket and placed it on top of Dillon's knapsack. After the guard turned on the lights, Jon guided Dillon inside and clicked the door shut behind them.

Dillon pointed to the painting. Jon stepped toward the easel, which was illuminated by track lighting. Brushes, tools, and solutions littered the table next to it. The image of the little boy seemed to jump off the canvas.

"I'll be damned." He pointed to Dillon and mouthed, "*You* did this?"

Dillon nodded.

A notepad drew Jon's gaze to the table. He searched for something other than a paint brush. He found a pencil and wrote, *This is the fake?*

Dillon nodded.

Prove it.

Dillon stepped to the table and pulled the magnification lamp over the painting. He clicked on the light. Picking up a thin brush he pointed to the lock of hair on the boy's head.

Not sure what he was supposed to see, Jon peered into the light and studied the area where Dillon was pointing. He didn't notice anything. Dillon tapped the brush on the canvas again. Frustrated,

Dillon took the pencil.

I painted the word 'Collins' on the wave in his hair. I also put words on the buttons of his britches—Nec Spe Nec Metu. Means "without hope, without fear" in Latin. A phrase used by Caravaggio.

The words, barely visible, jumped out at him.

"Unbelievable," he whispered. He took the notepad and pencil back from Dillon.

Do you want to work for the FBI?

CHAPTER 20
The Visitor

Jon sat in his office the next morning and stared at the blank computer monitor while he tapped his pen end over end on his desk. He couldn't get the image of the painting out of his mind. He now understood how somebody like Dromov could become obsessed with the Old Masters.

Logging back on his computer, Jon pulled up the bookmarked page. He studied Dromov's picture again. "No happy ending here. All this jerk needs is someone with a pulse and a checkbook . . . " he muttered. He raised his eyes, surprised to see his assistant standing in the doorway.

"Some old guy's in the lobby. Says he needs to meet with you," Jenny announced.

"Who? Nobody's on my schedule today."

"Said he has something important—'key to the case', whatever that means. He wouldn't say his name." She wiggled her fingers in front of her face. "Ooh . . . I love a good mystery."

Jon grimaced and studied his ficus. He followed a leaf's path to the floor. "Okay, but throw some water on the tree. And get me Dromov's client list."

"I'm on it." She disappeared to the lobby.

"What I need today," he grumbled and attempted to straighten his desk. He gave up and stared at Dromov's picture.

Jenny escorted the man to his doorway and went back to her cubicle, but not without giving Jon a he's-all-yours smirk. The man removed his wool hat and walked into the office and stepped toward his desk. *Who wears hats anymore?* Jon had never seen this man before but was reminded of his childhood dentist back in Rhode Island. After his first filling, gentle and painless, he'd never again been afraid of going to the dentist. But something else . . . a little bit odd, like his image was a fraction out of time. And . . . he was odorless. Everyone gave off some scent: dry-cleaned wool, aftershave, breath mints, shampoo, even the car he'd driven in to get here. This man might have smoked a pipe with the delectable aroma of dried cherries. Nothing—there was absolutely nothing.

"What can I do for you, Mr.—?"

"Mr. Segert?

"Yes? You are?"

"I am Dr. Beaumont Gaines. Thank you for seeing me." An odd delay led this man's movements, a smoky trail as he reached out to shake Jon's hand. "You can just call me Doc, like everybody else. Been called Doc since the end of the war—Civil if you're wonder-ing," the man said and winked. "You don't know me, but I certainly do know you."

"How so?" Jon reached across the desk and gasped as their hands touched—cool and too soft for his age. *Again . . . no aroma. His voice sounds echoed. Did he say Civil War?*

"Mind if I sit myself down? I won't stay long."

"Please . . . do."

Doc sat and leaned back in the chair in front of Jon's desk, relaxed and comfortable with himself. He fingered the edges of his hat, nearly completing a full circle before he spoke again. Jon stared at him, transfixed, with no clue what would happen next.

"You must protect this child, Mr. Segert. Dillon is quite special. He's a might special to Jean and Spencer too."

Jon froze. *Jean and Spence?* All his alarms went off when the man walked through the door, but now they were blaring. "What are you talking about?"

"The impossible *is* possible. I can help you if you'll let me, son. Mr. Machelli switched my—I mean, the Collinses'—painting at the museum. Impressive museum, by the way. I believe Dillon's copy can help you solve your case against the untoward man on that box." Doc pointed to the computer screen. "We are both aligned, my friend. Seems you want to catch this Mr. Dromov, and I want to help Jean and Spencer and the young man too. We can come together for a united purpose."

"How the hell can you do that?"

"Follow the money, Mr. Segert. Follow his money." Doc smiled as if he'd thought of private joke. "Well, I guess I mean partly *my* money, when you get right down to it."

Jon sat quiet. An odd feeling coursed through his body. Absurd, but he wanted to ask if this man was real. At first, he thought about his needing glasses when he noticed the slight illuminated outline, but now he was positive his eyes weren't the problem.

"What money? Dromov money?" he asked, unable to take his eyes off the man.

"Yes, precisely—very perceptive. Mr. and Mrs. Collins have most of their inheritance from my Mary invested in the Dromov Fund. You see, I'm Mary Coulter's stepfather."

Mary was eight-six when she . . . so he must be—

"The Collinses don't know as of yet, son. Not for me to say, but you certainly can. Ask them to investigate those funds. Like medicine, this is a puzzle. Use your imagination. I will help you, but you must believe."

"Believe in what?"

"Pull that talon out of your drawer and set it on the desk here. Go on, now."

Jon wasn't used to taking orders from anybody, but he wouldn't dare question this man's instructions. Only a handful of people knew about the talon. He pulled out the top drawer of his desk and plucked the talon from its hidden compartment. He set the claw on the desk.

The man's hand left faint strands as he placed his sure fingers on the talon.

"Now put your hand on mine, Mr. Segert. Just for a moment."

The man's spotted hand drew him forward. As soon as Jon touched his skin, electric energy coursed through his veins that sparked flashes of visions: The Dancing Boy *on the bedroom wall in Richmond . . . Doc and a black woman with their hands on a large dog . . . Jean falling down the steps at the V&A museum . . . The hawk tearing into Raleigh in the back of a London taxi.*

Jon pulled his hand from Doc's. "You are immortal, aren't you? Are you real?" he asked, unable to believe he'd said the words out loud.

"I'm as real as you want me to be, son." The man faded in front of him, his words trailing in the mist. "I will help you, if you help me . . ."

The man was gone. *He was right there.*

Jon paused, his mind in a whirl. He lunged for the phone. "Couldn't be," he whispered. "Dammit!" He punched in Jean and Spence's number.

"Hey, hi, Jon!" Spence said.

"Do you have investment money in the Dromov Fund?" Jon asked. He heard the shaking in his voice, from his meeting Dr. Gaines, and he cleared his throat.

Spence cleared his throat too.

"Kind of weird question, Jon, but yeah. A good portion of the stock money we inherited from Mary Coulter is in that fund."

"How much? I'm not asking because I'm being nosy. This could be important."

An uncomfortable silence hung on the line before Spence answered. "About half a million. I've been trying to call Mr. Dromov. I need to make a withdrawal to fund the opening of my store since we've identified some good locations—"

"Okay—here's what I want you to do," Jon said, cutting off Spence. "Get your last statement out and call every single one of the companies where it says you own stock. Call them directly, Spence, don't call Dromov—I mean it. Check if these companies have your account on file. If they do, then verify the balance. You've got to verify if the money is there. Call right away. Also, scan and e-mail a copy of the last statement to me ASAP."

"What? We haven't touched any of that money. The fund's returning such great interest."

"There's a reason. Make those calls."

"What's going on, Jon?"

"Just do it! Call me back when you're done!"

Jon slammed down the phone. His hand clenched the receiver so hard he might have crushed it to dust. With every passing second his will galvanized to iron.

"Say this isn't so, Doc," he whispered. "But if it is, then the Collinses are going to help me nail this guy." He raised his eyes to the ceiling. "Jenny!"

"Yeah?" she said, popping her head around the frame with a pitcher of water in her hand. "Hey, where's the guy who was meeting with you?"

"He had to go."

"I didn't see him leave." Jenny strolled over to the tree and dumped the water into the container.

"I did. We're taking this Dromov thing to the next level."

CHAPTER 21

Where's the Money?

Spence hung up the phone and dashed into the den. The pit in his stomach contracted as he rifled through the files in the cabinet. "Honey, come in here!"

"What's the matter?" Jean asked, following him. "Who was on the phone?"

"Jon. We need to check each of the accounts Mary's money is in. He thinks there's a problem."

"Did somebody hack into our account? Isn't the Dromov Fund insured?"

"No, a bigger issue." Spence plunked down in one of the leather chairs.

"Let me check the statement." Jean leaned over Spence's shoulder and inspected the paper in his hand. She flicked the corner and relaxed. "Honey, these stocks are all Blue Chips. They're legit companies. Why would he question them? It's not like we have start-ups of Jazz Hands Technologies or anything."

"No, the money might not be in them—who's the most despicable financial guy sitting in a jail cell right now?"

"A bunch—Good God! A Ponzi scheme?"

"I think *that's* what Jon's talking about . . ."

"It never occurred to me to check these companies directly. We always called Dromov." Jean glanced at her watch. "Almost one o'clock. We still have time to call, barely, if any of them are on the East Coast. Let's start. I'll stand right here."

Spence scanned the statement, trailing his finger down each stock name. The combined balance stated $503,452. "Honey, pull up every one of these company's websites and give me the number for investor relations. You feed me the numbers and I'll call them." He grabbed the phone.

"I'm on it."

Over the next forty minutes, Spence called four of the five com-panies. Each conversation yielded same results. He put his hand over the receiver as he sat on hold. "Here's the last one. We're hosed." He jumped when the voice came back on the line.

Jean sat at the desk and held her head in her hands.

"May I have your account number?" the voice asked.

Spence gave the name and account number as the paper shook in his hand. The corner curled from dampness.

"I'm sorry, sir, but no account is listed under that name. The number isn't even one of ours. Can you verify your social security for me?" the voice asked.

Spence recited both his and then Jean's.

"No, sir, I don't have an account under either one. Could the funds possibly be under another name?"

"No. Yes! Wait! Try Mary Coulter."

Silence. The click of keys. He rubbed his knee.

"I'm sorry, sir, nothing under that name either."

"Thank you for checking." Spence ended the call. He stared at the bookshelves in the den; the titles blurred. Not just a violation of their money; a violation of Mary.

Jean stood in front of him, switching her weight from foot to foot.

He looked up at her in disbelief. "No money in these accounts, Jean."

"Let's call Jon back right now."

Jon hung up the phone from Spence and put his head in his hands. "No . . . no, no, no," he moaned. The Collinses' money wasn't there. The deposits were never recorded, except in Dromov's personal account. He didn't need the call from Spence. He already had the proof. Dromov stole the funds. He'd promised an insane rate of interest and made up false balances.

Without a doubt, statements had been mailed out religiously every month. Most people invested for the long haul, believing the printed page and went about their lives. And why would they check? If the statements showed up on time, then clients felt secure; they'd believe anything. Rules. Ethics. Naive trust. Investors might as well throw open their front doors and invite thieves to come in for a sit-down dinner of everything they owned.

Ponzi schemes were all the same. The only differences were how much was in them and how long they lasted. Phone calls wouldn't be returned, and the evidence ended up as shredded packing material for valuables sent to relatives and friends. Lives, too, would be shredded.

Anthony Dromov didn't know his game was up. According to his credit cards, the spending continued unabated. Time to make a move. And the Collinses' little painting was going to help take the charade down.

"Okay, Doc. I hear 'ya loud and clear." Jon picked up his keys. "Jenny, I'll be on my cell for a few hours if you need me. I'm going to see this Franco Machelli guy."

CHAPTER 22

The Seed of Doubt

Franco Machelli walked into his apartment and threw his keys and the shipping receipt on the glass coffee table. He wished he had more time to think this through. Too late to change his mind. The crated box, insured to the maximum, had just made the cutoff for overnight delivery to London. He poured a whiskey and downed the shot in one swallow. At least the painting was out of his possession. He set the tumbler down and eyed the receipt. A wave of nausea washed over him; his head pounded.

Gerrod might have a buyer in the wings. If the painting went to auction soon or was sold to a private party, then no one would be the wiser. If Dillon spilled about his fake, he'd only be implicating himself. The Art Loss Register would show nothing because neither the Collinses, nor the museum, knew the original was gone. He'd left the frame to give the copy even more credibility.

He stepped to the bookshelves. The thick book of Caravaggio's complete works drew him close. His hand had been on one of the legendary artist's paintings only an hour ago. *The Dancing Boy* came and went so fast; he didn't get a chance to roll around in its spell. He pulled the book off the shelf.

Franco jumped at the knock on the door. All his senses heightened to full alert. He set the book on the living room chair and stepped to the peephole: A man, official-looking, stood on the other side and pulled something out of his pocket: A badge. *You've got to be kidding.* This was probably about some robbery or a crime in the neighborhood. He'd look guilty, though, if he didn't answer.

"Can I help you?" Franco asked as he cracked the door. The chain pulled taut, stopping at a mere three inches.

"Special Agent Jon Segert, FBI. I'd like to talk with you regarding an investigation. I'll be brief, Mr. Machelli. I believe you may be able to help me with some information."

Be cool. Be cool. He knows nothing.

"Give me a minute. I've got something on the stove." Franco's gaze darted around the living room. His eyes fixed on the Caravaggio tome on the chair, bigger than life. He grabbed it, dashed to his bedroom, and shoved the book under the bed. Slowing his steps to regain his composure, he approached the door and took a deep breath.

"Come in. I'm happy to help. Fire away," he said, his eyes widening at the coffee table. *The receipt!*

Agent Segert stepped inside and sniffed. He leaned over to peer into the kitchen and smirked.

"Uh . . . I was getting ready to make something to eat," Franco said.

"What can you tell me about a painting at the museum belonging to the Collinses?"

Three words hit Franco in the face: painting, museum, Collinses. Not possible.

"Only . . . that one of my students, Dillon Davis, is cleaning the piece for them."

"Have you seen the painting?"

"Yes, last week. Palmer Norquist, the curator, and I inspected the work. Quite something." Franco crossed his arms and pulled his eyes away. The thump in his chest accelerated when he turned back and spotted the agent staring down at the coffee table.

"Is the Collinses' painting still at the museum?"

"I believe so. I saw it only once," Franco said, distracted.

"Exactly when was that?"

"I don't remember the specific day."

"Only once?"

"Yes."

"Have you gone over to the museum at all since then?"

"No."

"I hear the painting is a Caravaggio."

"No, I don't think so, Mr. Segert," he said, relaxing now to be talking about art. "Possibly in the style, but we're fairly sure the artist is Hendrik ter Brugghen. I helped Dillon do the research."

"Interesting. I have no idea who that is. Sounds expensive." The FBI agent chuckled and pointed to the receipt. "You shipping out some art?"

Franco slid his empty crystal tumbler on top of the receipt. The bottom of the glass only magnified the address.

"No, an art book. A Christmas present to a friend."

"A little late." The agent cocked his head and studied the inside of the glass. "Almost the end of January. Kind of expensive to overnight a book to London. The painting at the museum is quite something. Somebody stole a fake and may be passing it off as the original."

"What?" Franco's knees went weak and itched. He tried to keep his breath steady and even.

"Here's my card. Please call me if you have any information, or if the copy turns up. We're happy the original's safe."

"How do you know there was a copy made?" Franco eyed the card suspended between them.

"A tip. We're checking it out. We don't want a fake with a name that big to get on the market. Serious repercussions." The agent held the card closer.

"Yeah . . . will do." Franco plucked the card, with only his first two fingers, as if it would burst into flames.

"Enjoy your evening, Mr. Machelli."

Franco closed the door, stalked the coffee table, and scrunched the receipt into a damp ball in his fist. *Did I send the fake to Gerrod? Is the original still in the museum?* Right now, he wasn't sure of anything.

Jon sauntered down the hall from Franco's apartment, satisfied he'd planted the seed of doubt. The shipping receipt confirmed Machelli took the original painting, as did his classic body and eye movements signifying lies and guilt. Easy enough to check out. The crystal glass had magnified the name of the recipient: Gerrod Barnes Fine Antiques in London. This was fate. He might be able to use his previous relationship with Barnes to corner Anthony Dromov, get the painting back to Jean and Spence, and clean up another loose end of the Raleigh Coulter mess.

Technically, Gerrod had done nothing wrong. There was no proof of collusion, but Jon had scared the hell out of the antique dealer during the Raleigh investigation. The fact that Raleigh was tak-ing that magical fabric to Gerrod Barnes when he was killed worked in his favor. He needed cooperation to pull off the plan forming in his mind. And the chief would love this one too. Or, it might be the idea that finally makes him throw his silver pen at the door of his office.

Jon's next stop: the museum. He'd bet the moon the sign-in log at the security desk would show Franco Machelli signing in more than once since the Collinses' painting was brought in for the clean-ing.

CHAPTER 23

The Immortal Plan

"You want to what?" The chief said, glaring at Jon.

"I want to take the Collinses and this Dillon kid to London with me," Jon said. "We're closing in on Dromov. I think, together, we can wrap this up. They've got a stake in this too. Their money is caught up in this Ponzi scheme. I want to use their stolen painting to get Dromov's attention. I know where it is. The auction is next Saturday."

"You are wearing out my last nerve, sonny boy. What magic fairyland budget do you think this trip is coming out of, huh? I'm gonna get my ass chewed on this! The Collinses are under my eye right now. They know more than they're telling. What did you think of the tape of their interview? Brick tripped 'em up but good."

"C'mon, Chief, the Collinses didn't have anything to do with Raleigh's death, anymore than I did. I'll be right with them the whole way. You'll be a hero, and at the same time the Art Crime Team will be thrilled. We're doing them a solid. A new recruit might result from the deal. This'll be a chance for them to see Dillon in action."

"I'm not human resources for the other divisions." The chief blew out a breath and muttered something unintelligible. "Dammit! These Collins people need to pay their own way—and this deaf kid too. I mean it. I don't want you to even buy a hot dog in the airport, except for yourself. Do you hear me?"

"Loud and clear. Here's the requisition." Jon stepped to the chief's desk and set the paper in front of him. He pushed it closer with his forefinger for emphasis. After the Chief scrawled his sig-nature, grumbling as he did so, Jon made an exaggerated gesture of looking at his watch. "Hey, Chief, do you know what time it is?"

"What?"

"Time to round up some bad guys. I might need to use a little magic to get this done."

"Get the hell outta here. I got your magic."

Jon closed the chief's office door. He flinched as the silver pen banged against the wood and dropped to the floor. He whistled all the way down the hall. Time to call Jean and Spence and ask them to gather up Dillon.

The phone rang. Jean ran down the stairs and peeked into the living room. Spence was engrossed in a book, trying to get his mind off the Dromov Fund. Nothing could be done until Jon made the next move. Duke Ellington's version of "Diga Diga Doo" spun on the turntable. He must be reading Duke's new biography. She took a closer look. Yep.

"It's Jon!" she called out before she answered the phone. Spence raised his eyes; his expression said he wasn't up for any bad news. "Hit me with good news, Jon." She churned her hand in a circle for Spence to pick up the extension. He continued to stare at his book.

"Dust off your passports. Does Dillon have one?" Jon said, his voice sounding buoyant.

"Where are we going?"

"Back to London."

"London? Does this mean we're getting the painting back—and our money?"

"No guarantees, but we're going to serve up the guy who stole your money. I found out the painting is up for auction on Saturday night at Farnum's. Oh, and the chief says you and Spence need to pay your own way—and Dillon's too. Go get him and let him stay at your house until we leave. Don't tell anyone, especially not Machelli."

"Hellava guy, the Chief. Machelli too? We help you catch the jerk *and* we pay our own expenses?" Jean paused. "We're in. When do we leave?"

"In three days."

"Expensive, Jon. A little more lead time would've been helpful. What if Dillon doesn't have a passport?"

"If he doesn't, I'll get the paperwork expedited. Bring me Dillon's photo and a copy of his birth certificate. Go to one of those instant photo places today. Then go get that fake painting at the museum. We need to take it with us."

"Uh . . . okay. Dillon's not in any danger, is he?"

"I don't think so, but Franco Machelli stole your painting. If he's desperate, I don't want repercussions for Dillon. Pack him up and bring him to your house."

Jean hung up the phone. "Spence! Put down that book and take off your slippers. We need to get Dillon! We're going to London on Tuesday for an auction on Saturday."

"Okay . . . give me five minutes. This is a good part."

"You'd better get off your diga-doo right now. We gotta goo!"

Spence raised his eyes, what she said just dawning on him. "We're going where on Tuesday?"

"Why don't you drop me off here," Jean said, pointing to the tree-filled corner along the Park Blocks by the museum. "I'll walk to the school and get Dillon; you go pick up the painting."

"All right, meet me back here. Be careful. If you'll be more than fifteen minutes, call me on my cell." Spence said as the T-Bird idled.

She turned around and made a shooing motion for him to get going, then stuck up her thumb. Both Spence and the T-Bird were reluctant to leave her.

The school was quiet. A pungent mix of aromas wafted around

her as soon as she walked through the door: oil paint, solvent, and clothes in need of a wash. Jean tiptoed down the hall, trying to keep her wet snow boots from squeaking on the linoleum. She peered into each studio. Some were empty or had one or two students working; others were filled to capacity with classes in progress. Hopefully, Dillon had checked his e-mail and was aware she was on her way. She hadn't given specifics in her note, only that she needed to see him. She spotted Dillon sitting alone in quiet contemplation, staring at a sheet-covered canvas on an easel in an otherwise empty studio.

Jean stepped inside and tapped him on the shoulder. Dillon received her e-mail; he didn't even flinch. He'd been waiting for her. She pointed toward the door and made a walking motion with her first two fingers. Leaning over to the notepad on the worktable, she wrote, *Let's go back to your apartment and pack up some things. We're going to London to get the painting. Jon's found it. You need to go with us.*

What? When?

We'll leave on Tuesday and come back Monday. About a week. Jon wants you to stay with us. Let's go to your apartment.

I'm packed. This is all I need.

Do you have a passport?

No.

A birth certificate?

I guess we need to go by my apartment.

Dillon picked up his knapsack and jacket. He slipped his phone in his pocket. Jean waited for him by the door. Dillon lifted up the sheet and glanced at the painting of the Man for a few seconds. He followed her out of the studio.

"Uh, excuse me. Where are you two going?" a man's voice said behind them in the corridor.

Jean turned. The hair on her neck prickled as if a hairy spider had raced by her ear. *Machelli!.* She pointed to the door at the end of the hall, signaling for Dillon to keep walking.

"We're going to a celebration lunch. Dillon did such a good job cleaning our painting we wanted to do something for him."

Jean sensed Franco's eyes boring a hole in her back as the squeak of her boots quickened toward the door.

Once outside, she pointed for Dillon to walk to the T-Bird on the corner. Steam from the tailpipe melted a brown tunnel in the snow piled at the curb. Spence had been sitting in the spot for more than a few minutes.

Jean pulled the seat forward and motioned Dillon inside. She slipped into the front passenger seat. "Did you get the painting?"

"Got it. I had to sign a release, but it's ours. It's in the case in the trunk."

"I ran into Franco Machelli on the way out. I thought we were blown."

"What did you say?"

"We were taking Dillon to lunch. Let's get the hell out of here. We need to stop by Dillon's apartment to pick up his birth certificate, and then we'll have his photo taken.

Jean and Dillon waved at Spence after he dropped them off at the house. He continued on to deliver the photo and certified copy of the birth certificate to Jon. The three of them laughed when she asked Dillon to put that long strand of hair behind his ear. As much as the photographer wanted that hair out of his face, she too wanted him to pull back the curtain he hid behind. Not the best picture—Dillon seemed stressed—but something adventurous gleamed in his eyes too.

Once inside the house, Jean showed Dillon to the guestroom. She laid out a towel and a fluffy terry cloth robe, and then motioned for him to give her his clothes—all of them. While he changed, she pulled a new toothbrush from a pack of ten, a sample-size tube of toothpaste, and a travel-size shampoo and conditioner from the linen closet. Dillon cracked the door and held out his clothes. One of his angel eyes peeked out. She handed him the toiletries and pointed to the guest bath. For the first time in her life she felt like a mom.

As Jean came in from the garage, the machine harrumphed in

response to how hard the washer had to work to get those clothes clean. She turned on the gas fireplace and listened to the squeak of the shower knobs. Sensing a new source of potential warmth and another set of suitable hands for petting, Mycroft lumbered down the stairs.

Dillon needed to be fed. She doubted he'd slept very much since the painting was stolen. He'd crash after lunch. She smiled as she thought of Spence chiding her about washing the guestroom sheets every other week, even though they didn't have company coming.

The stairs squeaked as Dillon descended in the white terry cloth robe. The warmth of the fire drew him to the living room. Dillon's wet hair shined like dark silk. Jean set out a pan to heat up some leftover vegetable soup and grabbed a spoon. Dillon motioned for her to join him. He put his forefinger to his lips for her to remain quiet. Jean set down the spoon and followed.

Mycroft was sprawled out across the carpet in front of the fireplace. Dillon pointed at him. Something wasn't right. Mycroft's head was suspended in mid-air with his chin jutted out. He was sound asleep. Dillon turned to her and shrugged his shoulders.

Jean knelt on the floor and waved her hand around Mycroft. *Yes, there he is.* Resting her hands on the warm ribcage, she closed her eyes and whispered, "Wiley . . . show yourself. Who's a beautiful boy?"

The black Labrador materialized. Mycroft's back followed the contours of the dog's belly, his head resting on Wiley's paws. The dog gazed at her and Dillon, satisfied with his prize, and then dragged his tongue between Mycroft's ears. A shower of sparkles floated around his face and filtered through his long whiskers.

Jean nodded for Dillon to give Wiley a pat.

Yes, he is real. Yes, he is there.

Dillon reached out and pulled her up. He replaced her on the floor next to Wiley and stroked his rump. Jean watched him marvel at the ghostly trail his own hand made at the touch of Wiley's fur. He fanned Mycroft's long tail over Wiley's rib cage, combing it out with his fingers. The art of the image resembled a soft red phoenix feather against the black background. Mycroft's tail raised and lowered with

Wiley's gentle breaths. Dillon stared in awe.

Jean turned and went back in the kitchen to tend to the soup.

An hour later, Spence walked through the door with the art case containing Dillon's copy of the painting.

"We should have Dillon's passport by Monday," he announced. "Cutting it really close, but Jon's determined. He's going to meet us at the airport on Tuesday morning. What have you guys been doing? Where's Dillon?"

"Reading in the living room." She waited two downbeats before continuing. "Wiley's here." She slid the chicken in the oven to roast for dinner. "And Mycroft's totally smitten. You can't pry them apart. They've been fused together since I started the fire when we got home."

Spence raised his hand to Dillon and held up the art case. Dillon stuck up his thumb and pointed at Wiley and Mycroft, and then turned his attention back to his book, Spence's 1922 edition of Arthur Conan Doyle's *The Lost World.*

"Get a load of those two lazy louts," Spence said to Jean. "They're like newlyweds." Wiley lifted his head, as if to say *shush.* "What will Birdie and Jess think about this?"

"Oh, they'll be fine. If not, I'm sure we'll hear from them, probably from Doc too."

"Did you feed Wiley? What's he's supposed to eat?" Spence laughed.

"No clue. He's not asking for anything, though."

"I am. I'm starving.

"I'm trying out Birdie's recipe for roast chicken. It'll be least another hour. Get some Forever Kibble to snack on."

CHAPTER 24

Let's Go Get the Bad Guys

On Tuesday morning, Spence finished taping the straps on the art case that contained the copy of *The Dancing Boy* canvas. "This will work fine. It can hold both canvases when we get the other one back. And it'll fit in the overhead bin."

"Great. Now let's go. Gotta go! Gotta go!" Jean urged, waiting with Dillon by the front door. She watched Spence adjust the tension and secure both buckles—one more time.

Jean looked through the peephole in the door to make sure no one was in front of the house. "The cab's here. Uh-oh! If we'd left ten minutes ago, we would have made it. Now, there's a news van out there too."

"There. Done. Let's go. Did you warn Linda and Bill?"

"I did. In fact, I offered to bring Mycroft to their house instead of coming over here, but Bill wouldn't hear of it. He said he wants to see Sparkles again."

Spence opened the front door and motioned her and Dillon toward the waiting cab.

"Here we go. Eyes straight forward," Spence warned.

Jean looked at Dillon, who nodded and followed her out the door. The three of them scooted into the back seat of the cab.

"Let's go. And don't stop. Ignore that reporter," Spence said to the driver.

"You know, we're going to have to face these guys at some point," she said. "Maybe it'll be a good conversation if all this mess gets resolved in London. Finding the painting and nailing Dromov will deflect the spotlight from Raleigh—if we're lucky."

"Lucky is right. Brace yourself. Here he comes."

The muffled voice of the reporter on the other side of window shouted out her name. "Mrs. Collins? Jean Collins? What did the FBI ask you when they interviewed you? Can we have a few words?"

Jean smiled and waved. She pointed to her ear, acting like she couldn't hear the reporter. "Don't stop—keep going," she said, keeping her smile fixed at the window. The wheels squealed as the driver gunned the cab toward River Road.

As they drove up Highway 205 toward the airport, Jean turned to Spence. "At least this flight to London is going to be a lot calmer than the last one."

"Yeah, it would be hard to top the last one."

The driver looked into the rearview mirror. "That was some-thing I don't do every day. Are you guys famous?"

Spence met his mirrored eyes. "Hardly—fifteen minutes—tops."

Jon watched the three of them approach the gate. He waved and motioned to the seats he'd been saving for them.

"Well, this is kind of déjà vu, isn't it?" Spence said.

"No kidding, but let's hope the similarities between the two trips end here," Jon shot back. "Dillon doing okay?"

"Doing great. He's like family now," Jean said, her face flushing.

"Glad to see you have the painting." Jon eyed the case as Spence rested it against his knees.

"Speaking of the painting, why don't you fill us in on this plan of yours while we have some time before we board. I hate not knowing the full scoop."

"Once I get you settled in the hotel, I'm going over to talk with Gerrod Barnes. I'll take Dillon's copy here with me. I need confirmation from Barnes that Franco Machelli sent him that original painting. Then, I need to convince Barnes to get Dromov's attention, so he'll bid on the painting. Then, I'm going to have him switch the painting and put Dillon's copy in the auction. I want to leave with the original in my hands. Pretty simple."

Jean looked at Spence. "Simple? That's simple? Sounds like any one of those things could go horribly wrong. What if—?"

Jon raised his hand to cut her off. "The auction is on Saturday, which is why I want to move fast on this. We'll only have three days to get everything organized once we get there. I also believe that Dromov is a flight risk. From what I can tell of his burn rate, his funds are bottoming out. Once the rest of the clients find out they can't get their money, all hell is going to break loose."

"How much money has Dromov stolen?" Spence asked.

"Millions. Tens of millions, I don't know. From what I can tell, though, a few of the early clients are legit. Their money is safe. Dromov uses those clients as references to get new clients. It's the ones he acquired in the last three years who've been screwed. You're in that batch. We're still verifying. That's all I can say."

"And you think you can get all that done before the auction? Yeah, right," Jean scoffed.

"I do. I've had some help." Jon looked away. Jean and Spence looked at each other. Dillon scanned all three of them.

Dillon wanted the window. Jean took the aisle next to him. Spence was across the aisle, and Jon had the seat next to Spence in the center section. Jon really wanted the aisle, but Spence was adamant. He wanted a clear path to the restroom. At least Jon was able to get on the plane first to secure space in the overhead bin for the art case.

Jean wrote to Dillon, *Have you ever been on a plane before?*

No, Dillon wrote back.

Just breathe and feel the lift . . . to another world.

As the plane took off, Dillon grabbed Jean's hand and looked out the window. She squeezed it when the plane banked to turn north, more for her own peace of mind than Dillon's. She reached her other hand to Spence. He wrapped his fingers around hers, the three of them connected in a human chain.

Dillon pulled out his sketchbook after the plane leveled off. The page filled with a montage of faces: those of the flight attendants, businessmen, children, and a parade of passengers who stood waiting for the restroom. Each had a story. Each had been given a soul on the page.

During the layover in Newark, Jean handed Dillon a small ruled notebook with a cover patterned with Dalmatian spots.

Jean tapped the notebook *It's a long six hours. Tell me your story.*

For the next two hours, Dillon only looked up to acknowledge the flight attendant, nod for a refill of water, accept the meal, and shimmy out to go to the restroom.

Spence sparred with Jon about music. Jean closed her eyes and listened. Spence knew so many obscure details of the lives of great musicians—and so did Jon. They chattered about Chick Webb, Fats Waller, Louis Armstrong, Dave Brubeck, the Animals, the Kinks, Spencer Davis Group, B. B. King and, of course, the Rolling Stones ad nauseum. But it was Muddy Waters who dominated a good portion of the last hour of their conversation—his wives, his real name of McKinley Morganfield, his illegitimate children, his genius, his influence on the Rolling Stones, and all the musicians he inspired even after he died in 1983. She recalled that she and Spence were buying their first house when they learned Muddy Waters had died.

As their conversation swirled around her, Jean realized how much of her and Spence's own lives were marked with music. To-gether, they had seen in small clubs so many legends that kids today watch on television oldies retrospectives. When she skipped her music theory class in college to see U2 play with Romeo Void in the student union of San Jose State in 1979, she had no idea how famous the band would become. Of course, she'd listened to the same stories from her parents about seeing Duke Ellington, Benny Goodman, and Louis Armstrong at outdoor summer dances on Lake Winnipesaukee in New Hampshire.

Jean drifted in and out of sleep, thinking about Bruce Springsteen and Wiley snuggled with Mycroft in his immortal paws. Spence talked with Jon. Dillon wrote in the notebook. He grabbed her hand when the plane hit turbulence over the shoreline of Greenland on its trek toward Ireland.

Jean and Spence checked in and went to their hotel room; Dillon's room adjoined theirs and could be accessed through an interior door. Jon's room was located down the hall in front of the elevator.

"I'll come over in fifteen minutes," Jon said, his tone all busi-ness. "I need to get moving. Dillon is coming with me. We need to get to Gerrod Barnes's place before he closes in an hour."

"What about Spence and me?" Jean asked.

"No way, you talk too much."

"But, Jon—"

"You guys keep yourselves busy. Dillon can handle this with me. We'll be about an hour or two."

"Absolutely not! We're going with you. It's our painting, so not one more word about it." Jean all but stomped her foot as she said it.

"Dammit! Spence?" Jon appealed, pointing at Jean.

"You're outnumbered, buddy boy. We're going."

Jon turned and stormed down the hall. Jean leaned out of the doorway and watched him slide the key card in the door slot, and then disappear into his room.

"Well, how do you like that? He's trying to ditch us."

"Jon has his reasons," Spence said, pulling a pair of pants from his bag and looping them over a hanger. "Don't take it personally. He's trying to solve a case."

"Our case, by the way. He's not telling us everything."

"Plausible deniability. Isn't that what they call it?"

CHAPTER 25

Are You In or Out, Mr. Barnes?

The taxi pulled up to the elaborate storefront of Barnes & Company Fine Antiques. The oak trim around the expansive front windows gleamed with shiny varnish. The building had been maintained with meticulous care over the past two centuries. Displays of antique writing desks, bookcases, breakfronts, and sparkling cut-crystal punch bowls held the lure of history from those most fortunate. The wood furniture had been freshly polished and exuded the patina of age and lemon oil, even in the cold, gray light.

Jon hopped out of the taxi and zipped up his jacket against the bitter chill. He opened the back door and out poured Spence, Dillon, and Jean. Jon took charge of the art case. Leaning through the front passenger window, he told the driver to wait at the corner, or to make sure he was back in an hour.

Turning to Jean and Spence, he said, "You two have to let me talk to Barnes with just Dillon. Wander around the shop. Keep your-selves busy. We can't gang up on him or he'll shut down, especially if he's coming face-to-face with the owner of the painting."

"We understand, Jon. We would've been tearing ourselves up waiting for you both to come back to the hotel," Jean said. "We'll be on our best behavior, right, Spence?"

"Yes, *you* will."

The heavy wood and glass door swung in without a sound, except for the soft click of a motion light. A long bong was triggered at the back of the shop. A tall, dark-haired woman of about sixty walked toward them with a gracious smile. Given the volume of her hair, she had an extended morning session with a blow dryer and a large can of spray-on shellac. Either she rolled around in baby powder before she got dressed or her perfume was antique too.

"May I help you?" the woman asked.

"Is Gerrod Barnes here? I'd like to speak with him, please," Jon said.

"Do you have an appointment?" In an instant, the woman's tone changed from gracious to protective. She gave Dillon a dubious glance and then sized up Jean and Spence as to whether or not they could afford to buy anything.

"No, but I need to talk with him. My name is Special Agent Jon Segert. I'm with the FBI . . . in the US."

"One moment, please. Mr. Barnes is in his office. I must consult with him to—"

"He's available. I'll go with you, if you don't mind." Jon waved at Dillon to follow him toward the back of the shop. He motioned for Jean and Spence to stay put. The woman peered over her shoulder as she walked in clipped steps. Jon and Dillon kept pace.

"Gerrod, an FBI agent is here for you," she said, stopping in the doorway of Gerrod's office. The expression on her face was equal to that of taking a deep whiff of spoiled clotted cream.

Jon noticed Barnes had changed his hair since he'd interrogated him after Raleigh's death. Last fall, it had been longer and somewhat gray, but now the cut was short, a solid color, and precision-buzzed close to the scalp. That particular shade of dark brown didn't seem right for his age, mid-sixties, nor did it go with his bright-blue eyes. But he still looked every bit the part of a decorator of manor houses with outrageous tax rates.

Recognizing Jon, Gerrod stood and glared, preparing himself for a duel. He buttoned his bespoke suit jacket and barked out a nervous cough, but didn't offer a welcoming hand. His gold pinky ring, with a blood-red ruby in the center, glinted in the light from the art-glass lamp on his desk.

"Mr. Barnes. Agent Jon Segert, FBI—in case you forgot my name." Jon flipped open his wallet and showed his ID. "This is Dillon Davis, a soon-to-be colleague of mine." Dillon studied Ger-rod's face, as if he couldn't quite decipher his expression. He reached out his hand. The gesture was not returned.

"Yes, I found it rather difficult to forget you, Agent Segert. What might I do for you *this* time? Please say this is not about that Raleigh Coulter unpleasantness." Gerrod took another distrusting glimpse at Dillon and, with an air of defiance, settled his gaze on Jon. "Who is that couple who came in with you?" Gerrod leaned to his left and spotted Jean and Spence meandering around the shop with his assistant. They all turned as Jean's lilting voice said, "Objects have a life of their own."

"I believe you're in receipt of an oil painting from a Franco Machelli in Portland, Oregon."

An uncomfortable silence hung between them.

"I will neither confirm nor dispute such a statement. I do not discuss my clients, Mr. Segert."

"Oh, Mr. Barnes, you can. It was sent to you last week. I saw the receipt myself. Franco stole that painting."

"I have no knowledge of the circumstances, I assure you."

"Let's step back for a moment." Jon turned and glanced out the office door. Jean picked up a crystal bowl that threw off colored lasers in the light from the front window. He tapped the door closed and motioned for Dillon to take a seat. "This feels like a repeat performance, Mr. Barnes—someone stealing something and then coming to you to sell."

"I harbor no small amount of anxiety, or many sleepless nights, about that situation. Haunts me to this day. Terrible business. Yes, terrible business." Gerrod pulled a monogrammed handkerchief from his breast pocket and wiped the top of his lip. His eyes shifted be-tween Jon and Dillon, as if the young man was going to snatch something from his desk and run off.

"I cleared you once, Mr. Barnes, but I now assume you accept stolen items for sale."

"I . . . I have never knowingly accepted such items. Not then and not now."

"May I sit?" Jon sat without an acceptance. "Personally, I think you have a proclivity for greed, wrapped up in the so-called respectability of foo-fooey antiques. I don't know a whole lot about these things, but I do have you pegged for an opportunist. And I'm here to give you an opportunity—keep your reputation, your fine things, and the ability to continue your business without interruption. And at the same time, we might put the whole Raleigh affair behind us." Jon's eyes settled on the wall behind Gerrod's desk: a painted scene depicting a white-capped sea with boiling storm clouds. He pointed to it. "That's interesting. Who did that?"

"Turner, Mr. Segert." Gerrod wrinkled his nose as if Jon, of course, should have recognized the artist. "This is highly irregular."

"The case I'm working on is highly irregular. I'm here to request your help."

"I will certainly do what I can." Gerrod sat at his desk and made a steeple of his forefingers against his bottom lip.

"I'm so glad you said that. There is something you can do." Jon turned to Dillon and motioned to the art case next to his leg. "My young colleague here, Dillon Davis, understands more about fine art than all the fancy folks you know, combined. I bet he could even piss off Caravaggio." Jon threw his head back in an exaggerated laugh. "In fact, I'm sure he has."

Not amused, Gerrod stared at the case as Dillon lifted it to the desk. Dillon made a slow production of loosening the buckles and pulling back the straps to remove the canvas. He set the painting on the desk in front of Gerrod.

"Good Lord. Is this the original?" Gerrod whispered.

"Better than the original," Jon said, and then pointed to Dillon. "The artist is right here."

"What? Surely not." Gerrod gawked at Dillon with his mouth open.

"Don't judge people by their appearance. Not a good thing to do."

"This is the copy? Why—"

"Mr. Barnes, please bring out the original. Let's put it side-by-side with this one."

Pulled from his trance, Gerrod stood. "Yes . . . right here. I've been keeping the painting in my office closet." His eyes glinted with the thrill of a discovery. "As soon as Mr. Machelli mentioned Caravaggio—well—I had no small amount of excitement. When it arrived, I was overwhelmed. Farnum's was quite enthusiastic to add the work as a late entry in Saturday's auction."

Gerrod fished a set of keys from his jacket pocket, paused for another glance at the copy, and slipped an antique-looking one into the lock. An expensive waft of oil paint and aged wood fanned through the air as he opened the oak door. He pulled out the canvas and set it on his desk, next to Dillon's copy.

"I can hardly tell the difference. In fact, the copy appears richer. The light plays on the skin in a most animated way. Something about the ears . . . yes . . . more detail in the ears. Bravo young man! Bravo!" Gerrod realized he'd gotten carried away and composed himself. "Even the wood on the back of the canvas appears authentic, the edges match up perfectly. You are a singular talent, my young man." He studied Dillon, waiting for a response to the praise.

"He can't hear you, Mr. Barnes. Dillon is deaf. But I want you to put Dillon's copy in the auction on Saturday. I'm going to take the original to Farnum's myself. A man will want to bid on this painting because you're going to call him and convince him to come to London to attend the auction. His name is Anthony Dromov." Jon slid his FBI business card across the desk with Dromov's contact information. He turned it over and tapped the back. "This man is a thief—not of art—but of people's money. And you *are* going to help me catch him. Right, Mr. Barnes?"

Gerrod narrowed his eyes at Jon. He had too much class to voice the question, but Jon knew the look.

"Don't worry, you'll get your ten percent commission when the painting is sold," Jon said, annoyed. "Consider it a finder's fee. And, as I mentioned, your reputation will remain intact."

"But my normal fee is fifteen percent."

"Like I said—you'll get your ten percent."

Dillon poked Jon's knee and pointed to the notepad. Jon clicked the end of his ballpoint pen and handed it to Dillon with the ruled paper, still staring down Barnes about the fee percentage. Dillon started to write.

Can you bring Jean in here? I want to try something.

Jon hesitated and met Dillon's gaze. *Why?*

I can convince him, but I need Jean's hand.

Jon turned to Gerrod.

"What? What did he say?" Gerrod said and leaned over to glimpse of the notepad.

"Wait."

Jon left the office to search the showroom. He found Jean and Spence inspecting a marble Deco clock with a panther lunging after fleeing elk. The assistant hovered over them with her arms crossed, sporting distrustful pursed lips.

"Guys," he whispered, tapping Spence on the shoulder. "We need you in Barnes's office. Dillon's asking for Jean's hand. What's he talking about?"

"Oh, *now* you need us," Jean said. "C'mon, dear, Jon *needs* us."

Spence chuckled, "What? You running low on ooga-booga?"

"Yeah, yeah. Get in there—both of you."

Jean and Spence followed him to the office.

Jon pulled Jean forward, while Spence stood at the back of the room.

"Hi, I'm Jean Collins, Mr. Barnes." She held out her hand. Gerrod's eyes widened when they touched. "And this is my husband, Spence."

Spence dipped his head in acknowledgement.

"Jean . . . Dillon said he wanted your hand." Jon was uncomfortable with not being able to anticipate the next step.

Jean's expression softened. "Sorry I was snippy, Jon." Her gaze locked on Dillon, who reached out his hand to her. She wrapped her fingers around his. Dillon closed his eyes.

"What's going on?" Jon asked.

"Dillon knows." Jean let go, winked at him, and stepped to the back of the office. She turned to Spence. "Why don't you give Dillon your hand too? Maybe you can do the same thing."

Spence stepped forward and held out his hand. Dillon turned, confused, but grasped it. Dillon sucked in a breath. "Amazing!" Spence grinned and released Dillon's hand.

"What were you two doing?" Jon said, frustrated.

Jean and Spence stayed quiet as Dillon wrote a note. He handed the pad to Jon.

"Mr. Barnes, Dillon wants you to set your hand on top of his, and then on the original painting." Jon had to admit he was curious as hell at what was going to happen.

"Well, I—an absurd request," Barnes stumbled.

"Not really. I'd do it if I were you."

Dillon held out his small hand and waited for Gerrod Barnes to rest his on top of it. Gerrod's fingers shook as they made contact with Dillon's skin. Both hands lowered on the torso of the figure in the original painting. Golden light sprayed from beneath their fingers.

Jon's mouth gaped. Gerrod gasped and closed his eyes. Dillon did the same. Jon wanted to rush in and set his hand on the painting too, but stayed still.

"Jean, do you think they're seeing the same thing you did?" Spence whispered.

"I haven't a clue."

Caravaggio's brow dripped with sweat. He hadn't washed in days. Familiar demons chased him in fever as he crawled across the sand on a Tuscan beach in Porto Ercole. The shaking was uncontrollable. Lead from the fumes of his paints coursed through his veins. Alone. All alone.

Tortured images from his paintings rolled by his mind's eye on an imagined, stained scroll of canvas: Caravaggio's own face on the head of *John the Baptist*; his eyes peering over a shoulder in *The Taking of Christ*; his mouth gaping on the severed head in *David with the Head of Goliath*, his face instead of the angel's in *The Seven Works of Mercy*; his head turned toward the light-filled window in *The Calling of St. Matthew*; and the final stomp of the horse's hoof on his own body in *The Conversion of Saint Paul.* Caravaggio raised his hands to the sky and moaned for absolution. He collapsed in the sand. The last sound was the crash of waves as they rolled over him, washing away his pain. The world went dark.

Dillon lifted his hand. Jon watched tears well in the boy's eyes. Gerrod's misted, too, from the vision. He leaned forward for more.

"I had no idea," Barnes said, struggling for a breath. "Such skill and talent should never have been so shattered." He plunked down in his antique desk chair. The leather groaned as he held its polished wood arms for support. "My God. What on earth *was* that, young man?" Gerrod swallowed hard. "Was that really M?"

Dillon picked up the pen. *You must do what Jon says.*

"Yes . . . I will."

"Who's M?" Jon asked, perplexed. "What did you see?"

"The demise of Michelangelo Merisi da Caravaggio, Mr. Segert," Gerrod whispered. "He was called M by his closest confidents."

"M . . . Well, I can tell you it means *make* the call—right now, Barnes. You need to convince Anthony Dromov to attend the auction in person, not by phone or Internet. The auction is in"—Jon glanced at his watch—"I'd say about sixty-eight hours from now. He needs to be on a plane by Friday morning." Jon moved to pick up the original painting.

"Wait—please! Once more?"

"No, this goes with us after a brief stop at Farnum's on Saturday night. It belongs to these folks here, Jean and Spencer Collins, not Franco Machelli, but you should submit Dillon's copy to the auction under Franco Machelli's name, as you originally planned. Can you give me the receipt for delivery? I need it as evidence."

"Yes, but what happens to that painting?" Gerrod pointed to the original.

"Home. It's going home. But take a magnifying glass to the hair and buttons on that dancing kid's coat and britches. Look at them before you deliver the copy to the auction." Jon pointed to Dillon's copy.

Dillon secured the original canvas in the art case and tightened the buckles of the straps. He offered his small hand to Gerrod, who smiled and grasped it with both of his.

"You have a gift, son. A privilege."

"Gerrod, thank you," Jon said. "If this all works out, you'll be helping a lot of people. We'll talk again after you've called Dromov. You'll be able to see this one more time. The original is the one Dromov will buy, but not take home. I'll leave you alone after this. Right now, though, I appreciate your willingness to help." Jon shook his hand. An electric charge ran up his arm. He heard the echo of ocean waves and a distant scream of agony as he released his hand from the shake.

CHAPTER 26

I Want It!

Gerrod stood in the doorway of his office and watched Jon, Dillon, and the Collinses walk out of the shop. His sales assistant nearly bumped into him as they both raced to the display window as the front door shut. Agent Segert hailed a taxi. One pulled up, as if the car had been waiting round the corner the whole time. The art case disappeared with the gifted young man.

"What on earth was all that about, Gerrod?" the assistant said, stretching to gawk out the window. Her pearls clattered against a lead-crystal bowl, the prisms resonating with a deep ring.

"What did the couple say when you showed them around the shop?" he asked, eager for the answer.

"Quite odd, actually. They had to touch everything. Touch this. Touch that. Went on and on about how antiques have soul and other such nonsense."

"They were right. Please, no interruptions for the next half hour. Business I must attend to." Gerrod turned and marched back to his office. He slammed the heavy wood door, tinkling a set of delicate Venetian goblets in a display case.

Gerrod pulled a magnifying glass from his desk drawer. He held the disc over the painting and inspected the velvet buttons on the boy's waistcoat. The Latin words emerged into his enlarged view. "Nec spe, nec metu," he whispered. It had been years, maybe dec-ades, since he'd uttered those words—Caravaggio's words. The tiny word *Collins* appeared in the hair; faint, but visible. Gerrod had to remind himself he was looking at the copy. He sniffed the wood on the back; perhaps not quite the same.

Gerrod plucked Jon Segert's business card from his desk blotter. The contact information for this Anthony Dromov stared at him. He typed a note to the e-mail address, attaching Franco's JPEG pictures of *The Dancing Boy*. He hit the send button, reached for the phone, and rehearsed his first words.

The paper shredder whirred in Anthony Dromov's office on Wednesday morning, high in the skyline of New York's financial district. The panoramic view of steel and glass from his window was clouded with fog, under which a bustling crowd of shoppers picked through the winter-wear sale tables in the local shops. He would miss this view and also the view of the mountains from his office out in Portland. Both had given him years of constant inspiration to turn thin air into something big.

All traces of his accounts needed to be destroyed, except those in the Cayman Islands. He'd already moved the cash under his new name, but the largest stash was hidden in the value of his Vermeer. The focus was now on grinding away the trail, and he wanted to be methodical and organized. Haste resulted in mistakes—stupid mis-takes. Dodging his clients' requests to withdraw their funds signaled the end of the line. He wouldn't have to do this much longer.

The intercom buzzed with a Bronx accent laced with disrespect. "Tony, a Gerrod Barnes is on three."

"Don't know him. Take a message," Anthony snapped, leaning into the speaker.

"Says it's important and personal."

The name didn't sound familiar. This guy wasn't a client. "Find out what he wants." Anthony inserted a handful of account statements into the shredder. They transformed into tortured ribbons.

A sigh preceded an answer from the intercom. "Something about a painting coming up for auction."

Silence.

Dromov shot a glance at the phone as if he could see the woman's voice coming out of the speaker. She was a looker, but her low wattage couldn't even light up a birdhouse. "All right. Put him through." He tossed a folder on the side chair and stepped back to the green blinking light on line three, hesitating before snatching up the receiver. "Dromov."

"Yes, good afternoon—or rather, good morning—Mr. Dromov. My name is Gerrod Barnes of Barnes & Company Fine Antiques in London. I'll be brief, but I wanted to alert you to an extremely important painting which has come to my attention. The piece will be offered at auction on Saturday, here in London at Farnum's Auction House."

"What painting?"

"A previously unknown Caravaggio, Mr. Dromov. Actually, it is a Hendrik ter Brugghen but was finished by Caravaggio. Quite stunning. It has never been to market . . . before now."

"Provenance? What's the history?"

"This piece was commissioned by the Mini family in Rome before 1610. The painting is called *The Dancing Boy* and was in the family until 1881, and then went to the Gaines family in America. An estate piece. I doubt the work will ever be offered again. If you don't purchase it, a museum will—most likely."

"Why are you calling me? What's your advantage, Mr. Barnes?"

"Competition, Mr. Dromov. The curator who wants to buy this painting outbid me on another work I, myself, wanted very much to acquire not too long ago. I would be quite disappointed if they were to get *The Dancing Boy.* Of course, I am the agent for the painting and will earn a commission when sold. And it *will* be sold, I can assure you."

"E-mail me a picture. I'll take a look."

"Review your e-mail. Photos are already waiting for you."

"Hold on."

"I'll be more than happy to."

Dromov shook the mouse to awaken his computer. He'd not checked his inbox for several hours. Above the unopened messages from his clients was an e-mail from Gerrod Barnes with three attachments. He downloaded the first image. As the photo appeared, his eyes widened and his stomach contracted. Magnificent.

He liked happy, upbeat subjects in his paintings, not depictions of tortured souls and retribution. This one would do quite nicely over the fireplace in his new apartment in Amsterdam.

"I'm looking at it now," Dromov said. "What's the estimate?" The familiar twinge of want crept in. A parting gift. After this pur-chase, he'd wave goodbye to himself.

"The opening bid will be £250,000, but given how infinitely rare this is, the sky is the limit, as you say. I highly recommend you attend the auction in person," Gerrod pressed. "I anticipate a spirited crowd when this lot comes up for bid. The photos certainly don't relay the exquisite detail and richness of the hues. You won't regret being here in person to see for yourself. Might you arrive by Friday afternoon? Remember, the auction is at Farnum's on Saturday and begins at five thirty."

"I'll be there. I want this painting. But I need an authentication in writing."

"Very good, sir. We shall meet on Friday. We can inspect the painting together during the preview in the afternoon." Gerrod recited the address of the auction house and hung up.

Dromov set the phone in the cradle, his mind racing. Change of plan. He'd have to get his assistant to take over the shredding project. He could tell her these files were duplicate and unnecessary copies. He stacked the folders on his desk.

"Diane! Book me a ticket to London for Friday morning," he shouted.

"Return?" The increased edge in her voice had become tiresome.

"Wednesday afternoon." Nobody would know that he wouldn't be on the return flight back to the US. "I'm spending a long weekend with a friend," he said, spewing more cover story into the intercom. He'd need to book a separate ticket from London to Amsterdam under the name of Arthur Williams.

"I'll make the reservation, but you have to take Mrs. Hite on line two. *Please* take Mrs. Hite on line two."

"Take a message."

"Don't do this to me, Tony."

"What did I say? Are you deaf?" *God, he hated when she called him Tony.* "And do something about this damn Internet—moving at a crawl again. Are dim-witted gerbils spinning the wheels?"

He hadn't planned for it to happen so soon, but opportunity was opportunity. The ability to move fast had made him a rich man; a lesson he heeded well. The time was right. If only one of his clients complained to the authorities, the Feds would crawl all over him.

Dromov threw two passports on the desk. The name inside one of them was Arthur Williams. He thumbed through his new birth certificate, driver's license, and social security card. On the flight to London, he'd practice saying his new name. *Arthur Williams . . . Arthur Williams.*

The painting was tangible, unknown, and desirable—and important. The perfect addition to his house in Amsterdam. Yes—he'd fly there from London after the auction. Fine art was insurance, like cash in the bank.

Selling the painting wouldn't be a problem—if he called the right people—but only if necessary. He wanted to live with the work for as long as possible; a perfect mate to the Vermeer. *The Dancing Boy*—he liked the title. This young boy in the painting would dance in his living room, celebrating his successes while the young girl played her piano. Even one stroke of a Caravaggio in his home was more than he could pass up.

"Tony, do you want the car service or drive your own car to the airport?"

"Car service!" he bellowed as he stuffed folders in his briefcase. Leaving his cars behind was a shame, especially the yellow Lamborghini. *C'est la vie.* They'd be found eventually, but he'd be long gone. He'd already made arrangements for the Vermeer to be packed and shipped.

This big-deal auction was his perfect public ending. Smile for the cameras, make the news, and then go. Smart to have a visible pres-ence to the last minute. He'd be sipping Lillet over ice, with a twist of orange, in Amsterdam by the end of the week.

Right now, though, he had a painting to buy.

CHAPTER 27

Ow . . . Quit It!

At four o'clock on Saturday afternoon, Jean applied the final touches to her lipstick in the hotel bathroom mirror. She turned to check the back of her black pant suit and adjusted the top button of her aqua silk blouse. "Jon will be here any minute, Spence. You ready?"

"Almost. Just doing my tie," Spence called back.

"Can you slip a note under Dillon's door? Hopefully he's ready too."

Spence straightened his vintage Jerry Garcia tie, the one with the saturated blocks of neon colors in geometric shapes.

Jean shook her head, laughing. "Jon told us to stay low-key."

"What? This tie is art. I bet Graham wishes he had one of these in his collection at the V&A."

The day before, she and Spence had taken Dillon to the Victoria and Albert Museum to meet with Graham Hollingsworth, the director of the textiles department. Graham had told them his experience with the magical fabric had been the highlight of his career, if not his life. The three of them shared a private and important moment in the retelling of the story. Afterward, they'd rummaged through the sale tables at Harrods for new clothes for Dillon.

A knock on the connecting door—Dillon had beaten Spence to leaving a note. Dillon seemed self-conscious but raised his thumb when he spotted Spence's tie.

Dillon had on his new wool sweater and slacks from Harrods. The colors had drawn Jean in: dusky gray with broad splashes of ochre, electric blue, and black. The design reminded her of the art in Nefertari's tomb. Dillon looked hip with the new black gabardine slacks, although finding dress pants with a twenty-eight-inch waist had been a challenge. Jean had to admit this outfit for Dillon was about as low-key as Spence's tie.

Spence had insisted on picking out Dillon's new scarf: cream-colored cotton with random pattern of black triangles. The pattern didn't quite go with the sweater, but Spence thought Dillon would be more comfortable maintaining some semblance of his Bohemian appearance. Plus, Dillon's beat-up Keds popped out of the bottom cuffs. Not a complete makeover.

Jon tapped on their door and announced himself.

"Hey, Jon! Aren't you FBI-suave in your dapper blue suit. And your tie is so subdued." Jean dipped her head toward Spence.

Jon laughed.

"You guys leave this tie alone," Spence said, grimacing. "Hey, honey, did you bring a lint roller? Mycroft's hair is on my jacket."

Jon glanced at Dillon and rolled his eyes. "While you three gallivanted around London, I was making progress on Dromov. Barnes confirmed he's coming, so now we're tracking him. All the dominoes are set to tip as soon as Dromov gets on the plane. Spent the afternoon at Farnum's with a colleague, and I even had a chance to arrange a surprise for Dillon." He clapped his hands together. "Okay, time to get serious. We have work to do. Grab the painting and let's go. I'll need it when I talk to Dromov."

"What do you want us to do while you're talking with him?" Jean asked.

"I'll tell you in the taxi, but you three will sit in the back with me and look pretty. Hmmm . . . we may have to fend off potential buyers of Spence's tie."

Spence picked up the art case and nudged Dillon's shoulder to follow Jon and Jean out the door. "Here we go, kids!"

Dillon wrapped his arm through Jean's as they sat with Spence and Jon in the last row of the auction room. Jon held his hand out flat, signaling for them to stay quiet.

As he scanned the crowd, Dillon marveled at such an obvious show of wealth in one place. The recessed lights weren't meant to flash the diamond rings on attendees' fingers, but they did so anyway.

Along with anticipation, disappointment sunk in too. After reviewing the catalog, Dillon wished this fine art was going to be more accessible. Many of these pieces should go to museums, where everyone could enjoy them. Private homes were a waste.

The auction was about to start. He sensed the tension as bodies stilled and mouths stopped moving. People opened their catalogs; hands poised on their paddles. He froze. *What the—? The Man!* Dillon studied the figure in the last seat of the row in front of him. Jon leaned forward and patted his shoulder, like they were acquainted. He caught the number on the Man's paddle: eighty-six. After the auction, he would approach him. Dillon needed to touch the skin of the Man's hands again, to study those wide brown eyes, and to run his hand through his wavy hair. If he could find out the Man's identity, maybe he would give him the portrait when he was finished.

Jon's gaze followed Dromov as he sauntered into the auction room with a tall, slim woman in a short, sleeveless black dress, its neckline beaded with shiny gems. He'd bet anything Dromov picked her up from some high-class escort service. The pair gravitated toward two seats in the third row. The woman seemed pleased with herself; a fur coat was draped over her arm. *Lynx?* He felt like calling PETA.

Dromov controlled paddle number forty-two, though the woman physically held it—gripped in her elegant hand as if someone were about to snatch it.

Jon leaned forward and tapped the shoulder of the man in front of him; he gripped paddle number eighty-six.

"Thanks for coming. You ready?" he whispered.

The man reached up and patted his hand.

Jean dug her nails into Spence's leg as a hush settled over the capacity crowd in the auction room. She didn't realize she was doing it until Spence winced and plucked up her fingers.

"Sorry, I'm so nervous. I want to punch Dromov's lights out," she said, a little too loud.

"Me too, but don't cut off my blood supply." Spence scrunched his eyes and rubbed his thigh.

"He's got such a smug face. I bet he bought all that jewelry for that hussy with *our* money. Hey, what if someone else buys the painting? Then we're screwed."

"They won't. Dromov and Miss Gotrocks want our little boy at any cost. Jon's got it all under control. And, by the way, it was *Mary's* money, not ours."

"How did Dillon's copy get by Dromov's inspection?"

"Jon said Farnum's arranged for Dromov to inspect the original, but they're putting Dillon's copy in the auction. Farnum's is cooperating with the FBI, and so is Gerrod Barnes."

"But what if—"

"Ladies and gentlemen, welcome to Farnum's," the auctioneer announced as he stood behind the podium. "This evening we have a very special collection of important paintings, furniture, and *objets d'art.* Many pieces in tonight's sale have never before been offered to the public. A unique and rare opportunity, I can assure you. Without delay, let us begin."

"I'm not sure this was such a good idea." Jean grabbed Spence's knee and dug in her nails.

"Shhh . . . We're starting." Spence gritted his teeth. "Ow . . . quit it."

CHAPTER 28

The Auction

The copy of *The Dancing Boy* emerged from behind the curtain, stage-left, between a pair of white-gloved hands. Dillon's eyes fixed on the image. Whoever was holding the painting wore a dark suit that blended with the curtained backdrop so that the gloves appeared to float, unattached to anything but the unframed canvas. The image did a backward jig across the stage and came to a rest on the polished wood easel. This was *his* painting, holding court with the best of the best. One day, maybe his paintings would be sold like this—with his name, his pedigree, and with collectors coming from all over the world to bid on them.

Dillon broke his concentration to catch a glimpse of the Man. Jon was in the way, leaning forward with his elbows on his knees, pressing his forefingers perpendicular to his lips. Jean covered her eyes with one hand but peeked through her fingers and dug the nails of her other hand into Spence's thigh. Spence studied his tie for comfort in between pop-up glances to the stage. Behind him, Gerrod Barnes leaned uncomfortably against the oak-paneled back wall with his arms across his chest, glued to his phone. They were all as nervous as he was. *Follow the paddles. Dromov is forty-two.*

"Lot 123," the auctioneer boomed. "A previously unknown Hendrick ter Brugghen, believed to be finished by Caravaggio between 1605 and 1610. Part Caravaggio, ladies and gentlemen. Historic piece. Possibly the last strokes of Caravaggio's brush before he left Rome. This work was originally commissioned by the Mini family in Rome and has been in private ownership for its entire history. The first time it has come to market. We will open the bidding at £250,000, with increments of £10,000. Let us begin . . ."

The audience members shifted in their seats, their necks strain-ing to get a better look at *The Dancing Boy*. Hushed whispers released like a flock of swallows taking flight.

"£250,000! Thank you, sir. We are off and running. Two sixty, two seventy, two eighty, two ninety on the phone.

"I have £300,000 on the Internet. Excellent! This is quite exciting ladies and gentlemen!"

In rapid succession the bids climbed. Jean bounced her gaze at a rate resembling a match at Wimbledon. Spence's eyes bulged as he tried to get Jon's attention. Jon only had eyes for Dromov's paddle forty-two.

"New bidder—£400,000! Thank you, number forty-two in the third row."

"It's worth more than this, I can assure you. Caravaggio touched his brush to the canvas. Never been offered before."

Silence.

"New bidder—£410,000. Number eighty-six, the gentleman in the back. Thank you, sir."

"Number twenty-one, £420,000."

"Number eighty-six, £430,000."

"Yes, quite exciting—£440,000. Number forty-two."

"Down to only two bidders? Do I have £450,000 . . . £450,000? Don't let it go, sir. To you, number eighty-six? No, sir? All done? Last chance!"

"Once . . . twice . . . Excellent!—£450,000! Number eight-six in the back has changed his mind. Back in it, I see. Thank you, sir!"

"One of a kind. Do I have £460,000?"

Silence.

"Thank you, number forty-two! Gentleman in the third row. Exciting, indeed."

"Do I hear four seventy? Four seventy? All done? Last and final bid is £460,000 once, £460,000 twice. Sold!" The hammer banged. "Well done! This amazing painting goes to number forty-two in the third row for £460,000. Thank you. Congratulations, sir!"

Enthusiastic applause erupted as Anthony Dromov stood and waved his paddle to the crowd. He beamed, triumphant.

Jon punched in a number on his phone, motioning for Dillon to follow him out of the back door with the art case. Gerrod stepped from behind, whispered in Jon's unoccupied ear, and slipped out of the room. Jean and Spence jumped up and followed Jon and Dillon, having no idea what was going to happen next.

Dillon turned and scanned the back row of chairs. The man at the end, paddle number eight-six, was gone.

"What's happening, Jon? What do we do now?" Jean asked, breathless, even though Jon was still on the phone. "Oh God, I thought I'd have a stroke. Outrageous."

"Honey, do you know how much that is? That's about seven hundred fifty thousand in US dollars." Spence swung his fist as if pulling a long-haul truck horn. "Score, baby!"

"You do remember that wasn't a real sale, right?" she laughed. "And we're never selling our beautiful little dancing boy."

Jon waved to someone across the lobby, the phone still pressed in his ear. A tall woman with long blond hair waved back and marched toward him. Jon turned to Jean and said under his breath:

"We wait until Dromov completes his transaction. I'll intercept him before he picks up the painting. I want you and Spence to go with Dillon to meet with this woman who's coming over to us. When I make the call, someone from the Farnum's staff will come and get you to bring the painting in. Go be parents."

"But, Jon—I thought we were going with you."

"Do as I ask. Please, Jean. Dillon needs you both."

The woman arrived and shook Jon's hand. Her navy-blue suit screamed FBI, but her bright-yellow silk scarf became airborne behind her. Maybe she wasn't *all* business. Her peaches-and-cream complexion made her smile warm and genuine. The slight overbite appeared to make her mouth bigger than it really was. She shook each of their hands as if they were in a receiving line at a wedding. Lingering the longest at Dillon, the woman analyzed every detail of his young face.

"Jean, Spence, this is Laura Reed," Jon said. "She's a special agent with the Art Crime Team. She's crossed the pond to meet Dillon, and inspect his copy of *The Dancing Boy*, of course."

"Hello, hello! Jon has told me quite a bit about all of you," Laura said. "I think Dillon has some gifts we should discuss. Please, let's go to a private room. The auction house was kind enough to give us space in one of the viewing rooms down this hall." Laura motioned for the three of them to follow her. Jean could tell Laura's perky shell masked a ruthless underbelly. This woman got what she wanted and compelled you to thank her.

Jean's eyes pleaded with Jon, torn about staying with Dillon or fighting to go to the ugly meeting with Dromov. She wanted a ring-side seat to the ugly meeting. Spence pulled her arm.

"C'mon, Jean. You're no FBI agent, sweetheart. Dillon needs us."

Jon gave her a determined look. "Jean, you and Spence go with Dillon and Laura until I send someone in for you. Don't worry—you won't be left out."

As Jean turned to follow Laura, Spence, and Dillon, she heard Jon say into his phone, "Move in on Machelli." Now she really wanted in on that meeting.

Franco Machelli's knee bounced up and down as he downloaded the video software from the Farnum's website. He couldn't wait to watch the auction in real time. He completed the user registration and stared at the computer screen. The knots in his stomach tightened as the image of the auctioneer approached the podium. He had some time before Lot 123 would come up for bidding. He popped two antacids for the burning in his chest. Even though it was only eleven in the morning, he needed a drink. The ice cubes clinked in the glass. He poured a whiskey, with an extra tip of the bottle. Returning to the screen, he followed the bidding on Lot 117, a kidney-shaped Chippendale desk and chair set. A refill was needed for Lot 119. *Getting close.* His chest went tight; his heart pounded in his ears. Adrenaline coursed in his veins with every pumped thump.

He tapped the computer screen through Lots 121 and 122, reminding himself to breathe. Finally, *The Dancing Boy* jerked with the video delay as gloved hands moved the canvas across the stage to the easel. He rushed to refill his tumbler, spilling the whiskey on the glass coffee table. He returned to his desk and grabbed the edges of the monitor. A wave of nausea rolled over him as he attempted to focus.

Every increase of the bid fed the pounding in his chest. *God, what a beautiful painting.* The image blurred. The auctioneer appeared to be talking in slow motion.

"Dillon . . . I'm sorry," he slurred, glancing at the book on Caravaggio, open to *The Seven Works of Mercy*. "So . . . sorry." He turned back to the screen.

Bid!

"Take . . . it . . . back!" he shouted. The glass tumbler fell to the floor as he swept his arm across the desk. The whiskey splashed to the carpet; puddles of amber disks soaked into the woven fibers.

Bid!

"I'm a rich . . . man." His voice trailed off as he grabbed his left arm.

His eyes blurred. *Pain . . . in . . . chest.*

Franco slumped to the floor. He clawed at the wet fibers, as if crawling through sand to the oasis of the phone. Images of art scrolled past his eyes: Dillon's copy of *The Dancing Boy*, followed by those of

Whistler, Turner, Velázquez, Michelangelo, and the out-stretched hand of Da Vinci.

The world went dark. The last sound was waves . . . thunderous waves of applause.

Franco never saw the pulsing alert at the bottom of the com-puter screen, signaling the arrival of a new e-mail.

No one answered the relentless knock on the door.

Two FBI agents approached the door of apartment 4D with the building manager in tow.

"Mr. Machelli? FBI! Mr. Machelli?" shouted one of the agents, and then put his ear to the door. "TV's on."

Heads poked out of apartment doors on each side of the long corridor. The other agent swept his hand, a signal for the residents to go back inside. He nodded to the manager.

"Smells like liquor in here. There he is—on the floor by the desk! Call the paramedics!" As the agent rolled Franco over on his back, a string of froth trailed from his mouth. The agent pressed his hand to Franco's neck and raised his eyes. "Nothing, but he's still warm."

"CPR?"

"I'll give it a try, but I can already tell he's gone."

"I'll call Jon." The agent stopped short when his attention was drawn to the computer on the desk. "Hey, look at this—" As he dialed Jon's number, the agent stepped over to the screen. "The auc-tion Jon's at," he said, viewing the live video. He clicked on the flashing e-mail alert to open the new message.

Good news! The painting hammered at £460,000. Congratulations!
Gerrod

CHAPTER 29

Horus Gets Noisy

Jon waited outside the auction room for Anthony Dromov to complete the transaction for *The Dancing Boy.* Once the staff verified his payment information, a young gentleman from Farnum's shook Dromov's hand. "We'll bring the painting out to you, Mr. Dromov. Please wait in the lobby as the sale is still in progress."

A slight nod of the head and a quick smile from the employee signaled Jon was free to make the next move.

"Anthony Dromov?" he asked, approaching the man from behind.

Dromov turned, indignant about the violation of his personal space. The woman next to him ignored Jon as if he were the epitome of trash. She inspected her freshly polished crimson nails.

"Yes?"

"May I talk to you about your painting while you wait?" Jon kept his voice smooth and calm.

Dromov laughed. "You want to buy *The Dancing Boy* from me? Why didn't you bid against me? No use, though, because I'd have outbid you."

"Is that so? Using which of your client's money?"

"Excuse me?"

"I need you to come with me." Jon made a sweeping motion toward a room down the hall, the room next to where Jean, Spence and Dillon were meeting with Laura Reed.

"I don't need to do anything of the sort." Dromov turned and took his escort's arm. "C'mon, sweetheart. A loser with regrets." The woman glared at Jon.

"Yes, I most certainly can make you come with me. My name is Special Agent Jon Segert, FBI. I need to talk with you—right now." He allowed his words to sink in.

"Wait here, dear. I'll only be a few minutes. A mistake. This jerk is going to owe me an apology."

Dromov's steps were stiff as Jon followed him down the hall. Jon stood in the doorway of the viewing room, relishing the worry on the man's guilty face.

"I want my painting," Dromov said. "What is the meaning of this?"

"Sit . . . please." Jon closed the door and pulled out a chair at the polished walnut conference table. He thumped the back of the seat. "Make yourself comfortable. We'll have a chat." The small room was lined with oil paintings depicting somewhat violent hunting scenes. Jon fingered the talon in his pocket—his support team on stand by. He sat across from Dromov and gazed around the room. "These paintings in here are beautiful, aren't they? Does art speak to you, Mr. Dromov?"

"What? Is this normal."

"What's normal?" Jon turned and fixed his gaze on Dromov's muddy eyes. "Your clients scrambling to figure out how they're going to pay the electric bill? Buy birthday presents for their grandchildren? Not being able to get medications to keep them alive? Maybe they have to choose a frozen dinner while you gorge yourself on Kobe beef. I think you did more than steal their savings to buy paintings or drive fancy cars. You stole your clients' lives."

"Pfffft. What are you going on about?"

Jon reached for the phone on the conference table and made a call. "Send Mr. and Mrs. Collins in here with *The Dancing Boy*, please." He studied the receiver like something might come out of it.

"The painting is mine," Dromov snapped.

Jon remained silent. He set his hand over the talon in his pocket. He smiled to himself at the image of it being a gun in a holster. The talon vibrated under his hand.

"Where did you get the money to buy the painting?" Jon stared into Dromov's eyes; they shifted to the right. *Scrambling to make something up.*

"I owe you no explanation. My personal financial situation is nobody's business but mine."

"I think you do owe me, and a lot of other people, an explanation." Jon set the talon in the center of the conference table. "Meet my partner."

"This is absurd." Dromov leaned forward to get up but stopped as the talon started to vibrate against the wood. He studied the claw, curious at first, and then fear and disbelief washed over his face. He grabbed the chair's arms and lowered his substantial rear back on the seat.

The talon grew: feathers, claws, a second foot, legs, a body, and a menacing head emerged and took shape. An enormous hawk stood in the center of the table. The predator let out a screech that tore through the air in the room, announcing his rebirth. Jon sat back in his chair, satisfied, but inside he was a horse pushing against the starting gate.

"Horus," Jon said, making a sweeping gesture to the bird.

The fully formed hawk clawed at the wood, etching deep, ragged grooves with each swipe—a tortured sound. Shiny cream-colored feathers ruffled on the hawk's head as it bobbed in anticipation. Horus screeched again.

Dromov's eyes went wide. They darted to the handle on the door. His chest heaved as he tried to get a breath.

"Stay right where you are," Jon ordered. He turned to the hawk. "Shhhh. Horus, come." He made a production of stretching out his arm. Horus dismembered Dromov with his glare, anxious for the kill, but then whipped his head back to Jon. The massive hawk climbed up his arm, buckling it under his weight, and settled on his shoulder. From his perch, Horus stared at Dromov as if he were a juicy rodent.

"What the hell—is that?"

"This is truth. You are going to tell me and my partner the truth. You stole your clients' money, didn't you?"

Dromov went silent. Finally, he said, "You're full of—"

"Do these names sound familiar?" Jon interrupted him and pulled a piece of paper from his inside breast pocket, trying not to jostle Horus. "Salena Steward, age eighty, $183,422; Lawrence Flanders, eighty-two, $49,347; Vivian and Donald Hite, seventy-nine and eighty, $2,000,000; Judith Hawkins, sixty-three, $67,422; Jean and Spencer Collins, fifty-three and sixty-one, $503,452 . . . " He stopped and stared at Dromov. "Should I keep going? We're just getting started." Horus shifted in agitation, snapping and clicking his razor-like beak as Jon tapped the paper. "More names here—and we've talked with all of them. But they can't seem to get a return phone call from you."

"I've been busy. You're trying to make something out of nothing."

"Nothing? These are real people—with real hopes and dreams. I read their ages to make a point. They don't have time to earn back their money. Not that timing makes any difference in the severity of the crime. There are young ones too, who also worked hard and trusted you with their savings. We've checked. Nothing is in the accounts listed on their statements—statements *you* sent to them. And here you are, spending it, flaunting the spoils." Horus let out a shriek and stretched his massive wings, smacking Jon on the back of the head. He soothed the hawk. "Shhhh . . . I know. Stay calm."

"Those people are happy with their experience with me." Dromov attempted to be controlled, but his eyes told another story.

Horus lurched forward and puffed out his wings, anxious to tear skin. The hawk walked himself down Jon's outstretched arm to the table and stood in front of Dromov, poised to strike. Dromov began to shake.

The soft tap on the door switched Jon's focus.

"Let's see how happy, shall we?" The handle turned. Horus's head did a sharp turn toward the sound. Jean poked her head inside. Spence stood behind her with the *The Dancing Boy* balanced in his arms.

"Jon? You okay in here? They came and got us to bring in the—Whoa!" Jean's eyes went wide as soon as she spotted Horus. She recovered and nodded to Spence.

"Here's the painting they gave us to deliver." Spence set the canvas next to the deep scratches in the wood, never taking his eyes off the hawk. He glanced at Jon for further instructions.

Their eyes locked. "Spence?" Horus lurched over to Spence and nudged his arm. "Are you a happy client of Anthony Dromov?"

Spence turned and glared, stroking the hawk's back. He straightened to his full height and said, "Happy? If I didn't think Horus here couldn't do a better job, I'd rip your throat out. Did you steal Mary Coulter's money—*our* money?"

Jon could tell that Dromov wasn't prepared to be confronted by one of his clients. The truth was on his face, regardless of what he might or might not say. The man remained silent, but his expression screamed guilt.

"Spence . . . don't." Jean set her hand on his arm, the other stroking Horus's back. The hawk responded by moving closer to her without taking his eyes off Dromov. Jean's gaze followed Horus's and fixed on Dromov too. She couldn't heed her own advice to stay quiet. "You're a fake!" she hissed. "And you just bought a fake. But the money you spent on this painting is very real. It's going back to your clients." Jean pulled a magnifying glass out of her pocket and reached around Horus to hand it to Jon.

Dromov started to laugh; the peel sounded sinister. "You guys will stop at nothing, will you?" He ran his fingers through his greasy black hair. "I need to go. I'll take my painting now. My lady friend is waiting outside."

"Is she paid for by us?" Spence growled.

"Shall we?" Jon twirled the magnifier in his fingers.

"Shall we what?" Dromov seethed, failing to acknowledge Spence's sarcastic comment.

"Here, take this." Jon handed the glass disc to Dromov. "Check the hair and buttons on the coat and on the boy's britches."

Dromov snatched it from Jon's hand. He glared at the hawk, bent down, and viewed *The Dancing Boy*'s buttons. "Nec . . . Spe . . . Nec . . . Metu," He recited the words in a slow sequence. He shrugged. "Nothing. Just letters." The magnifying glass clattered to the conference table. The bird didn't even flinch at the noise.

"Art doesn't speak to you, does it? You don't deserve to have this painting," Jean said. Jon held out his hand for her to stay quiet. The last thing he needed was for her to lose her temper.

"Do you know what those words mean?" Jon continued. "Latin—'without hope, without fear.' You have no hope of getting out of this, and you *should* be very afraid. You need to come clean. We have your statements. We've checked the accounts. Where's the money?"

Silence. The air buzzed with an unspoken conversation. Dromov stared at the hawk and moved his hands in his lap, as if fingers might go missing.

"Do you recognize my name, Mr. Dromov?" Jean asked.

"No. Who are you?"

"I'm Jean Collins. My husband and I are one of your investor accounts—you ass! Does the name Mary Coulter ring a bell? How about Raleigh Coulter?"

The hawk went rigid at the mention of Raleigh's name. He inched his way across the table toward Dromov, stalking him. Horus spread his wings to their full span, a good five feet. Dromov sucked in a gulp of air as the bird went closer. His mouth attempted to say something, but only opened and closed—and so did Horus's.

"How many clients did Coulter refer to you, besides those I named?" Jon continued. "He's dead. Horus here didn't care much for Raleigh."

"I don't know a Raleigh . . . Coulter. But you've screwed with my business. You had no right—"

"Of course you did, you lying sack of—" Spence stopped when Jon held up his hand.

"Oh, come on." Jon opened his hands in front of him. "We know that Coulter put his clients' money in your fund. And you gave him a nice kickback for doing so. The bank has a record of those sweet transfers. I believe that adds collusion to a charge of criminal theft."

Horus screeched and lunged, snapping at the air with his lethal beak. The brown and white feathers on the bird's chest fanned in anger.

"I . . . It's gone," Dromov stuttered, holding up his hands to shield his face. Horus raised his right claw, splayed his talons, and stretched his wings. The bird lasered his eyes on his prey and opened his mouth to strike. "Nooo . . . stop!" Dromov recoiled.

Horus lunged at lightening speed. A gash opened on Dromov's arm, tearing his shirt. Blood blossomed at an alarming rate on his sleeve. He stared at his arm in disbelief as the red disk expanded.

"Better tell the truth. This bird is hungry and angry. Bad combination."

"I want my lawyer present. You can't do this! I'm filing assault charges!"

"Go ahead—call an army of lawyers. I'm more interested in what you have to say to your clients than what you tell your legal council."

Horus did one last screech and whipped his head around to Jean. He walked across the table toward her. "C'mere, Horus. You did good work, baby."

Spence reached over to stroke the thick feathers on the hawk's chest. "He's a chunker. No wonder he can do so much *damage*."

"Let him go, Jean. Make him come back," Jon said.

"Off you go, Horus." The hawk inched his way back to Jon, never taking its eyes off Dromov.

"You're in on this too? Who *are* you people?" Dromov stared at Jean and Spence as if they had snakes coming out of their ears.

"We're your worst nightmare," Jean fumed, "who also happen to be witnesses."

Horus screeched and disappeared. Only the spinning talon remained. All four of them watched it slow and finally stop. Jon made a display of slipping it back in his pocket.

"Where'd that hawk go?" Dromov demanded.

"I didn't see a hawk, did you?" Jon asked, turning to Jean.

"Nope. No idea what you're talking about."

Jon turned back to Dromov, whose mouth gaped open. "What makes a man, perfectly capable of earning a good living, *do* it? You're clever—note that I didn't say smart—you're educated, and clearly a man with excellent taste . . . in art. But you have extremely bad judgment."

Spence picked up his cue to continue. "Greed, right? Other people's lives don't mean anything to you, do they?"

Dromov remained silent.

"I still don't get it," Jon said, shaking his head. "But I'll tell you what I am going to get. I'm going to find the money." He tapped the paper in his hand and gestured toward Jean and Spence. "And tonight's auction was a pretty good start."

"How are you going to do that?" Dromov said, more curious than defensive. His shirtsleeve was now soaked with blood and had started to drip on the conference table.

"You're connected with Raleigh Coulter's death too. And you know why? He brought people to you who trusted you with their life savings."

"And my husband and me too, but it's not about us." Jean's voice nearly cracked. "You betrayed a woman who is dead—Raleigh's mother. She lived simply and helped people—that's all she wanted to do." Jean leaned into Dromov's face, eyes ablaze, and sneered: "But she's still alive and is watching you. I talked with her—*after* she died."

Dromov turned to her, his eyes filled with contempt. "You know what, Mrs. Collins? You're bat-shit crazy. All of you are." Dromov stared down Jean, and then at the blood pooling on the conference table.

"Horus should've torn you to shreds," Spence interjected. "He could, you know, like you shredded everyone who worked with you. But, oh, right—I didn't see a hawk in here either."

"Calm down, Spence. Enough." Jon turned and addressed

Dromov. "This painting comes with me. I just found $750,000 of the missing money. The Vermeer, which you enjoyed parading in front of the cameras, is being packed up as we speak, along with all the other paintings in your apartment. Over forty million is tied up in that painting alone, and we're going to liquidate it. And your assistant turned over the files." Jon paused when Dromov straightened. "Oh yeah, we have them. You should have been a nicer boss. Diane didn't shred them like you asked her to. In fact, she's been extremely helpful. We've gathered quite a bit of paper you were trying to turn into filler for Easter baskets. You could have been a raving success in that business alone." Jon waited for his words to sink in.

"I am a success!" Dromov shouted.

"If that's earning a living, then I'm not buying what you're selling. I don't think Scotland Yard will either. They're anxious to put the Raleigh Coulter mess to bed. 'Appened on their turf, mate." Jon used his best fake Cockney accent, which wasn't at all believable. "And we 'appen to be on it."

Jon stood and opened the conference room door. Two inspecttors entered, clipped Dromov's wrists in plastic straps, and escorted him out to the hallway.

"Oy, what's this about? His arm's a bloody wreck," one of the inspectors said.

Dromov jerked his head back. "That guy attacked me with a goddamned hawk! I'm gonna sue his ass!"

"Keep walking, sir; we've heard that verse before. Eyes forward.

Jon blew out a breath. Laura and Dillon were waiting in the hall. Jean and Spence stood frozen at the conference table.

"Be with you in a minute." Jon's phone buzzed for his attention. He shook his finger toward the hallway. "Yeah, what you got? In his apartment? Damn! Dromov's done, by the way. We have him. Tell the chief."

Jean tried to compose herself as she and Spence moved to the hall when Jon motioned for them to leave the room.

"I lost it, Spence. I promised myself I wouldn't, but seeing Horus—"

"I know. Pretty intense. You had every right to come unglued," he said, rubbing her back. "I was ready to rearrange that jerk's face. Not a word about Horus, okay?"

"What hawk?"

"I'm proud of you."

"That makes two of us. I mean, I'm proud of you too."

Jon poked his head out of the conference room. "Can that art case fit both canvases?"

"Yeah, no problem," Spence said. "Opens like a book. Holds a canvas on each side."

Laura Reed leaned toward Jon and whispered, "I don't think we should be walking around London with these paintings. Let's have the auction house store them in the safe downstairs. I'll arrange for Jean and Spence to pick them up tomorrow. I'll talk to the staff."

"Good idea. We'll wait in the lobby," Jon said.

"Let's all go to dinner. I'm starved," Spence chimed in.

"I need to meet with the inspectors at Scotland Yard. Not that I don't want to."

"Oh no, you don't. Not after this," Jean said, wagging her finger. "We need a drink, a meal, and details about what was going on in that room before we came in."

"Plus, you have to eat, Jon. I think Dillon has a lot to tell us too." Spence put his hand on Dillon's shoulder.

"C'mon, Jon. We owe you one. My budget, okay?" Laura said, smirking as she walked away. "Not every day that I find a recruit who'll change the future of our division."

"All right. All right. There is a certain satisfaction in letting Dromov stew for a few hours. Where do you want to go?" Jon rubbed his hands together.

"We're going to our favorite restaurant while we're in London," Jean said, eyeing Spence who nodded in agreement. "In Kensington—Ffiona's on Church Street. The best onion tart on the planet."

"Do they have dessert?"

"The sticky toffee pudding is to die for. By the way, you were wonderful in there. Your whole plan was brilliant."

"We make a pretty good team, the three of us."

Spence leaned over to him and whispered, "And Horus."

CHAPTER 30

Choices

"A toast!" Spence announced. "Here's to Dromov going behind bars, Jean and me getting our investment back, and—drum roll, please—Dillon's future career at the FBI."

"You pulled off your plan without a hitch. I'm impressed," Jean said, holding up her glass of red wine.

"Thank you!" Jon tipped his head, waving his hand toward himself to keep the compliments flowing. "So, Laura, tell me how your meeting went with these kind folks who are heaping me with praise."

"You were right; Dillon's knowledge of art is impressive. Once I saw his copy of *The Dancing Boy*, I was downright blown away. But he has more than talent . . . I can't explain it. He's got a higher sense or something, an intuitiveness that's pretty rare."

Jean pressed her lips together and glanced at Spence, brimming with pride.

"He didn't even sell himself," Laura continued. "He was just being Dillon."

Jean reached her hand and set it over Dillon's.

You're going to do important things, aren't you, Dillon? Spence wrote on the notepad.

Dillon shrugged and grinned at each person at the table with a hint of mischief in his eyes.

Laura took a sip of her wine. "He'll finish out art school. A job will be waiting for him after he graduates. We'll put the details in writing shortly. In the meantime, if we need his help, we'll pay him a consulting fee. He'll report directly to me."

"Incredible." Jon lifted his glass of iced tea to Dillon. He went serious. "You do know, the money, or the painting, are now part of Dromov's assets. If you keep the original—and Farnum's is aware *The Dancing Boy* is yours—the money Dromov paid becomes part of those assets. You don't get the proceeds, guys."

"But—" Jean stopped when Jon cut her off.

"Uh-huh . . . right. Take the money, and the painting becomes a physical asset—the real one, not the copy."

Spence put his hand on Jean's arm. "We should talk, Jean. The cash we were going to use to start the store was in the Dromov Fund. We'll be in line with all of Dromov's other clients to get our money back. Could take a long time."

"Hmmm . . . yeah . . . we need to make a choice. Not fair," Jean said, preferring to have the money, the original, *and* the copy.

"I'd take the painting," Laura chimed in. "The piece is only going to become more valuable with all the publicity. The liquid assets will be far better for Dromov's clients, including you, so you might get your money back faster."

"Maybe you're right. What do you think, Spence? We can still start the store, but we'll need to use our own savings if you want to stay on schedule."

"Let's have Dillon decide. He has a stake in this too." Spence wrote a note to Dillon. *Should we take the painting or the money?*

The Dancing Boy. *Definitely!* Dillon wrote.

"Well, there you go! We'll pick up both paintings tomorrow afternoon. The FBI keeps the money," Jean declared, and then turned to Jon. "So what about you? Are you okay with how this came out?"

Laura's cell phone rang out the theme from the television show *Get Smart.* Jean chuckled but got serious as Laura stepped outside the restaurant. She paced back and forth in the front window. Jean turned to Jon and leaned on her elbows.

"Okay, spill," she said in a low voice. "What was going on with Dromov before we came in?"

"Horus and I have . . . a kind of bond."

"Uh . . . yeah, I'd say," Spence quipped.

"The talon transforms for me, protects me." Jon's gaze seemed to be far away, and then he snapped back in the moment. "And you both too. Horus's healing powers are as amazing as his ability to be lethal. I need to train him up a bit, though. The biting thing isn't good."

"Nice," Spence said, nodding his head. "We've got a hundred-year-old ghost dog that's in love with our cat, and you get a gigantic hawk with an anger management problem." Spence took a sip of his ale. "Next?"

Jean wrinkled her nose at Spence. "He's a lovely dog," she said and turned back to Jon. "His name is Wiley. He's immortal and we love him . . . and so does Mycroft."

"Who was bidding against Dromov?" Spence tried to keep his face deadpan but was having way too much fun.

"A friend of mine. That's all I'm going to say." Jon smirked as he sipped his tea.

"I'm glad I didn't know you had Horus's talon when we were on the plane. Weren't you the tiniest bit concerned?" Jean asked.

"Horus pretty much keeps in his talon, unless he thinks I need help."

"Only comes out when he's around bad guys?" Spence took a bite of his onion tart.

"Something like that." Jon's phone buzzed. "Segert. Confirmed? Let's do a complete debrief when I get back. Leaving tomorrow morning with Dromov in tow."

"Everything okay?" Jean asked.

"Franco Machelli's dead—heart attack. Happened during the auction, before our guys went into his apartment."

"Oh my God!" Jean's hand flew to her mouth.

"Look—don't tell Dillon right away." Jon acted antsy to leave. "Wait until you're home. I'm sure this trip's been overwhelming. He may not take the news well. I gotta go."

Jean watched Dillon studying Laura on her cell phone outside the front window. He seemed to be pondering the prospect of having a boss. As Jon stepped out the door, she turned to Spence. "Ugh."

"Ugh is right."

CHAPTER 31

The Man Returns

All was quiet and dark in the basement of Farnum's Auctions. The Man waited for the security guard to make his final round for the night, check the doors, and jiggle the handle on the vault. Locked. The guard scanned left and right all the way down the hall before climbing the stairs.

Getting inside that vault would not be an issue. The guard disappeared. Time to move. He stepped to the thick steel door. He adjusted his glasses and reached for the dial. The blue haze of the basement light made the numbers gleam and sparkle along the edge.

The Man checked the identification tag on the black case in the vertical slot labeled Lot 123. The straps pulled away at his touch. He opened it and smiled as the twin *Dancing Boy* canvases unfolded in front of him. He set his hand on the left one . . . *Dillon's copy.* On the right one, beams of golden light burst from his palm. His own hand trailed in a wispy blue wave as he lifted away the painting.

The interior elastic straps thronged back into place as he slipped the canvas out of the case. The painting was released to his custody.

The Man and the painting were gone.

"I'm glad we had the morning with Dillon at the National Portrait Gallery. He was taken with Joshua Reynolds," Spence said. "Next time, we'll go to the Tate Modern."

"The extra day was wonderful. I wish we could be here another week," Jean said. "I'm sorry we didn't get to say goodbye to Jon. I think he checked out before we even got up. We'll be getting up at the crack tomorrow, ourselves, so we should go over to the auction house and pick up the paintings now. Then we can grab a bite to eat and turn in early." Jean cracked Dillon's door open and waved. He motioned her to come inside his room. She wrote a note: *Time to go get the paintings.*

Dillon swung his thin legs off the bed and set the museum catalog on the nightstand. He grabbed his scarf and jacket.

Jean stood at the hotel room door, grasping the handle. "Let's go. I won't relax until we get those paintings home."

Spence held open the heavy glass door of Farnum's Auctions for Jean and Dillon.

"We're here to pick up a case with two paintings. Jean and Spencer Collins," Spence said to the prim woman at the reception desk. "Arrangements were made by Laura Reed from the FBI."

"The artist, sir?"

"Brugghen-Caravaggio. I think that's how the catalog labeled it—Lot 123. Two paintings: the original and a Dillon Davis copy. Both in a strapped black case."

"Ah yes. One moment, please." The woman turned and handed a note to a young gentleman on the auction administrative staff. The smartly dressed man of about thirty-five walked around the desk and offered Spence his hand. His lengths of wavy hair resembled those of a subject in a Caravaggio painting.

"Pleasure. My name is Nicholas Larabee. I'll retrieve the paintings straight away. You are correct; Laura Reed did inform me of the details. Excuse me for one moment."

Spence turned to Jean and Dillon, who had taken a seat on an antique couch that appeared to be highly uncomfortable, and swished his eyebrows up and down. He leaned on the counter, admiring both of them. He turned and smiled at the receptionist.

"Please take the liberty to have a seat, sir." She nodded to the Victorian couches, a signal for him to step away.

"Oh . . . sure."

The three of them waited. After about ten minutes, Jean started to fidget. "What's going on? How long does it take to retrieve a case?"

"I don't know—let me check." Spence walked back up to the desk and spotted Nicholas coming around the corner with the case in his hand.

"Mr. Collins, may I speak with you in private?"

"Okay . . ." He turned back to Jean and shrugged his shoulders. Her eyes bulged with inquisition. Spence motioned for her to stay put and followed Nicholas into his office.

Once inside, Nicolas closed the door. "Appears we have a slight problem, sir."

"What kind of problem?"

"One of the paintings is missing." Nicholas set his hand on the art case and rubbed the surface, as if a genie might make it magically appear inside.

"Open it. I need to know which painting was removed—the original or the copy. Do you have a magnifying glass?"

"Of course. Can you distinguish which is the original, sir?" Nicholas set the case on the conference table.

"Just get the magnifier." Spence inspected the painting inside: Dillon's copy. Too perfect. He had to verify with evidence. His stomach did a flip, but nothing compared to the flip-out Jean was going to have when she found out. And this would only pile more on top of Dillon. He blew out a breath to calm down. He could just imagine Jean sitting on that couch, running an internal Indy 500. Yep, she is going to completely lose it.

Nicholas came into the room and handed Spence a magnifying glass. He placed the disk over the wave in *The Dancing Boy*'s hair, squeezing his left eye to focus. There it was: *Collins*. The buttons contained tiny letters too.

"Call Laura Reed immediately," Spence snapped. "The original is missing. This is the copy."

"Straight away, yes." Nicholas pulled up Laura's number. He pressed the button.

"When she answers, hand the phone over to me." Spence stared at the can lights in the ceiling. As his eyes swept around the wall of fine art, the burned-in spot trailed like Tinker Bell's light—or the immortals'. Larabee's voice broke the spell.

"Laura, hello, this is Nicholas Larabee at Farnum's. The Collinses are here to pick up the paintings. Appears that one of them—the original —is not in the case. I'm not sure. No. Locked in the vault since yesterday. Yes, he's right here." Nicholas held out the phone to Spence. "Laura would like to speak with you."

"Yeah, Laura. Seems we have a big problem. Okay . . . Okay . . . But we're on a flight tomorrow morning. Well, do your best and keep me informed. Call me on my cell, or e-mail me, as soon as you can." He handed the phone back to Nicholas. "This is going to get complicated. We're leaving London tomorrow."

"I need to talk to my boss straight away. A full investigation will be conducted, I assure you, but until we have more information, I'm not sure what to say."

"You'd better think of something quick, because you're going to be the one to tell my wife."

Jean set the case on the bed in the hotel and started to unbuckle it. Dillon had gone into his room and closed the door. She could hear him sobbing inside.

"How can this happen twice?" Jean said, the strain in her voice evident. "They knew what they were taking, Spence. That young man is devastated—*devasted*!" She pointed to Dillon's room.

"I know. Laura's got a stake in this too—her reputation."

"Why did we ever bring that painting home from Richmond? I had no idea the firestorm this would create."

"Think of it this way—we at least have Dillon's copy, and we'll eventually get our money back. We'll be compensated. We have the best of both worlds."

"Don't count on it. This is not their problem." Jean put her head in her hands. "A piece of us is gone. The painting is magical. It was *ours*."

"C'mere. Not gone. We're right here."

Spence held her tight, letting her cry. He knew he needed to go into Dillon's room and let him do the same thing.

CHAPTER 32

Losing It

The flight home was quiet. Jean leaned against the window with a book, wallowing in Jonathan Harr's *The Lost Painting*. Dillon alternated between sketching details of *The Dancing Boy* and taking copious notes for Laura. Spence tried to focus on the biography of Duke Ellington but wasn't reading it. Laura Reed had called twice before they left London to say she had no new information, except a suspicion the theft had been an inside job. Spence's goal was to keep Jean, Dillon, and himself calm.

They floated toward the snow-capped peak of Mt. Hood. Spence patted Jean's knee. "We're almost home. We'll be fine. Dillon's got his first case."

"Hmmm . . . yeah, okay. Another person is dead because of us, Spence. We haven't even told Dillon about that yet."

"Wait just a minute. We can't take responsibility for Raleigh being a greedy bastard and screwing over his mother. And we can't take responsibility for Franco having a heart attack."

Jean went quiet as her eyes welled again. She was running on empty.

The cab turned right on River Road. All three of them were tired, hungry, jetlagged, and grim. Their mood matched the cold, gray drizzle outside. They had gone from pure elation to complete dejec-tion in one day. Dillon took responsibility. Jean was frustrated. Spence wanted everyone to feel better. It was going to be good to get home, take showers, and put their feet up by the fire. Spence sug-gested that Dillon spend a couple days with them. Jean and Dillon jumped at the opportunity for the three of them to stick together.

"Turn left at the next intersection. Ours is the modern-looking house on the left," Spence said to the driver. He pulled out his wallet. "Almost home, kids."

The taxi made the turns. Vans with large satellite dishes on top lined the street.

"Oh God. Now what?" Jean ran her hand through her hair

"Don't get out of the car while I pay the driver."

Dillon threw them each a questioning look.

"This is not good, not good at all." Jean gathered her bags and swung her purse over her shoulder, ready to dash.

The taxi pulled into their driveway. Several reporters with microphones ran up to the cab.

"Okay, you and Dillon go inside as fast as you can. I'll get our bags from the trunk. Don't wait for me. Get in the house. I don't know if this is about the painting, Dromov, or Raleigh. I'll call Jon when we're settled."

Jean swished her first two fingers, signaling for Dillon to follow her. Then she held up one at a time. *One . . . Two . . . Three.* She opened the taxi door and tugged on Dillon's jacket.

"Has Farnum's found the missing painting yet?" a reporter shouted, sticking a microphone in Jean's face.

"I don't know. They're working with the authorities," Jean said, pushing away the microphone.

"Are you going to sue? Do you think the theft was an inside job?" shouted another reporter.

"No information!"

"Is that the Caravaggio in the case?" asked the first reporter.

"No. Please leave us alone."

"Were you involved in the Dromov Fund? Were you there when he got arrested in London?"

"No comment! Stop harassing us!" she shouted and motioned Dillon to follow her up the steps.

Jean fumbled with the keys as her hand shook. *Won't go in.* "Dammit! Why didn't we drive our own car?"

"Were you working with the FBI to trap Dromov?" The re-porter shouted as he came up the steps after her. Dillon held out his hand in a *stop* motion.

Go in. Key, go in! The key slid in the lock, and she pulled down the handle. Jean pushed Dillon inside ahead of her. She did one last peek over her shoulder to see if the hounds unleashed their fury on Spence. He had his head down and his hands full. She waited with the door cracked and opened it to suck him inside. She turned the lock.

"Thank God there aren't any eye-level windows on the front of the house!" Spence said, breathless. He dropped the bags on the floor in the entryway. "How did they find out about all this so fast?"

"Dromov's arrest must have made the news. And the sale of the painting was pretty high profile, Spence," she said, rummaging through the kitchen drawer for a notepad and a pen. She wrote Dillon a note.

The painting made the news!

Dillon's shoulders slumped. Spence pointed to the railing along the catwalk upstairs. Mycroft and Wiley stuck their heads through the rails, waiting to be noticed. Jean and Dillon stopped and raised their eyes.

Mycroft leaned in and rubbed Wiley's chest with his muzzle. Wiley bounded down the stairs, followed by Mycroft, to the living room. They both waited in front of the fireplace for a warm blaze.

Spence shook his head. "It's official. We now have a dog."

CHAPTER 33

What Is That?

Laura Reed's eyes were so fixed on the video screen they started to water. Her reputation was on the line, just as much as was the staff's at Farnum's Auctions. Every precaution taken; every protocol followed. Who on earth would be so brazen and stupid to try a stunt like this? The hazy blue video showed no one in the basement from nine to eleven o'clock on Saturday night.

"Next one, please," Laura said in a measured voice. Nicholas Larabee handed her a disk. "Hmmm . . . Saturday night from eleven . . . to midnight." She inspected the label and pushed the CD in the slot on the side of the computer. The blue security light in the base-ment appeared on the screen. The digital read-out on the right corner whirred in tenths of a second. She took a sip of her Darjeeling tea as she studied the image.

"Stop! Stop, stop! Back up! Did you see that?"

"No doubt. Right there," Nicholas said, pointing to the left corner of the monitor.

"Time?"

"11:57 P.M."

"Play the sequence again, and slow it down."

The slow-motion image showed a security guard climbing the stairs, each step painfully sluggish, until he disappeared. From the left corner, tiny blue sparkles left a trail as they bounced across the screen toward the door of the vault.

"I can't make it out, but there's definitely somebody, or something there. Is the security light causing those fuzzy reflections?"

"Perhaps the slowing of the image?"

"Again—in real time."

The sparkling blue lights whirled faster, organizing themselves in the shape of a shimmering human form in front of the vault. The door didn't open. The shimmer disappeared.

"Stop, stop! Switch! Give me the disk for this exact same time span from the camera *inside* the vault."

Nicholas thumbed through the stack. "Here—camera three—from midnight to two in the morning."

"What I can't figure out is"—Laura hesitated and took another sip of her tea—"why the alarm wasn't tripped if someone went inside? If the door was opened, without a security code, then the siren would have gone off. Yes? No?"

"Yes." Nicholas slipped the CD into the slot. As it buzzed and clinked to load, Nicolas turned to Laura. "But . . . the vault never opened."

"Ridiculous."

They both leaned closer to the computer, waiting for an image to appear. The screen flashed white. Completely white.

"What the hell! Fast forward! This disk is blank!"

Laura reached for her phone and called Jon Segert. He answered right away.

"Jon! Laura here. You're not going to believe this. Is Dillon back in Portland with the Collinses? I need him."

Dillon sat in the Collinses' den and reviewed Laura Reed's e-mail one more time. He printed out two attachments: one was his employment offer, to be executed upon his graduation from art school, and the other outlined the project consulting contract for his assistance with the recovery of *The Dancing Boy*. He signed both documents and inserted the pages in the scanner. The move to Washington, DC upon graduation meant leaving Jean and Spence. Difficult, but he had a year to get used to the idea.

He jotted down his temporary password into the private site of the NSAF—the National Stolen Art File. Laura had also forwarded links to several major auction sites for upcoming sales. Time to find *The Dancing Boy.* The morning flew by in silent contemplation.

Hundreds of beautiful paintings, sculptures, and etchings appeared with each click of the mouse. Some were stolen a hundred years ago; others had just been entered yesterday. Only one piece came up under *Caravaggio*: an enormous canvas of *The Nativity with St. Francis and St. Lawrence*, also known as *The Adoration*, stolen in 1969 from the altar of the Oratory of San Lorenzo in Palermo, Sicily. It was painted right around 1609, roughly the same time as *The Dancing Boy.* Dillon stared, transfixed by the image; an angel floated over Mary Magdalene in a stable with the infant Jesus illuminated in a bed of straw. The perspective of the angel was similar to *The Seven Works of Mercy*, painted two years earlier, in 1607. Duplicitous. How could such a brute of a man paint scenes so tender and emotional? He wanted to understand. Dillon made a note to examine a better image of the painting in a reference book on Caravaggio at Powell's Books.

Unthreading the past held a sensual lure to explore unrevealed secrets. Perhaps he would uncover this masterpiece. One right step to correct time's ignorance. An heir of a long-dead thief might not know a painting that graced the wall over a fireplace, maybe for decades, was the one waiting for a chance to go home.

He did one more search. He typed in several key words for *The Dancing Boy.* When the screen flashed *No Results Found*, he shut down Spence's computer. Feeling sorry for himself wouldn't accomplish anything. Get back to the school; the Man waited for his finishing touches. Tomorrow morning he would resume his search for a little boy who told him his only wish was to dance.

CHAPTER 34

Doing Doughnuts

Early on Wednesday morning, Jean and Spence dropped Dillon off at the art school and went to the museum to meet with Palmer Norquist. Distraught about the death of Franco Machelli and the missing original painting, Palmer vowed to jump into the search. The next stop was their debriefing with Jon.

"If we get our money back, we should do something special." Jean said as they drove up to the FBI offices. "What about all those other clients? Some of them can't recover from this."

"I know—maybe set up the Wiley foundation." Spence hesi-tated. "I mean, after I start the store."

"The Mycroft Foundation, remember? But I don't want to make it dependent on finding *The Dancing Boy*. Dillon will find our painting; just a matter of when. I'm concerned about timing. A lot of these people are elderly."

"Let's talk this over with Jon. We can't write a check to anyone if we get our money back. There are messy tax issues."

She turned and smiled. "You're giving me a look. I keep thinking about what Mary would do in this situation . . . or Doc."

"I think we're both well aware of what they'd do, Jean."

Jon reviewed the complete list of clients in the Dromov Fund one more time: names, addresses, fake account balances, and their ages. He tried to separate the information on the page from what the numbers meant to their lives. Faceless names until he'd talked with many of them. The anguish in their voices twisted his gut. Dromov had targeted the elderly, which made his crime even more heinous. Did these people have time for this to be sorted out? Was this going to be an estate matter? No doubt the money would be tied up in the courts for months, if not years, and siphoned off in legal fees.

At least the Collinses could get their money back from the proceeds of the painting. He'd almost convinced the chief to approve the plan for their help in getting the case to this point. Using the painting to corner Dromov eliminated months of work. He'd thwarted Dromov's plans to flee the country by only one day. Twenty-four hours would've changed the outcome of the whole in-vestigation. Now he had a shot at undoing the damage.

Jenny appeared in his office doorway. "The Collinses are here."

"Can you bring them in?" Jon scooped up the papers into a haphazard pile and threw a half-eaten chocolate chip cookie in his waste basket.

"Weren't they brought in before to be interviewed?"

"They're not visitors any more. They helped me stop Dromov."

"Well, this is a first. You never want to meet anyone without grumbling like an old man. Clean up your desk, Jon." She smirked and pointed to the carpet under the ficus tree.

Jon ignored the leaves but attempted the desk. He brushed the cookie crumbs to the floor.

Jean's head peeked through the doorway. "Is the coast clear? No Agent Brick?"

"Clear. How're you holding up?" he asked.

"Tired," Spence said, stepping in behind her. "We just met with Palmer Norquist at the museum. We filled him in on what happened. Depressing."

"Sit. Take a load off."

Walking around the office, Jean stopped at the window to assess the view. She glanced at the carpet. "Jon . . . this poor tree needs water and attention." She picked up the leaves, crushed them in her palm, and held out her hand to Jon. "Here, throw these away. You need a mirror so you can enjoy the outside view on two walls. And file all those piles of folders. How do you find anything?" Jean took a seat and scooted the side chair to the desk.

"Prime wall space," Spence said, inspecting the bare walls. "Not much on them. Why don't you personalize your office? I'd be taking advantage of all this natural light. I could get you a BG-289 . . . Rolling Stone's *Tumbling Dice* . . . right here." Spence put his hands up in the shape of a frame on the empty white wall across from Jon's desk. "Bill Graham—Winterland—1972." Spence glanced over his shoulder at Jon. "You do know, *Tumbling Dice* was only printed twice."

"Okay, what is this? A surprise makeover?" Jon chided. "I like my office."

"No, you're an important man. You need to make your space important too."

"Sit."

Spence joined Jean and took a seat. They both sat at attention in front of him like they'd been given a time-out.

"I've got three things to talk about. Here's where we stand. One—no painting yet. But Laura and I talked, and she's cleared Gerrod Barnes. He wasn't involved. She's found something interest-ing, though, on the security tapes. We're discussing it and Dillon is doing the research. The piece is too hot, and the media is all over this story. Whoever stole your painting will never be able to sell it on the legitimate market."

"Uh . . . yeah. About the media part," Spence added. "We're being hounded. There was an ambush when we came back from London. Can you do something?"

"Don't say anything for now—and not to your friends, either. The formal indictments were filed. We're going do a press conference this afternoon. The laundry list of charges against Dromov will give them another shiny object to chase."

"Okay, what's *two*?" Jean asked, pulling one of her own notepads from her purse. This one said, *When All Else Fails, Hug the Cat.*

"Two—the money from the painting is sitting in escrow ac-count at Farnum's. The sale's been rescinded, as agreed. Farnum's fully cooperated with Laura and me."

"Who gets the money, Jon? We don't have the original," Spence said. "Are we hosed on this? No painting and no money?"

"Yeah, Jon, this was *your* plan," Jean added. "We're *double* screwed. Did you forget the little nugget about our investment being in the Dromov Fund too? We wouldn't even know who to sue! We're not litigious people."

"The money is now part of Dromov's frozen assets. Farnum's will turn the funds over to us. This looks like we screwed this up—and okay, maybe I did." Jon brushed the top of his crew cut and wiped his face with his hand. "Was the painting insured?"

"Of course not. We had no idea it was worth so much."

"What about Farnum's?" Spence offered in an attempt to cool Jean down. "It was stolen on their premises."

"Yeah . . . about that. Technically, Dillon's copy was auctioned, so the original wasn't covered under Farnum's policy. Contractual issue." Jon felt his face turn an odd shade of rotting raspberries. "Okay, here's *three*—I'm working on a compromise. If I can make this up by giving you restitution on your missing money in the Dromov Fund, then will we be square? And if you get the painting back, all the better. Consider it a thank you for helping to get this case solved."

Jean nosed the air and turned to Spence. "I think that's fair. What about you?"

Spence nodded in agreement. "How soon could we have our money back? And we get to keep the painting when Dillon finds it?"

"Forty-five days—tops!" Jon straightened with renewed enthusiasm. "And yes, you keep the painting if it's recovered. We have Dromov's money to give these people something once we get a conviction. His accounts in the Cayman Islands have been found since we confiscated his fake passport."

Jon flipped a page on his notepad and pulled out small calculator from his desk drawer. He hesitated, and then reached into his breast shirt pocket for his new half-moon reading glasses. "Based on the current conversion rate, the total amount in the escrow account, coming to the FBI from Farnum's, is about $750,000." Jon thumped his pencil and wrote out the numbers. He then clicked the keys on the calculator. "Take off 10 percent for Gerrod Barnes . . . $75,000. He earned his fee. The auction house is waiving payment of their commission since the transaction was rescinded. You get your $503,452 and the painting if it's found. That leaves about $171,500 that the FBI will retain to add to the assets we recover. And you guys come off the plaintiff list." He raised his eyes and set down his pen as if his plan was a done deal.

"I want to move forward with my record store," Spence said. "We have Dillon's copy. That's magic, too, in a way."

Jean had been tracking along with Jon's numbers on her list pad. "And how long until the rest of the clients get their money?" She tapped her fingernails on the desk. Spence mouthed *Stop it.*

"It's going to take a while to unravel this mess. All of the physical assets we've been able to seize are in a warehouse, but the case still has to go to trial. Those assets can't be sold until after Dromov's convicted. We need some time to sniff out this hidden cash. And the lawyers clog the process with appeals . . . you know how *that* goes."

"Will these people ever see their money?" Jean said, her tone softening.

"Because of you two, they will. Not all of it, but a good amount. We got to Dromov before he fled and liquidated. Unusual in a case like this. It'll take some time, though."

"Is he miserable?" Jean clicked the end of her pen, retracting the tip in and out with a rapid-fire rhythm.

"Completely." Jon grimaced and snatched the pen out of her hand. "In a cell with none of his normal conveniences. He's on anti-depressants and antibiotics. The gash on his arm won't heal."

"Won't heal? That's odd, given your experience. Good. Can you show us Dromov's client list? I mean—without violating too much confidentiality?"

"Not kosher, Jean." He handed her the pen with narrowed his eyes.

"Okay, how about this—" Spence said, trying to neutralize the air. "Who's the oldest client and how much do they stand to lose?"

Jon hissed air in and out of his teeth, deliberating on whether to give them the information. He stopped when Jean smirked at the noise. He pulled the bent corner of a sheet of paper from the top of a three-inch stack in a recycled manila folder. At least four labels layered the tab. He scanned the list of names, suspicious.

"Why do you want to know this? This isn't—" He went silent when Jean reached across the desk and set her hand on top of his. His wedding ring tingled. A vision of Meg and his daughter, Amy, on the camping trip they'd taken in New Hampshire flashed in his mind.

"Spence and I have talked. We're thinking of something."

Spence plucked at his front tooth with his fingernail. There was a moment of silence, except for the plucking. Jean and Jon stared at him in unison.

Jon ran his finger down the list. "Lawrence Flanders, age eighty-two—stands to lose $49,347."

The office went still as his words settled over them. Spence snapped up his head and leaned across the desk, trying to see the list. Jon pulled the paper away.

"Legs?" Spence said, almost to himself.

"What?" Jon gawked at him.

"I know who that is! Legs Flanders. He played horn with Louis Armstrong back in the '50s, maybe the '60s, and I think he blew harmonica with some of the greats too. Legs got his name because he's nearly seven feet tall. All legs and thin as a rail. Incredible blower." Spence rounded the desk and tapped the computer. "Google him."

Jon typed into the search field. They all stared at the screen and waited for the list of links.

"Click this one."

Spence and Jon scanned the article on Leg's life retrospective out of a music magazine. Jean stood and leaned over the desk.

"I think he's the same guy. Says here he lives in DC. The address on my list says Huidekoper Place." Jon pulled up the internal FBI database to verify the information.

"Jean, isn't that where your grandparents lived?" Spence shot her an animated look.

"That settles it!" Jean smacked the top of the desk. "Jon, can you add Legs—I mean Lawrence—Flanders to be paid out from our portion of the proceeds from the painting? Then, your leftover pool doesn't take a hit."

"Wait, will ya? This information has to be verified. A lot of red tape."

"C'mon, you can do this. The amount's not huge, but it might be a fortune to Legs. I have full faith in you. Pay him out directly, so we don't get into a tax mess."

"Better make it happen, Jon. She's determined, and I agree with Jean on this one." Spence sat and drummed his hands on his knees.

"Let's book a trip to DC this afternoon and give the check to Legs in person." Jean acted as though wanted to burst out the door and go straight to the airport. "You need to hand over two checks, one for us and one to Legs—I mean Lawrence Flanders."

"Cool . . . your . . . jets, missy!" Jon said, pointing his finger at her. "We need a minimum of thirty days to get that money trans-ferred from Farnum's. Then there's the internal investigation with Laura and Dillon."

Jean's shoulders slumped. "Thirty days could be a long time to Legs."

The office door flew open. All three of them jumped. A barrel-chested man marched in like he owned the place. The skin of his thick neck flushed as it bulged over his unyielding white collar. A strong waft of Old Spice *whooshed* through the door behind him, as if trying to catch up. The stiff silver brush of his crew cut stood ready to restore a barbeque grill to a shiny gleam. The dark, baggy circles around his eyes made him look like a raccoon ready for a fight over spilled trash in the driveway.

"Jon! Do you have—" the chief stopped and stared. "Who the hell are you?"

"Chief, these are the Collinses. Jean and Spence."

"Oh, *you* two. *You're* my budget busters. We've got a file on you two."

"We . . . uh . . . nice to meet you . . . too." Jean strained to move her mouth, stumbling on her words like she had a Jujube stuck in her teeth.

"I hope you brought a damn magic wand to fix Jon's expense account. He's got one helluva hole to claw his way out of!" The chief burst out laughing at his own joke. "Thanks for your help on Dromov, by the way." The chief pointed at Jon and bellowed, "In my office as soon as you're done! Now wouldn't be too soon. The vultures are waiting in the press room."

The door slammed and four leaves fell from the ficus.

Jon pressed his lips together. "Sorry. The doughnuts in the kitchen ran out, and his favorite celebrity didn't win at dancing last night. I'm giving the media an update on Coulter and Dromov—" he glanced at his watch—"in twenty minutes. Go home and relax."

Jean turned to Spence and nodded as if they shared an inside joke. She turned back to Jon, her eyes practically pouting. "What about a check for Legs?"

"Yeah, what about Legs?" Spence echoed.

Jon went quiet. They resembled two abandoned puppies in a shelter, trying to guilt him into taking them home.

"You heard the chief . . . thank us for our help." Jean cocked her head and batted her luminous aqua eyes.

"All right. Let me see what I can do. I'm not making any promises. Go on . . . git."

CHAPTER 35

Handwritten Letters Mean Everything

I think I got him. Dillon smiled as he stepped back from the canvas. Once he the finished the details on the Man's right hand, he'd be done. The fingernail on the thumb needed a more arched moon, but the shine and ridges of growth were exactly right. He swished the end of Mycroft's whisker in the paint. He moved to the wisps of hair on the knuckles. The whisker achieved the realistic variations from gray at the skin to brown on the ends of each thin hair. Upon making the last tiny stroke, Dillon heard a voice, a distinctly powerful man's voice. It filled him from the inside out.

I am here.

Dillon stared into the eyes of the Man through the mellowed glaze. *Who are you?*

You've done very well, Dillon.

No more?

No more. Make me a gift.

Dillon fluttered Mycroft's whisker to the palette. The Man was right; stop futzing with him. An overnight drying; check him again in the morning.

The following Saturday, the scrambled clack of thick toenails against the bamboo floor was followed by knock on the front door. Spence opened it and waved Dillon inside, attempting to corral Wiley. The immortal dog's tail sparkled in a blurred fan as it banged the edge of the door.

"Back, back! C'mon, now!" Spence scolded. "Yes, Dillon's here for you."

Dillon reached down and patted the dog's head and handed Spence the art case.

"Wow, this is heavy!" He motioned for Dillon's knapsack and jacket. Wiley turned his attention to the case, his snout puffing as if he'd picked up a familiar scent.

Jean gave Dillon a hug. She placed a notepad and a pen on the counter and resumed layering the enchilada casserole for lunch. "I'm ready to shove this in the oven. What's Dillon got there? You don't think—"

"I don't know, but we're about to find out."

"I'll be right there. Mycroft will want to visit with Dillon."

Spence heaved the case to the living room. Already sitting on the floor by the fire, Dillon stroked the long fur of Mycroft's heavy Elizabethan bib. Dillon leaned down to kiss Mycroft's head as Wiley licked his face, leaving a glistening trail of animated glitter on his cheek. Mycroft rolled on his back in an effort to compete with Wiley for attention.

"You come on over here, boy," Spence said, clapping his hands. "Leave Dillon alone." Wiley trotted to him and sat, but whined at Dillon and Mycroft with no small amount of jealousy.

Jean joined them and handed the notepad to Dillon.

Okay . . . you have our attention. What's in the case?

A present. Dillon crawled over to it, unhooked the buckles, and pulled away the straps. He appreciated the audience. With great ceremony, e lifted out the canvas and leaned the framed piece against the wall.

Spence gasped.

"Doc!" Jean beamed.

"And he's so real. He could reach right out and take my hand.

Look, Wiley—who do you think that is?" Wiley bolted to the painting and licked the face on the canvas. A glittery shine trailed behind. Wiley's tail thumped the carpet as he sat in front of the portrait. Mycroft sauntered over, conducted a thorough sniff inspect-tion, and batted at the kicked-up shower of sparkles.

How do you know Doc? He became immortal in 1945, Jean wrote. Tears filled her eyes as she wrapped her arms around him.

Confused, Dillon pulled away from Jean and reached for the pen.

I painted a dead man? He sat for me. He's a real person. At the auction too.

Silence loomed around the room. Finally, Jean turned to Spence, and said:

"We need to book another ticket to DC, and then we're driving down to Richmond—the three of us. We'll go over spring break. Dillon needs to meet Doc again, I guess."

Spence nodded and stared at the portrait of Doc. He found his voice. "You could ask that man any question in the universe, and he'd make you think *you're* the one who came up with the answer." He turned to Jean. "We have a Dillon Davis."

Jean gazed at him like he, too, had the same wisdom as Doc.

"I want to keep this painting," she said. "But let's take Dillon's copy of *The Dancing Boy* to Richmond with us. It belongs there over Doc's bed. Done its work, I think."

Spence tipped the notepad and stared at the calligraphy-like handwriting. "What did Dillon mean, Jean? I didn't see Doc at the auction."

After lunch, Spence pulled several albums from the den cabinet and stepped to the living room. He eyed Dillon sharing secrets with Mycroft on the couch. Spence sat next to him in one of the leather chairs, and taking an intermittent glance at the young man, flipped through the pile in his lap. This decision was a big one: The Clash, Iggy Pop, the Kinks, Bruce Springsteen, Art Tatum, Muddy Waters, or John Coltrane. Difficult to decide. After much deliberation, he made his choice. He took a deep breath. The Clash's *London Calling.*

Spence held out his hand to Dillon. Their fingers entwined. The familiar current raced, their souls connecting. Dillon raised his eyes and gasped. They smiled at each other, and then Spence handed him the album. Next would be Bruce Springsteen's *Human Touch.*

All the way home from dropping off Dillon at the school, Spence drove on air. It worked. Dillon bobbed his head to the music, and continued to bob on the drive back to the art institute. Not until they were in the car did Spence realize the weight of responsibility he'd assumed for Dillon's musical discovery. A piece of his soul had been imbedded with the notes. Riffs and lyrics spoke the words he, him-self, couldn't form. Is that what Dad's were supposed to do?

"Where's Wiley?" Spence said, coming through the mudroom. "I'm missing my sparkle assault."

"Well, take a gander at the painting. Wiley kept staring—and just like that—he was gone," Jean said and snapped her fingers.

Spence stepped to the portrait, still leaning against the wall. He laughed out loud. Wiley sat next to Doc in the image on the canvas. Doc had his hand resting on Wiley's head, between his ears.

"Can you believe that?" Jean joined him and stared at the canvas.

"Well . . . there you go."

"I'll get the mail," Jean said, turning and bouncing toward the front door. "You missed the mailman, by the way. And then let's have some private time with Mycroft."

"Dillon's going to be famous one day."

"Yes, he is."

The house was quiet when Jean closed the door. The only sound was the low *whir* and *whoosh* of the dishwasher. Spence stood in front of Doc's portrait. The two-foot-by-three-foot canvas was framed in an aged, pitted pecan wood. It showed him seated, with his left leg crossed over his right. One hand rested in his lap, the other on Wiley. Healing hands—so relaxed and confident. Spence admired the per-fect play of light on Doc's face. The folds of his gray, striped vest replicated the feel of smooth wool gabardine. Like sculpture, Spence was compelled to touch the canvas but didn't. The delicate links of Doc's watch chain gleamed as it hung with the weight of real gold from his vest pocket. Dillon captured that subtle twinkle in the man's eyes behind the glass of his wire-rimmed spectacles. The skin of Doc's face was exquisite and imperfect. Each line and crease had been etched from worry about everybody else. His gray hair was thick, wild, and wavy; needed a cut. This was the man who inspired him and Jean to do what they were going to do in Washington, DC.

Spence shook himself out of his trance when Jean came in with a pile of mail under her arm. "Anything good?"

"Bills, begging letters, and some fancy catalogs. I can't stop thinking about Doc. He's right here with us."

Mycroft searched for Wiley. He found his new best friend in the painting next to Doc. He stared into the man's eyes, his wild hair appearing to move, and then focused on the soft hand resting on his lap. That hand. He snapped his long, feathery tail. He rose up on his hind legs, stretching his right paw and lightly grazing the skin of Doc's hand. He pulled back and waited for a flinch, a reaction, any sign of movement.

Doc's fingers patted his knee.

Mycroft glanced at Spence, but he was busy with his book. He set his paw on Doc's hand to still the movement. At the touch, shafts of silent golden light erupted from beneath the tufts of fur between his toes. His tail puffed. He closed his eyes tight and took a leap on Doc's lap. Turning two circles to find the right spot, Mycroft settled himself and draped his paws over Doc's knee. The gentle hand stroked his ears. His eyes disappeared under the Man's touch. He lowered his head, vibrating the painting with a heavy, contented purr.

Jean flipped through the stack of mail that she'd tossed on the kitchen island. Her hand stopped on a white number-ten envelope that obviously hadn't been mailed. Addressed only to Jean and Spence, nothing else, she couldn't mistake Dillon's exquisite hand-writing. Her pulse quickened as she stuck her thumb under the flap. The lined pages inside, ripped from the notebook she'd given to him on the plane to London, released Dillon's thoughts like butterflies on a warm day.

January 21st
Over Maine
Clouds

Dear Jean and Spence,

I am overwhelmed. Everything with you both has been a first. I had no idea that life held such secrets. Mine aren't nearly as magic.

My parents were killed by a drunk driver when I was thirteen. We lived in Lawrence, Kansas. New Year's Eve of 1999 was a pivotal year. My father was the publicity director at the University of Kansas. My mother worked in the ticket office for sporting events. I was raised by my aunt, my father's brother's wife, after they were killed. She was a wonderful woman named Margaret Davis. My uncle died from a heart attack at a fairly young age. Aunt Margaret passed away last year from cancer. Just me now. I have a little money in a trust from her life insurance, which I use to get by. Nothing big.

I haven't always been deaf. I did all the normal kid stuff in a small town, but the world became quieter after every ear infection. Even after several surgeries, sound remained a phantom of the past. Maybe some day they won't be just memories..

Aunt Margaret always believed in my art. I started drawing pictures of my parents as soon as I moved in with her. I'll never forget the details of their faces, especially their hands and eyes. I got better. I kept them alive. That's when I started studying portraiture of the Old Masters. Every time I painted my parents, they became more real.

My work was entered in numerous competitions. That's how I came to get a scholarship at the Art Institute in Portland. Franco Machelli made that happen for me. I owe him a lot, even knowing what he did.

My goal in life was, and still is, to perfect the technique of creating a living being on canvas—to make them come alive. You've shown me the possibility of that happening. My father told me once that you don't have to talk if you want to say something. Write. So I write and talk through paint, instead of using sign language. Keeps me from blabbing about nothing.

I love you both,
Dillon

Update: February 10th

The portrait of the Man proved to be more complicated and difficult than I ever thought he'd be. There's something quite special about him: I think it's wisdom. He spoke to me. He came alive. I did it! I got an A+ on this project. I showed the Man to Palmer Norquist, and he wanted the portrait for the museum. The Man is for you. You decide where he belongs.

I still have a hard time believing Mr. Machelli would betray me like he did. There's no predicting human nature, I guess. Maybe I'll be able to paint the emotion of betrayal some day. Right now, it stumps me.

I will find The Dancing Boy*—I promise. But, I'm finding out a lot about myself in the process. I'm already getting attached to some of the missing pieces that are waiting to be discovered. Thank you both, and Jon too, for the opportunity. I won't let any of you down.*

Dillon

Jean stared at the pages, her heart bursting with pride. *Doc was right—one person at a time.* She wiped her eyes and drew in a breath. She folded the letter back into thirds and stepped to the living room. Spence had his head buried in the last few pages of *The Maltese Falcon.*

"Spence?"

"Hmmm?"

"You should stop reading for a minute. Read this instead."

Spence raised his eyes from his book as she handed him the folded letter.

“Where did Mycroft get off to, anyway?” she asked. “I thought he was in here with you.”

“I don’t know—probably up on our bed—but weren’t you going to hang Doc’s painting?” Spence unfolded the pages.

“Right now.”

Rummaging through the storage baskets in the mudroom, Jean pulled out a hammer, nails, and two heavy hooks. She grabbed the step ladder. She made two pencil dots on the wall and stopped.

“Does this height seem right?” she said, twisting around to Spence. He was lost in Dillon’s letter. He didn’t answer. She banged the hooks into the wall and came down the ladder. Turning to pick up the painting, she gasped. “Spence?”

“Hmmm?”

“I found Mycroft.”

With his eyes glistening, Spence looked up without focusing on anything. “Where is he?”

“On Doc’s lap.” She leaned down to the painting and wagged her finger. “Mycroft! You sneaky bugger!”

“Honey, leave him alone. He’ll come out when he’s ready.”

CHAPTER 36

The Checks Have Arrived

"I'm getting tired of traveling with this case. Stuff happens," Jean said as they walked through the concourse of Dulles Airport.

"Honey, you're not the one carrying it," Spence said. "I am."

Dillon scanned the faces in the crowd as he swung his knapsack over his shoulder. The rhythm of his lumbering gate made the triangle pattern on his cream-colored scarf bob as he moved toward the escalator.

"I can't get over Legs Flanders living on Huidekoper Place. My grandparents lived on that tiny street forever. You think they knew Legs?"

"Doubtful. Legs wouldn't know anybody who had old-lady lavender hair. Your grandmother wasn't exactly a jazz kind a gal. But I appreciated her doo matching her outfit at our wedding. She was the oldest punk rocker at the reception."

Still laughing about her grandmother's unbending lilac locks, they all piled in and buckled up in the rental car.

"Aren't the cherry trees beautiful? They're just budding." Jean wrote a note to Dillon. *When you get here to start work, you have to go to the Smithsonian to check out the portrait of Lincoln.*

Dillon nodded.

"Spence, we need to leave no later than two thirty if we want to be in Richmond before dark. The traffic getting out of here will be horrendous."

"No rush. The Old Gaines House isn't going anywhere," Spence said, savoring Washington's historic Georgian architecture. "And I want Legs to sign something for the store."

"Looking familiar. Turn here on Tunlaw Road." Jean pulled out her phone and opened the navigation application. She typed in the street number. The robotic female voice kicked in: *Turn left in two hundred feet on Benton Street.*

Spence turned. "This is a beautiful neighborhood."

"The trees have gotten so big. These townhouses are pretty pricey now," she said, rubbernecking.

In one hundred feet, turn left on Huidekoper Place.

"You can get turned around. The streets are narrow."

"Drive slow. There it is."

"Honey, that's not the number."

"I know, but it was my grandparents' house. Legs's place should be right here. Stop! Can you believe it? He's only two doors down."

Spence pulled to the curb in front of the brick townhouse. Most were the same style, except for the individual colors of the shutters and federal-style appointments around the front doors. The white spindles above Legs's door were in need of a paint job.

"Here we go," she said and blew out a breath. "I have no idea what to expect."

"Me neither." Spence waved for Dillon to follow them up to the house.

The scrolled aluminum screen door squealed in protest. Spence knocked with the knuckle of his forefinger.

Jean bounced on her knees in anticipation. Dillon acted nervous and uncomfortable. They waited. She craned her neck and spotted a shadow on the ceiling in one of the three windows along the top of the door.

"He's in there," she whispered.

Spence knocked again, a little harder.

She heard wrestling to unhook the chain. The wooden door

groaned open.

"Yeah? What you got?"

The man soared above them with a watery gaze. His alligatored, rich-brown skin was worn like a guitar case that had seen more gigs than he remembered playing. Even Spence had to raise his head, and he was nearly six feet tall. The man's blue checked shirt was clean but wrinkled. She wondered where on earth anyone found jeans that long. Until today, Joey Ramone, the lead singer of the Ramones, wore the longest-legged ones she'd ever seen.

Spence's gaze rose to the top molding on the doorframe. The man's hands rested on the inside edge for support. "Are you Lawrence Flanders? Legs Flanders?"

"What if it is? You got music, come on in. If you ain't, then don't come in. Don't sell me nothing, 'cause I ain't buyin' nothin'," Legs muttered in a deep voice, lumbering back into the shadows.

Jean stepped inside. Spence and Dillon followed her. Legs bent way down to the knob on the ton-a-tron television. He silenced *Judge Judy*, who buzzed the cabinet as she gave somebody the business about being stupid.

"Mr. Flanders, we tried to call you several times that we were coming, but you don't have voice mail," Spence said.

"'Cause I don't like talkin' on the telephone. Somebody want to talk to me, they can come to my door or put a pen to paper and write me a letter. They don't, then I don't talk to 'em. Either way jus' fine with me. Mr. Flanders was my daddy, by the by. You call me Legs like everybody used to do."

The living room was tiny. A metal TV tray had been set with a foiled disk of pot pie and a clean fork waiting for its diner. Trails of steam dissipated from a tear in the crust.

"We're sorry. We've interrupted your lunch," she said.

"Pay no mind. Pay no mind. Why you so anxious to talk to me?" Legs decided to turn off the television altogether and sit in his well-worn chair.

Medicine bottles and framed photos lined the top shelf above the cabinet: Ella Fitzgerald, Billy Holiday, and one of a beautiful black woman with her arms around a much younger version of Legs. The frames had been angled with care. Two others, each containing a different young black man posed heroically in Navy uniform, could have been twins. Both were tall and of approximately the same age. Thoughtful expressions; just like Legs.

"Mr.—Legs, I'm Spencer Collins and this is my wife, Jean. And this is Dillon Davis. We're here to tell you something."

Jean thought Spence's voice sounded nervous in front of such a legend.

"What you got to tell me I don't know already?" Legs stopped his fork in the long trek from the pot pie to his mouth.

A wave of nostalgia washed through her as Jean gazed around the small living room. She turned and addressed Legs. "This town-house is a complete flashback for me. My grandparents lived two doors down from you many years ago—from the 1930s. You may even remember them. My grandfather was the chauffeur for a prominent family here in DC. He worked in service for the colonel and his wife for over forty years. In fact, the colonel's wife made me a Christmas ornament, a little partridge. Still graces our tree every year. I barely remember her, but she had fat arms—but that's not why we're here."

Legs gave her a stunned expression, like a stray cat had slipped through the door and was scratching on his furniture. He turned to Spence and said, "What she goin' on about?"

Glancing at Legs, Spence offered a slight shake his head, as if to say, *She's working something out.* Legs caught on.

"What he look like—your granddaddy?" Legs asked. "I been here since sixty-four. Not too many folk like me around this neigh-borhood. But when people know who you is . . . well. I keep to myself, yes, I do." Legs studied her, his eyes reflecting a lifetime of music that conquered unspoken struggles.

"My grandfather was short—old before his time," Jean said, thoughtful. "Bald, with full cheeks and a kind face. A good man. A bulldog with angel wings." She laughed and touched the center of her right cheek. "See this scar? I was sitting in his lap in a wing-back chair, just like yours in the same spot by the front window, except with teal upholstery . . . and little dots. I was about five or six. He was telling me a story out of this big book, *Caroline and Friends*. The head of his cigarette brushed my cheek and stuck there. Caused such a ruckus, but I didn't care. I only wanted him to finish the story." She remembered every detail with vivid clarity. She suddenly felt ridicu-lous when Spence gave Legs an apologetic glance.

Legs nodded his head as if he only caught every other word. "Well, that's sayin' something. Got my own share a brands—markers on the map, they is." Like flipping a switch, Legs became engaged. "And, you know, I think I remember who you talkin' about. That old man wave at me when I get the paper while he's gettin' the paper. I was a travelin' back then—picked up gigs outta town—Chicago, Kansas City, New Orleans—but I catch him once and awhile. Uh-huh."

"Who'd you play with, Legs?" Spence asked.

"Aw, I played with 'em all." Legs pointed to the photos. "Ella my favorite, though." Her photo was inscribed, *To Legs, Keep on running!* "She from Richmond, you know. Voice like honey. All gone now."

"I . . . I'm in awe." Spence stepped to the shelf and gawked.

"What you doin' here?" Legs asked. "You didn't come here to pick my brain or talk about you grandpa."

"Do you mind if we sit?" Jean joined Spence on the couch. Dillon continued to browse the markers of Legs's life.

"Yeah, all right by me."

"Well . . . we have a surprise for you," Jean said, now eager to do what they came for. "You had an investment in the Dromov Fund. It went bad. Bad for us too."

"What you talkin' about? I got a bit a scratch. A countin' man get me in somethin' good. Every day a rainy day." Legs put on his thick-framed reading glasses and turned in his chair. He rummaged through a stack of papers on the side table and pulled a dog-eared one out of the middle. "Here, yeah, here it is . . . the Dromov Fund." He inspected statement. "Got this last month, it was. You think he a Commie or somethin'?"

Jean stifled a smirk. Dillon studied the framed family photographs on a shelf above the television.

"No, not a Communist, but the guy who created the fund took the money, Legs. He's under arrest for running a Ponzi scheme."

Legs turned and fluttered the statement back to the top of the stack. "A what? Sound like a fancy car."

"You could say that. He bought fancy cars with your money," Spence added.

"The authorities have probably been trying to reach you," she said, eyeing a pile of unopened mail on the coffee table next to an open newspaper. "But we're here to make this right."

"Make what right?"

"The money," Spence said "We've been fortunate. We want you to have it back."

Jean dug in her purse and pulled out the folded check, pre-printed to the order of Lawrence Flanders. "Spence, maybe you should—" She held it out to him, thinking Legs might be somewhat old-fashioned about accepting money from a woman. She also sus-pected Spence would want to do the honors.

"Legs . . . here." Spence gave her an appreciative glance.

Confused, Legs studied the amount: $49,347. He went quiet. His lanky frame had a slight rock as he hunched over the thin piece of paper in his long fingers.

"You know, I used to get excited when I got two Jacksons for a gig. Rich back then." Legs shook his head. "Why you doin' this for me?"

"Because we were able to work with the FBI to recover what you lost. I'm a big music fan. I recognized your name on Dromov's client list."

"You're pretty famous," Jean added. "The agent who uncovered Dromov's Ponzi scheme is a friend of ours. And when he told us you were eighty-two . . ." Her voice trailed off. "Let's just say it'll take a long time for the case to go trial."

"Some kindness right there." Legs tapped the check, gazed at each of them, and then settled his eyes on Dillon. "A story; I can feel it in here." Legs made a fist in the hollow of his chest.

"Yes, he's a special young man," Spence said, nodding. "He's an artist like you, only in paint."

"He your boy?"

"No, but we're beginning to think of him as ours." Spence's eyes locked on Jean's. She pressed her lips together.

Jean's gaze rose to the elaborately scrolled leaves in the medal-lion of the ceiling. "You have two bedrooms and one bath upstairs, don't you?"

"Yeah. Small. Salt-and-pepper tile. One of those bedrooms was hoppin' for a lot a years." Legs chuckled but watched her. "Don't be casin' the place, now."

"Oh no, nothing like that. The little tiles reminded me of dice. Full basement downstairs?"

"Uh-huh. Every day a gamble, yes it is. Nothin' down there 'cept records. Nobody play 'em anymore. They all gone . . . my friends. Why, hell, wife been gone over twenty-two years. I even outlive my kids." Legs glanced at the pictures of his boys in uniform.

"Who else did you play with, Legs?" Spence interjected, attempt-ing to brighten the mood.

"Louis . . . Armstrong that is. Genius man he was. Still is . . . out there somewhere in music land. Hear him blow that horn in my head at night. I stop playin' my horn and got me a harmonica later on. Wife said it made lips too rough for smoochin'. No good lookin' back; not good to eat the dust behind the bus." Leg's moved the fork around on his try, but didn't pick it up. "That all a mouth is for, any-way—makin' music and makin' my woman. Blow my harp with Muddy, I did . . . uh-huh."

"Waters?" Spence's eyes widened as if Legs had handed him a backstage pass. "I didn't know you played with him!"

"Oh, yeah, he a scoundrel, but the man could sing a lick. He had some mojo . . . mmm-mmm. Hit you in the gut he did." Legs closed his eyes and shook his head, remembering. He smiled, showing his yellowed teeth. "Aw, listen to me pushin' the air around. Some cool cats, you people. You do this for me; I do somethin' for you." Legs stood to his full height. Dillon's eyes traveled upward in amazement. Legs stretched but couldn't get quite straight; he resembled a seven-foot archery bow. Lumbering toward the kitchen, Legs waved his long arm like windmill. "Come on with me."

Spence jumped from the couch and motioned for Dillon to follow him. He turned to Jean and whispered, "C'mon, honey. He's going to show us his stuff in the basement."

"Go ahead. I'll wait here for you guys," she said. Spence's face filled with light. Dillon beamed too.

Jean stood and stepped to the wing-back chair. She slumped into the dip of its faded maroon upholstery. Motes of dust puffed and swirled in the hazy sunlight pouring through the clouded front window. The stuffing popped out of one corner of the cushion under her knees. Spence studied her from the doorway in the kitchen, his anxious grin melting to concern.

She made a shooing motion with her hands. "You better hoof it if you want to catch up with Legs."

"We'll be right back." Spence put his hand around Dillon's shoulder and pulled him out of view. Legs was already clunking down the creaky steps to the basement.

The living room went quiet. Alone, Jean listened to three pairs of feet thump down the stairs. The boys' gaits matched Legs's as they were led to the musty boxes of his rich life. Voices muffled and faded to a mere vibration. Legs's legendary friends might be released from their unplundered tomb, their genius wafting on a current of cornflake-coated oven-fried chicken her grandmother used to make in the same small kitchen, just like Legs's.

She rested her head back in the chair, her gaze arcing around the ceiling. *Eighty-two and a legend. Still famous to a few, forgotten by many.* A mosaic of images rolled through her mind of all of the things Legs must have seen and done in his long life. *Legs knows . . . magic.*

The chair creaked as she leaned forward, the upholstered wings seeming to wrap around her, not wanting to let her go. She stood and browsed the room. The glass-fronted hutch below the banister of the stairs drew her forward. Two old tarnished keys, tied with a frayed piece of kitchen twine, hung from the cabinet's door. One of them rested in the lock. She grazed the dangling one with her forefinger. The key swung with the rhythm of a pendulum in an old clock. The glass, unlike the front windows, was squeaky clean and maintained with care. She could see what was inside. The top shelf held several scratched shot glasses with the names of jazz clubs: the Blue Note, the Green Mill, Club DeLuxe, the Triple Door. The second shelf held guitar picks stacked like coins, belonging, no doubt, to other legends. A gleaming Indian Head nickel sat, all by itself, in a place of honor. Her eyes popped wide when she spotted the folded and yellowed handkerchief with two sweeping cursive letters embroidered along the edge: an *L* and an *A*. Next to it, a pair of luminous pearl earrings, carefully placed, glowed in the filtered light. Her gaze lingered on them and then lowered to the bottom shelf. A long, thick harmonica, perfectly centered, rested there, as if waiting to be played. The corners were smooth, polished like sea glass tumbled over and over in the pounding waves of riffs never to be repeated. The mouth side was worn differently than the rest of it. On each end of the harmonica was a letter, crudely scratched into the silvered metal; must have been done with a pocket knife. She leaned closer to the glass, her breath creating a halo of steam. She could barely decipher the upside-down letters: *M* on the right side, *W* on the left.

Turning from the hutch, Jean stepped toward the front door—eight steps for a six-year-old, from one end of the living room to the other. Today, she counted off four steps—probably no more than two for Legs. She pulled the handle, surprised that the door wasn't as heavy as she remembered, with its three clouded windows running across the top. She lowered herself on the cold concrete stoop, leaned her elbows on her knees, and gazed at the row house two doors down. A neglected newspaper sat on the walkway. Maybe—just maybe—her grandfather would come out to pick it up.

After an hour or so, maybe longer, Jean heard the door crack open behind her.

"Honey?" Spence asked. The concern in his voice snapped her out of the trance. "Sorry we were down there so long, but you should see this. Come inside—chilly out here."

She glanced at her watch. *Two o'clock. Where did the time go?* Jean lifted her head and twisted around. "Yeah, whatcha got?" She stood, rubbed her lower back, and stepped inside.

Spence beamed with excitement and pointed to two book boxes stacked on the maroon wing-back chair.

"I told Legs about the store. He gave me these. They're all original pressings. Many of them are on the old Victor and Okeh Record labels. You wouldn't believe who's in here—Ethyl Waters, Louis Armstrong, Duke Ellington, Buddy Bolden, Ella Fitzgerald, Dinah Washington, and even Bix Beiderbecke!" He rattled off the names as he flipped through the albums. "They're all in perfect condition. They smell like old records are supposed to." Spence talked a mile a minute. Dillon peered into the box. His eyes, too, were filled with music.

Jean stared at Legs, trying to find the appropriate words. "We'll never forget this day. You're a wonderful man."

"You two take those out to the car," Legs said, shaking his long finger at the boxes. "You, Miss Crazy Eyes, stay right here." He had a touch of mischief in his rich voice.

Spence and Dillon each picked up a box and headed for the door. Curious, Jean studied Legs as he turned the key in the glass-fronted cabinet.

"C'mere. I got some things for you too." Legs took two long steps toward her. "Give me your hand and close those wild-lookin' eyes a yours."

The vines of his fingers wrapped around hers like ivy as he pulled her forward. Her own hand seemed fragile and naive against the wisdom and skill of his. She sensed Legs leaning way down to whisper in her ear. The wisps of hair on her neck tingled when his breath floated over her skin. The soft words that followed sounded as if they were coming from everywhere.

"These'll look good on you. They Miss Ella's. She said I blew wisdom from my harp one night and gave 'em to me. Wife wore 'em for years."

Two small, smooth orbs. *The pearls?* "Can I open my eyes?" she said, a Mardi Gras party pounding in her chest.

"No, keep 'em close."

Legs turned the same hand over and opened her fingers. He placed something cold and round in her palm. The metal warmed with his voice.

"This is for the boy. The nickel I saved after my first payin' gig. What I had left. Blew my horn with Dizzy and Trane in 1950. Only twenty, I was. Give it to him when the time is right. Possibilities."

"Dizzy Gillespie and John Coltrane?"

"Doesn't get any better. Now gimme your other hand."

Her face flushed with heat; tears welled. Her left palm shook as she raised it from her side. She kept her eyes closed.

"This for you and your man together. Could use good blow. He a good man, that one." The cool, weighty metal slipped into her hand like a Popsicle. Legs's fingers folded hers over the harmonica.

Jean wrapped her arms around Legs, her fists squeezed tight to not drop the stuff of legends. She never wanted to let him go. Her right cheek pressed against the middle button of his checked shirt. She felt as small as a six-year-old.

"You have no idea," she choked.

"C'mon now. That's 'nuff. Your man is out in the car with all his new friends. He liable to run off and leave you at the curb."

Jean pulled away and opened her hand. "They're beautiful. These were Ella's?"

"Sure as I'm standin' here. Put 'em on. I notice you ain't got nothin' on your ears."

Setting the coin and harmonica on the coffee table, Jean wiped her eyes. She hummed "Fascinating Rhythm" as she inserted the pearl studs and snapped the backs in place. "How do they look?"

"Fascinatin'," Legs said, releasing a low chuckle.

Jean pressed her fingers to her right cheek. The raised ridge of Legs's button left an imprint on her skin, eclipsing the scar of the long-faded cigarette burn. She slipped the harmonica in her purse and tucked the Indian Head nickel inside one of the inner pockets. As she moved toward the front door in a trance, she glanced down at the curled ends of the newspaper on the coffee table.

"Are you done with this? I need something to read in the car."

"Go on. I don't take the paper myself. Somebody left it on the stoop this mornin'. One less thing I gotta throw away."

"You're not totally alone, are you, Legs?" she asked, anticipating an answer she didn't want to hear.

"Naw . . . I got a buddy, not too far from here. Wheezy Beevers, uh-huh. He a piano man, and a real good one. Me and Wheezy play the road for years. We keep an eye out for 'tother, yes we do. Don't you worry yourself 'bout me."

"Spence left a card next to the pictures over the television. You have all our information. If you need anything, drop us a line."

"I will."

"Promise?"

"You better breeze now . . ." Legs nodded his head toward the door.

Folding the newspaper, just like her grandfather showed her, Jean tucked the end over to keep it together. She hesitated and waved the paper at Legs, blowing him an airborne kiss. Legs wiped his eyes. He raised his hand and curled his long fingers at the air to catch it.

She pulled the door shut—odd there was no squeal—and held the handle so the screen didn't bang.

The boys waited in the idling rental car. Jean slipped inside and buckled the seat belt, her pulse still racing. "Wow—incredible," she said, shaking her head.

"Wait until I tell you what we talked about in the basement," Spence said, tapping the steering wheel. "And I was able to give Dillon a taste of some of the music. I'm blown away. Bill is going to freak when he sees those records. We'll stop by a shipping place before we go home. We can't take them on the plane."

"I'm still trying to wrap my head around the past two hours." She turned to the backseat, wrote a note, and handed it to Dillon. *Wasn't he fabulous?*

Amazing, Dillon wrote back.

Kind of like getting art lessons from M—a nice M?

Yep!

Moving her head from one side to the other in the mirrored visor, Jean admired Miss Ella's pearls. She flipped it up with a *pop* and checked her watch. "Perfect timing for a perfect day. Two forty—only ten minutes over schedule. We're crossing the river on 395 to pick up 95 south—right into Richmond. Easy-peasy."

"Nice earrings." Spence threw her a cagey smile. "Where'd you get those?"

"Oh, these old things? Legs gave them to me. They were Ella Fitzgerald's. I may never take them off."

"Pretty special," Spence said, nodding.

Jean pulled out the newspaper she'd stuck between the center console and seat. She snapped down the full length of the front page of the well-read copy of the *Washington Post.* Her eyes went wide at one of the headlines on a news story—*McCarthy Wins Support as Ad for LBJ Backfires.*

"What the—" She inspected the date on the masthead. Today's date, all right—March 9. But the year was 1968. Might her grand-father have delivered that newspaper to Legs's house this morning?

CHAPTER 37

Doc? Can You Hear Me?

"Here we are!" Jean announced. "Let's go in!" She pointed to the house and handed Dillon a note. *You ready to meet the family?* Dillon nodded and grabbed his knapsack.

"Janet and Doug are doing a wonderful job of keeping the place spit and polished," Spence said. "Let's take Dillon's painting in first. We can get our bags later, after we check in."

Jean didn't see any movement through the beveled glass oval of the door. She pressed the latch on the long brass handle.

"Helloooo! We're here!" she called out.

All was quiet downstairs, but the air was thick with the savory aroma of roasting meat and freshly baked bread, with overtones of something sweet.

"Well, look what the cat dragged in!" Doug Parson said, as he rounded the corner from the hall. "Been waitin' for ya."

"Glad to be back!" Spence said.

Jean turned to introduce Dillon, but he'd set down the art case and wandered to the parlor. He stopped at the tall, arched window next to the fireplace and gazed at the bird bath, setting his hand on one of the panes of rippled glass. Jean smiled as she studied his reac-tion. On the drive down, she'd written out the story of Wiley's passing, as Mary Coulter had relayed it to Spence and her. Wiley had passed in this room, with the three phoenixes appearing as he became immortal.

Wiley would be waiting for them when they got home to Portland in a few days, or maybe he was here with them now. They'd find out soon enough.

Doug marched them right past the front desk. "What do you mean you're not checking us in?" Spence said, pretending to be indignant.

"Oh no, I'm not charging you in your own house," Doug shot back.

"Yes, you are! I want to make sure you can still pay the rent."

Rolling her eyes at the banter, Jean stepped up to the registration desk in the hallway. "Doug, you're charging us. Not one more word about it."

"About what?" Janet Parson said, coming down the hall with a wooden spoon. "Check 'em in, Doug. Take their money. Don't argue with the guests. They'll give us a bad review on TripAdvisor." Janet winked and made a beeline to the kitchen. She called over her shoulder, "And thanks for sending both those things back, guys."

Spence narrowed his eyes. Jean stared at him, confused.

"What else did you send out here?" she whispered.

"I only had the chest put on the truck."

Jean shrugged her shoulders. "Let's take the painting upstairs. We'll hang it and not say anything."

While Spence finished the paperwork at the desk, she strolled into the parlor and tapped Dillon on the shoulder. He turned and gazed at her with dreamy eyes. Jean patted the art case and pointed to the ceiling.

The three of them climbed the stairs. Mary Coulter stood on the top landing. She looked the same as when she appeared in the kit-chen of her house in Portland. "Doc's been waiting for you—and I have too. He's in your room. *Shhh* . . . be surprised," Mary whispered. "I'm thrilled you're here." She smiled as her image faded.

"Well, so much for surprises," Jean said, turning back to Spence. The smoky trail dissipated as she stepped through it on the landing.

She stood in the doorway and froze, in shock. *The Dancing Boy* was already hanging above the headboard. Her gaze traveled from the painting to the rocking chair in front of the window. She hurried Spence and Dillon into the bedroom and lunged at the door.

"Belongs here," Doc said. The white strands around his image trailed in a syncopated beat behind him as he rocked.

"Doc? You found it!" she said, stunned.

"I never dreamed the little dickens was so important. Art is a funny thing, you know . . . the way it makes you feel inside."

"But—" Spence stopped when Doc put up his hand. Dillon stood with his mouth open, unable to move.

"I'm a might pleased Mr. Segert is going to get the attention he deserves from his boss. I believe a warm heart resides under that chief's porcupine skin. I must say, though, Jon has a mighty unique relationship with that bird. A bond I'd best stay out of. But I did agree to help him. I kept my word."

"You were working with Jon? So . . . you . . . at the auction bidding against Dromov?" Jean's hand rose to her cheek, putting the pieces together in her head.

"Risks, remember? I wanted to get the price of that painting as high as I dared, so this family didn't lose our investment to that untoward man. I do believe Dillon knew I was there. He recognized me from my sitting for his school painting. He did a right fine job too." Doc turned and waved Dillon to him. "Come here, young man."

His steps tentative, Dillon approached Doc. Their hands wrapped around each other's as Doc drew him to his chest in a long embrace. He patted Dillon's back, his hand creating a wisp of mist. Dillon pulled away to study the Man's face. Doc held his gaze and placed his firm, haloed hands on each of Dillon's cheeks. Dillon's expression changed. Golden light undulated and boiled around them as they moved to cover Dillon's ears.

"Inspiration for painting the 'real' can come from something 'unreal.' You, son, are smart and quite talented. But talent doesn't make you wise. Only years of riding life's train will get you to wisdom. I thought I'd help to put some dust on the soles of those worn-out shoes of yours. Shoes wear out from going somewhere, not wandering around admiring the scenery." Light poured faster from Doc's hands as he talked. "I posed for you to close the gap, you might say. You wished for wisdom and I showed you. Now, I stumbled plenty . . . and lifting that painting was a skosh under-handed, but I wanted you to have confidence in your decision to follow this new course. You must not be pushed, or obligated, out of gratitude. You should do this out of passion, and passion alone." Doc lifted his hands from Dillon's face. The light ceased.

"Doc—" Dillon whispered.

"Of course you can hear me, son. You already had the magic. I gave it some spice, you might say."

Realizing what Doc had done, Jean sat on the bed. She traced the swirls of green vines on the spread as Spence wrapped his arms around her. The afternoon with Legs, plus this, was almost too much. They both turned to Doc when he addressed them.

Dillon didn't speak. He listened.

"And you two . . ." Doc removed his glasses and squeezed his eyes. The flashes of sunlight bounced off the lenses, leaving luminous threads dancing behind them. "Jean and Spencer, you wanted to do lofty things. I believe you are not yet done. How do you put a price on the gifts of compassion, determination, and purity of art?" Doc gazed at *The Dancing Boy* hanging over the bed. "That painting has had quite the adventure since being in your hands. You took it home only because you thought it was beautiful. That is what art is sup-posed to be, you do know. A man's passions cannot be measured by the size of his billfold. No, siree, not the same. My dancing boy didn't get better with a hefty new price tag. Here you are, quite satisfied to have Dillon's copy. You knew that he was meant to dance right in that spot."

"I don't know what to say. Did you just give Dillon his hearing back?" Jean said, her words breaking into pieces.

"He did. I listened to you ask him the question," Dillon said, as if not recognizing his own voice.

Doc's hazy gaze met theirs, and then he smiled like he thought of something new. "Why, I believe there was a six-fold return for the one thing you and Spencer did." Holding up one finger at a time, he continued. "You helped solve Jon's case; saved the family's investment; took care of those other people's money; launched the career of a young man with impressive talent, and who will help many people to get their art back in the future, mind you; and gave me, an old ghost, a new lease on afterlife—I got another opportunity to heal. It is what I do best." Doc went quiet and thoughtful. He slipped his glasses back on and chuckled. "No—seven-fold! Wiley has never been happier. Send him home for a visit once in awhile. That is, if Mycroft is so inclined to share. Like peas and carrots, those two. Take the copy you have in the case with you. Be careful—a priceless Dillon Davis." Doc wiggled his eyebrows and slapped his knees. He stood and pulled his pocket watch from his gray, striped vest, the gold glinting when it snapped open. The cane chair continued to rock, leaving lazy translucent light trails behind him.

"I think my painting of Doc belongs here too. That way, more people can see him," Dillon said, turning to Jean and Spence.

"We'll talk. We want to live with it awhile," Spence said. "And Doc, you're not allowed to lure Mycroft away again."

Doc smiled and tapped is nose with his forefinger. "Turn about's fair. Come now, nearly five o'clock. Time to gather the family. Would y'all like to walk in the garden with us? Charlotte's hyacinths are coming into bloom."

Jean ran her hand through Dillon's long hair. "Yes. Lovely. Just what the doctor ordered."

"But first, you need to call Laura and tell her you've cracked the case . . . all on your own," Spence added.

Dillon inspected the bottom of his Keds as he listened to their voices. "I will. And I want you to tell me everything Legs said this morning too."

Doc stared at *The Dancing Boy* and scratched his chin. "On second thought . . . take the original home with you." He turned and pointed to the art case. "I think I'd prefer to have Dillon's version of the painting over the bed. Infinitely better and full of magic to me. I believe you are obligated. Its work is not done."

Doc faded and disappeared. A remnant wisp of him swirled and evaporated.

After dinner, Dillon retreated to his room. He needed some private time. The ability to fully participate in the discussion around the table had been overwhelming. The floodgates had opened. Strange. By the end of the evening, he'd almost lost his voice from overuse. The last verbal banter he'd had over a meal was when his parents were still alive.

He had called Laura with the news, dodging the details of how they'd found the painting, saying only that the piece was delivered anonymously to the inn in Richmond. Laura figured the perpetrator must have been spooked by all the publicity. Not unusual. Their vocal banter made focusing on the conversation difficult. She was shocked, too, by his voice. He'd explained to her that Jean and Spence had taken him to a specialist who had performed miracles with an experimental procedure. He didn't feel bad about the fib; pretty close to the truth.

Dillon jumped when the bed shook, realizing he'd resumed the comfort of being lost in his thoughts. Wiley materialized in front of him.

"Hey, Wiley. You sleeping with me tonight?" The dog licked Dillon's fingers, his tongue leaving a phosphorous residue. The sparkles left a pattern in the shape of constellations. "Canis? Apus? Aquila? Columba?" he asked, showing Wiley his hand.

"You know, you're a lucky young man," said a woman's voice. Dillon raised his eyes, transfixed, as the air rippled over the bottom corner of the bed. "Not many people can say they're a patient of Doc's anymore." Mary Coulter's image became stronger until she was sitting in front of him, her legs crossed at the ankles. The radiance of her face reminded him of Raphael's *La Donna Velata*, painted in 1516. Quiet. Calm. "You've made him happy, Dillon."

The slight ethereal outline framed her features. Her hazel eyes and the glow of her rich skin compelled him to sketch her.

"Can I do a painting of you?" he asked. "Just the way you are, right this minute." Her hair was swept up in a smooth twist, with a few errant wisps framing her oval face. It had so many variations of color: chestnut, white-silver, and mahogany.

Mary put her hand on her chest, embarrassed. "Me? There's nothing special about me."

"Yes, there is." Dillon stared at her face, attempting to mem-orize every detail. He reached over and touched her cheek. Like fresh cream. He rolled a loose tendril of her hair between his fingers. Soft as silk.

"You don't have any paint."

"Can I take your picture? I'll work from that when I get home." Dillon sprang off the bed and rummaged through his knapsack. He pulled out his phone and bounced back and sat cross-legged. "Okay, you ready?"

"Can Wiley be in the picture too?" Mary patted her legs. Wiley inched to her and rested his large head across her lap. The soft fabric of her wool skirt tickled Wiley's muzzle. The dog sneezed. She placed her hand between his ears.

Click. Flash.

Mary raised her eyes and smiled. Hazel . . . warm as clover honey. Maybe six or seven hues combined to make up the color.

Click. Flash.

She gazed at *The Dancing Boy* hanging over the bed. Her eyes turned thoughtful. Such a deep expression for a simple and beautiful face. *Wisdom.*

Click. Flash.

Dillon studied the three pictures and swished his finger across the small screen. The images could have been painted by Caravaggio himself. "The last one's best. That's the one I'm going to use. I'll come back and show you when I'm finished."

"If only my Raleigh had been like you," Mary whispered.

He raised his eyes. Mary was gone.

CHAPTER 38

The Office

Jean watched Dillon disappear into his apartment building with his knapsack. She wanted to lunge out of the car when the fringe of his scarf caught in the door. Spence pulled away from the curb.

"Wasn't it amazing to be able to talk with Dillon?" Jean said. "Our relationship has been raised to a whole new level."

"Like a son?"

"Kinda sorta . . ."

"Me too. You're going to save your stash of notepads from now on. You were blowing through those at a pretty good clip." Spence glanced at her.

"I have more, don't worry. Dillon's so articulate when he speaks. Grown up. His voice is much deeper than I expected."

"He is grown up. Remember, you were only twenty when we got married, sweetie. You thought you knew everything back then."

"Seems so young to me now. Funny thing about time."

The street was empty as they pulled into the driveway. The house was quiet too.

"What? No fanfare? Where's Wiley?" Spence set the art case by the stairs.

"Mycroft?" she called. Nothing. "We must be chum. I'll take the bags upstairs and find him. We need to do a load of laundry."

Jean found them on the bed. Mycroft lifted his head with a

contented expression and stretched, his back foot pushing against Wiley's chin. The dog took up over three-quarters of the king-size expanse. She lay down beside Mycroft and stroked his long ginger and white torso.

"Too much traveling. We're home with nowhere to go," she cooed and rolled off the mattress. She unzipped the duffle bags and gathered the laundry. Jean came down the stairs, clothes jumbled in her arms.

"Now we've got two bed hogs," she announced.

"I thought I'd open up the house. Let's check the painting." Spence eyed the art case.

"Wait! Let me start the washer get some hooks." When she came back inside, Spence had already unbuckled the straps.

"Beautiful!" She held up *The Dancing Boy* to different spots on the walls. "Maybe upstairs over our bed?"

"We can't hang it anywhere. This isn't ours anymore, Jean."

"I know, but—"

"But nothing. The painting goes to Jon. We talked about this on the way home."

"Can't we live with it for a couple of days?"

"Nooo . . ."

"I'm percolating on an idea."

"No more schemes."

"Mmm . . . One."

Jean set the painting against the wall and dashed to the kitchen. She opened the junk drawer and pulled out the address book and a notepad. This one said, *If Cats Could Talk—They Wouldn't.* After making a long list of items, she picked up the phone.

"Meg! It's Jean."

Jon stepped off the elevator and headed down the hall toward his office. Jenny ran up to him to block his path.

"What?" he snapped and raised his hands to his hips.

"Here. Hot—extra cream, two sugars." She handed him his favorite *Deny Everything* mug.

"Uh . . . thanks. Let me hang up my jacket. I usually beg and you give me back a bunch of rapid-fire guff. What are you up to?" Jon narrowed his eyes at her.

"You can't go in yet. The chief asked me to send you to his office as soon as you walked in."

"Tell him to chill."

"No can do, big guy. He's already pissed. Don't go poking a stick in his cage."

The closed corner door at the end of the long hall drew his gaze, a gateway to yet another ugly exchange. He turned back to Jenny; she had a smirk on her face.

"All right, dammit."

"Follow me."

"I know where it is."

Jon's jacket sleeves swished as he walked the long, carpeted hall. He took a sip of his coffee to stall. Maybe he should drink the whole damn cup before knocking on the door. He hesitated as he raised his knuckles. *Just get it over with.*

"Jon? Get in here!" The muffled voice roared.

The morning buzz kicked in as he turned the handle.

"Need me?"

"Hey! Nice work on finding that kid for the Art Crime Team. They're throwing points our way, even to me." The chief laughed, straining the buttons on his bright-white shirt over the beach ball in his stomach. "The kid—what's his name—Dillon? He's found that painting,"—he peered over his smudged reading glasses—"so I hear."

"How come they didn't call me?" Jon clenched his jaw.

"I'm the boss, that's why. And I'm apparently more accessible than you." A smile of triumph changed his face in a way that almost made him a nice guy.

"Yeah, Chief, you're the most accessible guy I know."

"Take a couple of days off. I don't care what HR says."

Jon stared at him, surprised. "Thanks. I was hoping my daugh-ter, Amy, was coming home for spring break." His eyes fixed on the window as a 737 climbed toward cruising altitude. "But she stayed back east with her new *boyfriend.* The old man is old news, I guess."

"Your buddies in Rhode Island taking good care of her?" The chief made continuous figure-eights on a notepad with his silver pen.

"Oh yeah." Jon studied the tufted squares on the beige carpet. "She's all grown now. I gotta back off."

The chief raised his eyes. The roll of thick skin on his neck turned an deep shade of pomegranate. "Who the hell made up that rule? Never back off, you understand me? That girl will need you till the day you die. Doesn't matter if she's three thousand miles away, has a billionaire husband, spoiled kids, or even a dog slobbering all over the foot of her bed. You got that? She's still your kid."

Jon let the words settle over him.

"Hey, change of subject"—the chief's expression turned serious—"I want this Dromov mess wrapped up—pronto! And clean up the Coulter fiasco too. Been dealing with *that* while you've been jet-setting all over the world. I've got the autopsy report right here. Says Coulter died of"—the chief adjusted his cheap, half-moon drugstore glasses and yanked the paper in front of him—"uh . . . a *brain* hemorrhage." He made a face like he'd been forced to swallow cold tapioca.

"Okay . . . that'll work," Jon said, with a little too much sarcasm. "But this isn't over quite yet. One more on my list: Kendrick Forrester. Goes by 'Kip'."

"How the hell does somebody get a brain hemorrhage in their thigh? How'd he die, Jon?" The chief's stare was a rope, poised to hog-tie him over the desk. "And Dromov's whining to everybody about a hawk tearing up his arm. Probably going to turn septic. What do you have—an aviary with mercenary hawks back there? Answer me!"

Jon winced. He blew out a breath and stuck his hand in his pocket. He took three steps from the doorway toward the desk. The talon made a high arc through the air and landed with a heavy *thud* on

Raleigh's autopsy report.

"Meet Horus. He's the newest member of our team. Doesn't eat much, has no expense account, and you don't have to pay him benefits. Budget impact is zero."

"What the hell?" The chief stared at the long, curved claw in front of him. "A flippin' weapon. You got a license for that thing?"

"You can't even imagine what it was attached to."

"Get the hell outta here. You're crazy! Ever think you need Amy more than she needs you?"

Reaching across the desk, Jon snatched up the talon. "Damn you!"

He marched to his office, the echo of the chief's laughter splashing on the back of his jacket like paint balls filled with disappearing ink. Jon glared at Jenny as he passed her desk. She pressed her lips together, trying not to laugh. He grabbed the door handle. A weird feeling churned in his gut. Every instinct in his body told him not to go in.

The office resembled a beauty snapshot from HGTV. The ficus had been pruned and was brilliant green from a weekend meal of fertilizer. The tree almost smiled at him. His computer monitor was void of sticky fingerprints; the letters on the keyboard were actually legible. File folders fanned in a perfect line on his clean and polished desk. The BG-289 rock poster of the Rolling Stones' *Tumbling Dice,* with its bright-orange lettering, was framed in ebony enameled wood and centered on the once-bare wall. The black background contrasted with the rounded corners of the stacked white dice. A wide, steel-frame mirror created a second window, a duplicate of the outside view. He stared into the reflection of the bright-blue sky. Dark, puffy clouds emerged from the edge and floated toward the other side. Three new pictures of Amy and Meg had been lined up on his credenza. In one of them, Amy had her head resting on the shoulder of her new boyfriend.

Jon sucked in a breath. Over the credenza, *The Dancing Boy* stared back at him in its thick, gold-leaf frame. The image was illuminated under a pin spotlight on a track in the ceiling. *Is this the real one?*

A cream-colored envelope, centered in front of his chair, waited for him. He stepped behind his desk. His hand shook as he lifted the flap and pulled out the card with a scrolled *C* on it.

Jon,

We couldn't think of any place safer to hang the original. Sell it with Dromov's assets and give the money to his clients. Doc has Dillon's copy, and Legs has his check, but they gave us back so much more. Doc had the painting, that scoundrel! The Dillon Davis hangs in Richmond. Set your hand on this one and see for yourself. Oh, by the way, give Amy a hug!

Smooch!

Jean, Spence, Dillon, Mycroft, Wiley . . . and Doc

Jon reached for the *The Dancing Boy*. Warm. A vibration, and then a prickling. Golden light erupted and rippled from beneath the fingers. He closed his eyes.

Doc hugging a still, dark-haired woman lying on a bed . . . Beautiful woman . . . Doc's hands on the fabric . . . The phoenixes taking flight from the tree outside a window.

He pulled away. No more. The light stopped. His body still vibrated as he turned to his desk. Yes, this painting had seen so much. His eyes felt swollen and ready to burst. He bowed his head and pushed the card back into the envelope. The Collinses presented him with a world he had no idea existed.

Jon slipped the note inside his drawer and placed the talon on top. *My world of magic.* Life became different after Jean and Spence became part of his life. They restored his faith in the human chain. Some things couldn't be analyzed or categorized. He gave the handle a tap, the tiny ball bearings gliding it closed with no effort. When he raised his eyes, his wife's face peeked around the doorway.

"Hey, honey! Somebody's here for you," Meg said and retreated.

Amy stepped into view with a wide smile and her long blond hair pulled into a loose ponytail. The diamond studs that he and Meg had given her for Christmas gleamed in her ears like two white search lights, guiding her home through the fog. She was angelic with no makeup, hands in the back pockets of her jeans, and wearing a teal oversized sweater. He held up his phone and snapped a picture. He'd frame it and give the photo a home on his credenza next to the others. He embraced her as if no one else in the world existed.

The chief leaned his beefy head past the doorframe. "Glad none of this fancy stuff is coming out of my budget. Thank those Collins folks for this. I'm getting to like 'em!"

"Yeah, me too," Jon choked. He couldn't hold it in. Meg and Amy wrapped their arms around him as his shoulders shook.

"Get the hell outta here. Spend the day with your family." The chief thumped Jon's shoulder three times, turned, and inspected the raised pattern in the carpet on his trek back to his corner office.

CHAPTER 39

The Staff Meeting

Spence watched Bill flip through Legs's albums. He'd finally managed to impress the unimpressible Bill.

"Okay, we're both set on the name of the store, right? Not Fade Away is good for you too? Are we final? Bill? Bueller?" Spence asked, trying to get his attention. "You'd better be fine with the location on Main Street because I signed the lease. We should still catch a lot of business from the farmer's market. Runs through October."

"When can we get into the space?" Bill muttered, inspecting the back of *Monk's Dream* by Thelonious Monk.

"In the next week or so."

"Yep, totally with you, buddy." Bill's voice sounded far away, his mind even farther.

"Good. I got our website domain and e-mail addresses, and it's what I put on the paperwork for the retail space. The logo design is done and the stationery is being printed. Jean has a budget mapped out for us."

"Oh man, check this out . . . Bix Beiderbecke? Damn!"

"These arrived this past week. Legs Flanders is the coolest guy ever. He just gave them to me. There's hundreds more in his basement. Did you know he played with Muddy Waters back in the sixties, and all the greats before that? Helluva nice guy."

"Do you think Legs would come out here for the opening?" Bill popped up his head and turned, the idea whirling around in his mind and radiating across his face. "How about we do a jazz event to thank him for all these records? People would flock from everywhere. He's big. We'd get a ton of publicity, especially if we can add some local blues bands to do cover sets. I want to meet him too."

"Not a bad idea. Depends on whether Legs is up to the trip. I'll write to him and ask."

"Why don't you just call him?"

"Oh, no, Legs doesn't do the phone."

"I'll leave that part up to you, but these are way cool." Bill pulled another album out of the box. "Whoa . . . Charlie Parker on Verve. 1953? This one alone is worth about four hundred bucks. Look at the David Stone Martin cover art!" The striking abstract image lit up the room with vivid gold, electric-blue, and black.

"Let me see that." Spence slipped the album from the sleeve and examined the label. "I'm not sure I can sell this one." He blew on the grooves and ran his hand around the edge. His fingers filled with the familiar tingle.

"Don't start with me, Spence. People won't come in the store if they can't buy anything. We're not opening a museum."

Spence rubbed his fingertips together. Still tingling. "Put these away for now. There's something Jean and I need to show you and Linda."

Bill erected his large frame to its full height of six-foot-five and eyed Spence. "What's up, buddy?"

Spence guided Bill into the living room and pointed to the portrait of Doc.

"This is Wiley's owner, Dr. Beaumont Gaines—goes by Doc. He's immortal too."

"Hey . . . Sparkles is in there." Bill stared at the painting, stroking his beard. "I'll be damned."

Spence stepped to the fireplace and turned the key in the wall. The flames danced to life. "Wiley! Uncle Bill's here!"

The dog leapt out of the canvas, ran in a circle, and sat at Bill's feet.

"Well, hey, boy!" Bill turned to Spence. "We need him as our mascot at the store." As he scratched Wiley's chin, he called into the kitchen. "Linda! You'd better come in here!"

Jean followed Linda to the living room and told the story of Dillon's painting of Doc. Linda studied the details of Doc's face. The soft light from the lamp animated his expression. Linda's, however, portrayed her anticipation of the man flying off the hook and sailing around the room.

Jealous, Mycroft wedged himself in front of Bill, forcing him to have two hands petting simultaneously.

Linda turned to Jean with her hands on her hips. "What do immortal dogs eat, anyway? We had no idea."

"A whole lotta love. He's always full."

CHAPTER 40

Spence's Birthday - May 18th

Sixty-one is a big deal; at least the day was a milestone for Spence. Jean figured he'd feel better after he read the AARP magazine article celebrating Bob Dylan turning seventy. She'd positioned the issue conspicuously on the counter. He couldn't miss it.

Jean left Spence lathered in the shower and dressed. He was about ten minutes behind her. She bounded down the stairs, switched on the coffeemaker, and hurried to one of the bookcases in the den. A separate section had been set up for Legs's albums. Spence wanted at least a few weeks of ownership before the store opened next month.

One special album eluded her fingertips as she deciphered Spence's system of organizational rules. Only a fellow vinylphile would know what those rules were. Not finding the title in the Ms, she flipped through the Ws in Blues. Paydirt! She dashed to the turntable in the living room. Slipping the album from the sleeve, she placed the thick vinyl disk over the spindle. The needle wouldn't be lowered until Spence came down the stairs.

While she waited, she pulled Spence's present from beneath the loveseat. She'd tucked the instrument away after they'd come home from Richmond. She turned to the window with the cold metal in her hand and wiggled her hips to the music in her head. The song would soon be coming out of the speakers. A dozen or so tiny birds picked at the suet ball that hung from the maple tree in front of the fence.

They reminded her of clip-on Christmas ornaments.

The shower knobs squeaked as Spence turned off the water in their master bath. The crunch of the floor upstairs signaled he was getting dressed. Drawers opened and slid closed in the tall bureau. His footfalls creaked across the catwalk.

Jean tiptoed over to the turntable and lowered the needle on the album with the faded Chess Records label—half blue, half white. The images of two chess pieces—a knight with a horse's head and a rook with a cross on top—exchanged places as the record spun, snapping and crackling at thirty-three-and-a-third speed.

Muddy Waters's 1956 rendition of "Got My Mojo Workin'" announced Spence's arrival at the bottom of the steps. He ran his fingers through his wet hair and listened.

"Excellent!" Spence bobbed and beamed. "Well, that was great this morning! Now—what's my second present?" He smacked his hands together twice. "You said I had two."

Jean turned from the window, twisted back and forth on the balls of her stocking feet, and bit her bottom lip. The harmonica's silver casing had warmed to the temperature of her hand.

"Just you wait," she said and pointed to the painting.

On the living room wall under the soft spotlight, the Man patted his knee in time to the harmonica solo soaring out of the speakers. Doc had his mojo workin'.

The harmonica sat in front of him on the desk in the den. Spence studied the surface. Jean always surprised him with her choice of presents, but this one was a socks knocker. He examined every scratch and dent under the lamp, forming the words he would write to Legs Flanders.

He lifted the lid on the box of fresh Not Fade Away stationery, handmade with the store's logo of three phoenixes in flight, and leaned in for a whiff of his future. The paper was an ankh, giving him the breath of life that would take him on to the last job he'd ever have. Not just a job; the realization of a lifelong dream that took over fifty years of intense study and passion to achieve.

Spence rubbed his fingertips together, as if deciding which petit four to pluck from the box. He took out the top piece and floated it to the blotter. The silver and onyx pen in his hand hovered over the blank page. It was the one he'd given to Jean when the company she worked for was sold, and which now had a permanent home in a wood stand above the desk. This pen was reserved for special letters.

He started to write—slow and careful—so Legs could read the words of his ragged penmanship.

May 18

Dear Legs,

You will never know the significance of the gifts you've given to me, Jean, and Dillon. Then again, maybe you do. The harmonica is more than an instrument; it represents the magic of a dream . . . your dreams that came true. I am honored for it to share mine too. Jean showed me the nickel. We think you should give something that special to Dillon yourself.

Not Fade Away *opens in four short weeks. My friend and business partner Bill Flannery and I would like to bring you out to Portland for the event on Sunday, June 19th. The concert will celebrate you and all your friends who are currently enjoying themselves in our den. The collection already has a place of honor waiting in the store.*

We plan to assemble some of the best jazz and blues musicians in Portland. The harmonica gave me a future vision of you playing it once again. Legs, I think it'll only play for you.

If you can't come, I'll understand. Please write me back or, if you're inspired to use the telephone, give me a call at the number on the card I left for you.

We hope to hear from you soon,

Spence Collins

Spence folded the paper in thirds, making sure the corners aligned with precision, and slipped the note inside the matching envelope. He addressed it simply to Legs, with his street address on Huidekoper Place. The commemorative *Jazz Forever* postage stamp had a hallowed place on the top right corner.

"I'm going to chase down Frank," he called out to Jean. "I bet his mail truck's in the neighborhood."

"Sounds good. I almost have this renovation budget done for Mary's house."

Spence stared at the harmonica and ran his fingertips across the reflective surface. Tiny sparks flew out of the holes of the mouth-piece: ignited dust. He shut off the desk lamp with a soft click.

Author's Note

Many thanks to all the great local businesses who I've mentioned in the book: GG's Delicatessen and Catering, Ray's Ragtime, Casa de Tamales, and the singular world of Powell's Books.

The Portland Museum of Art is a fictitious museum in the book, but the real one upon which it's based, the Portland Art Museum, is pretty wonderful. Their collections rival those of the best museums in larger cities.

The painting, *The Dancing Boy*, is based on a real work of art that has been in my family for over ninety years. Alas, it is not a Caravaggio, or even a Hendrick ter Brugghen—that I know of—but it's pretty magical to me.

The relationship between Caravaggio and Hendrick ter Brugghen was created for this book, although Brugghen was a prominent member of the Caravaggisti in real life. The Caravaggisti was a real group of artists who were so enamored with Caravaggio's technique that they studied, and subsequently copied, his style of painting. The mark of Caravaggio's influence is seen in a number of great artists of the time. With the exception of the relationship with Brugghen, the scenes of Caravaggio's life are based on facts as documented in a number of books about the artist. Specifically, *M: The Man Who Became Caravaggio* by Peter Robb paints vivid accounts of Caravaggio's self-tortured, hedonistic—and, yes, genius—life. Simon Schama's documentary, *The Power of Art*, is another great resource for snip-pets of Caravaggio's life story.

The Old Gaines House is a fictional bed-and-breakfast, but there are numerous beautiful, old B&Bs in Richmond, Virginia, that are quite similar. The historical facts about Richmond relayed in the book are accurate to what is documented in the city's archives. They were invaluable for this book's research.

My husband, a rabid collector of vintage vinyl, provided me with endless amounts of music trivia to include in the book. His encyclopedic knowledge was easy research.

Lastly, and sadly, I must say that Legs Flanders is a purely fictional character. You won't find him through a Google search, but I did want him to be real. And so he is . . . on the immortal pages. Legs is made up of an amalgam of the great jazz musicians from the '50s and '60s. The ten-part film series *Jazz* by Ken Burns provided me with a world of ideas for shaping Legs's character.

And, by the way, Legs lives on in the third book, *Riffs*.

About the Author

Courtney Pierce lives in Milwaukie, Oregon, with her husband and bossy cat. *Stitches* and *Brushes* emerged from her own magical history, which encompassed a twenty-year career as a sales and marketing executive in the Broadway entertainment industry. She became transformed by the magic of fiction from a theater seat in thirty-two cities for touring Broadway shows. The series is also a showcase for her other passions: music, fine art, international travel, ancient history, and sewing exquisite fabric. Courtney is active in the writing community. She is in the Hawthorne Fellows program at the Attic Institute and is Vice President of the Northwest Independent Writers Association.

Readers can follow all of Courtney's books on her website:
courtney-pierce.com

The magical journey of Jean and Spence Collins continues in the third book of the series, *Riffs*.

www.ingramcontent.com/pod-product-compliance
Lightning Source LLC
LaVergne TN
LVHW091034080826
845145LV00002B/494